AMISH HEARTS

COMPLETE SERIES

GRACE LEWIS

D1521430

BOOK DESCRIPTION

Betsie Hershberger's young life consists of family, Amish values, and honor. But the reality of their circumstances changes as time goes by. Follow this young woman and those she cares most deeply as they learn to navigate in an ever-changing world and face insurmountable odds.

The Amish Hearts series is one that will pull at your heartstrings, make you jump up and down for joy, and will leave you speechless as cultures collide, danger pays a visit, and love everlasting visits a small Amish community and refuses to let go.

Can the couple from humble beginnings with deep roots find their place in the world

without losing sight of their values and what it means to be in a relationship?

What readers are saying about the Amish Hearts series:

★★★★★ *Sweet and clean. A throughly enjoyable read by an accomplished author who never disappoints. Family values, biblical foundations, and a story line with just enough "problems" to be considered real. The characters are relatable and I would recommend this story for anyone.*

Book 1: The Heart of Innocence
★★★★★ *This book is the sweetest Amish book I have read, thus far. It is filled with love, joy, growing pains and has a pleasant ending.*

★★★★★ *This was such a great family book full of drama in the home and in the community. (...) Super good book and I recommend this book to everyone that loves drama.*

★★★★★ *This book made me laugh and cry at the same time.*

Book 2: The Heart of Longing
★★★★★ *(...) It was one of those stories that was*

hard to put down and sometimes brought a tear to my eyes. I would highly recommend it.

★★★★★ *This book combines complex characters who grow throughout the story, causing their interactions to shift and their true natures -- positive or negative -- to be revealed. A complex story with a satisfying ending.*

Book 3: The Heart of Perseverance

★★★★★ *Awesome. What a great story and such great writing. It's the kind of story you can't put down. Every page made me hope it would turn out good.*

★★★★★ *Great book- I am looking forward to the next book in this series . Thanks so much for such a lovely book.*

★★★★★ *Such a sweet, well written story that was hard to put down!! Looking forward to the next one!*

Book 4: The Heart of Forgiveness

★★★★★ *Loved it. Good writing. Family and their closeness and sticking together in time if need.I will reccomend to friends always.*

★★★★★ *Great love and faith story. This story is so well written. I wasn't able to put this book down. In fact I read it all at once.*

FOREWORD

This book is dedicated to you, the reader.

Thank you for taking a chance on me, and for joining me on this journey.

Do you want to keep up to date with all of my latest releases, and **start reading *Secret Love* and *River Blessings*, exclusive spinoffs from the *Amish Hearts* and the *Amish Sisters series*, for free?**

Join my readers' group (copy and paste this link into your browser: *bit.ly/Grace-FreeBook*). Details can be found at the end of the book.

THE HEART OF INNOCENCE

BOOK DESCRIPTION

Jamesport, Missouri, early 1980s.

Betsie Hershberger's whole world is her little Amish village and her small family. The youngest of four sisters, she is the apple of their eye, and privy to all their secrets. When the circus comes to town, Betsie's overactive imagination risks getting her eldest sister in trouble, and harming an innocent friend.

Sarah Hershberger is responsible for her sisters since their mother's death. Her father, Leroy, relies on her to keep track of the house and his willful daughters while he works on the farm, but Sarah fears this dependence will leave no room for her to make a family of her own. Proving this fear well founded, Leroy detests the only man Sarah loves and forbids marriage.

Will Betsie save the day? Will Sarah convince her father to grant her the love she seeks? Or will the sisters end up in more trouble than they bargained for?

"Behold, children are a heritage from the LORD; the fruit of the womb is a reward."
~ Psalm 127:3

TALL TALES

"People are convinced he will win the nomination," Benjamin Lambright said. "Can you imagine it? Ronald Reagan, the next President of the United States, a movie star!" He hooked his thumbs in his suspenders and gave Betsie a teasing wink.

"Ben," Sarah Hershberger said. "You're boring her with your political talk."

"He's not!" Betsie cried.

Betsie Hershberger was a lot of things, but she was not a stupid child, and she disliked being treated like one. At eleven she was the shortest girl in her class, but she could outsmart them all at mathematics. She hitched up her school satchel, her brown curls bouncing on her back as she tried to keep up with the large strides of her adult companions. It was early morning, and the woods were cool. The sun winked at them through the leaves, its warmth hinting at the heat they could expect later in the day. Sarah and Ben were walking her to school. Normally Betsie wouldn't have wanted anyone to walk her anywhere, but this provided Sarah and Ben an opportunity to meet, and Betsie couldn't deny them that.

Benjamin Lambright worked on an *Englischer* farm on the other side of the river that marked the boundaries of the Amish village, so he found time for Sarah only in the early hours before the day started, and late at night when the day had finally come to a close. It also happened to be the only time Leroy Hershberger couldn't spot them together. Father of the Hershberger girls, he disapproved of Ben, much to Betsie's confusion.

Betsie thought about what Ben had said. She had never seen a Ronald Reagan movie, but her sister Kathy loved him. She had a secret stash of magazines under her bed. He was certainly handsome, but was that enough to make a good president? She wondered if Ben was pulling her leg, but she didn't think he would make a joke at her expense. Ben wasn't like most adults, he was funny and attentive, and he took her seriously.

"Ben." Betsie frowned. "Can you vote?"

"*Nee.*" Ben shrugged.

"Why not?"

"It goes against the *Ordnung,*" Ben explained, scratching the back of his tanned neck. They walked out of the woods into a large clearing where a squat school building stood in the middle. Betsie saw her classmates milling about the yard. "Besides, I don't have any interest in politics. I just pick up a lot of news from my *Englischer* boss."

"Useless information," Sarah muttered under her breath, tucking a loose strand of blond hair behind her ears. Betsie giggled.

"Well." Ben tilted his head, a furtive smile on his handsome face. "Not all information is useless. I have one interesting thing you might want to know."

"Humph." Sarah rolled her eyes.

"Would you like to know, beautiful Betsie?" Ben asked.

"*Ja!*" Betsie bounced on the balls of her feet.

"The circus is coming to town next week. Would you like to go?"

"The circus!" Betsie clapped her hands. "Can we go, Sarah? Can we?"

Sarah bit her lip, a sure sign that she was reluctant to agree. Her pale oval face was still, but her heavily lashed eyes darted from Ben to Betsie, agitated at the decision she had to make.

"They have clowns, cotton candy, and all sorts of animals doing tricks. James was telling me they even have an anaconda from the rainforest."

"What's an anaconda?" Betsie asked, her eyes so similar to Sarah's, wide with wonder.

"It's the largest snake in the world. It can grow as tall as the length of your fields."

Betsie's mouth hung open in shock.

"They even have motorized rides and," Ben grinned down at Sarah, "they even have Twinkies."

Sarah loved Twinkies but could never buy any from town. *Daed* didn't approve of Twinkies, just like he didn't approve of Ben Lambright. Sarah tried not to smile, but Ben's grin demanded reciprocation.

"Oh, all right," Sarah said. "But you have to promise not to tell *Daed* we found out from Ben." She paused and added, "Because if you do, he'll be furious with me." She was serious now.

"You know I won't tell." Betsie was earnest.

"Now run along and learn something," Sarah said, pushing Betsie gently.

"Unless you want to be like Sarah here," Ben said, tapping his finger against Sarah's temple.

"Ben," Sarah protested, swatting his hand away, but she was grinning and there was a warm glow in her eyes.

Betsie ran off in the schoolyard's direction, her satchel bouncing against her thin hips. At the edge of the yard, she looked back at the woods. Ben and Sarah were walking back up the path, fractured sunlight bouncing off their heads, their hands – one pale and delicate, the other tan and firm – held firmly together.

Betsie smiled at the sight and turned to join her friends. She knew Sarah and Ben loved each other very much. It was a shame that *Daed* didn't approve. Because of that, Sarah had to pretend she wasn't walking out with anybody. Betsie didn't understand why *Daed* disliked Ben so much, but she knew it would be stupid to ask him to change his mind. The last time anyone had mentioned Ben in the house, their father hadn't eaten supper or breakfast the next day.

Shaking her head to dismiss her thoughts, Betsie walked into the schoolyard. The younger children were playing a game of tag, while the eldest sat in groups, looking about the yard as if they were too old for such behavior. A large group of pupils was crowded around one of the benches in the yard, watching something Betsie couldn't see. The only person not interested in the gasping crowd close beside them was Samuel King. He was busy fixing a yellow pinwheel, his chestnut hair glowing fiery bronze under the morning sun.

"Betsie! Look at what I found," Susan Hostetler, a tall girl with buck teeth, stood at the heart of the crowd. She waved at her. Betsie came closer and her heart stopped for a moment. A snake was twisted around Susan's arm; a line of turmeric yellow ran through its khaki green scales. Betsie recognized it as a garden snake. You could easily find one near the woods and the river where they feasted on frogs. It was beautiful.

"It's just a common garden snake," Betsie said, flipping her hair behind her shoulders. "What's so special about that?"

"You're just jealous," Susan accused her.

"Jealous? Me?" Betsie's laugh was high and melodious. "Why would I be jealous of a common garden snake when an anaconda nearly killed me?"

The crowd gasped. Betsie was enjoying the attention. That would show up prissy Miss Susan for calling her jealous.

"That's a lie! You're a liar," Susan said.

"*Nee*," Betsie said with grave dignity. "It's no lie. I saw one at the circus when I was a *kinner*." Everyone was staring at her, waiting for her to continue. She smiled a little to herself. "I was only four, but I still remember the lights and the clowns. *Daed* bought me a cotton candy, and it was so sweet. But I got lost and wandered inside a tent. It was dark, and no one was there... or so I thought."

They were hanging on her every word. Even Susan seemed to have forgotten to look skeptical. Only Samuel King seemed indifferent to the whole affair. He hadn't even looked up once from his pinwheel, but Betsie didn't pay him much thought; no one ever did.

"The first thing I felt were the floorboards trembling," Betsie whispered, and the crowd leaned in closer. "The slithering movement echoed in the darkness. Then, suddenly, something brushed against my legs; something cold and clammy and HUGE!"

They all jumped back. Susan clutched her chest, the garden snake still twisted around her arm. Betsie stopped herself from laughing out loud. She loved captivating an audience.

"Before I knew what was happening it had twisted around my legs, and its tongue was hissing in my face," Betsie said.

"Did it bite you?" Nancy, a girl from the first form, asked. "Did you die?"

"Of course she didn't die," Mathew, a boy from the seventh form, snapped. "She's standing in front of you, isn't she?"

"How did you escape?" Susan asked.

"I was very lucky," Betsie said. "The lion in the next tent roared so loudly that the snake stopped what it was doing, giving me enough time to jam my cotton candy in the anaconda's mouth and poke a finger in one of his eyes. Then I ran and ran till I found my *Daed*."

"You were so brave!"

"Did it hurt after?"

"What color was he?"

"Did they kill it for trying to eat a little girl?"

"How big was it?"

"Was it as big a liar as you are?"

Betsie's smile faded. Isaac Hilty, tall, broad, and unpleasant, was sneering at her from amongst the crowd. His friends, the two Marks, Wittmar and Graber, mirrored his expressions.

"You've never been to a circus," Isaac said. "You just couldn't stand not being the center of attention, so you lied. *Gott* is watching Betsie Hershberger, and *Gott* will punish your sins!"

Betsie felt a retort rising up her throat, but she knew better than to argue with Isaac Hilty. In the senior-most class, Isaac was a mean boy who took pleasure in condemning them all to damnation for as little as forgetting to clear pencil shavings off the schoolroom floor.

"Admit it!" Isaac said, pointing an accusing finger at Betsie. "Admit your sin of lies and pride!"

Betsie was hopping mad. How dare Isaac Hilty make a spectacle of her? She decided to throw caution to the wind and tell him exactly what she thought of him. Yes, Isaac would complain to a teacher and then to her father, but it was only a minor story. How bad could the punishment be?

"It's not a lie."

Betsie, along with everyone in the yard, swung her head towards the boy sitting in the grass fixing the pinwheel. Samuel wiped his sweaty hands on his pants and then blew; the yellow paper flower became a spinning blur.

"What did you say?" Isaac asked, taking a threatening step towards Samuel.

"I said she's telling the truth," Samuel said, shrugging his shoulders. "I was there that year. They even had fireworks on the last day. I saw the anaconda, and one of the clowns told me to stay away from the tent after dark because a girl had nearly gotten eaten a few days earlier."

Betsie stared. Why was Samuel King, the boy who seldom talked to anyone because he didn't have any friends, defending her?

"You filthy little liar!" Isaac roared. He made to shove Samuel, but Betsie rushed to stand in between them.

"Leave him alone!" Betsie shouted. "You wanted the truth, and we gave it to you. Now go away or I'll tell a teacher!"

Isaac was panting, his chest rising and falling. He reminded Betsie of their angry bull, snorting and pawing the ground in the barn every morning.

"Are you sure you want to defend spineless Samuel? You wait till I tell Leroy about Ben," Isaac's smile was cruel. "I saw him walking with Sarah in the woods. Did you think we couldn't see you that far away? You'll be sorry you stood up for the likes of him."

Betsie's heart sank. Would Isaac really tell *Daed* about Ben walking with Sarah? *Daed* would be furious. Betsie considered stepping away and letting Isaac have his way with Samuel. What did Samuel mean to her anyway? Sarah would be hurt and upset if *Daed* found out about Ben, and he would refuse to take her to the circus.

But before she could decide, the school bell clanged. The crowd of pupils dispersed, and Isaac Hilty gave her one last dirty look and went to join the throng heading inside. Samuel didn't wait for her to say anything but shuffled inside as well, his shoulders hunched.

Betsie felt sorry for him. She had always thought Samuel was odd and quiet. She realized that she wouldn't have let Isaac bully him, not because giving in to Isaac's threats would have given the bully power over her, but because it was the right thing to do. Samuel had helped her out when he had no reason to. This was the least she could do.

She kept glancing at Samuel throughout the morning lessons, but he never turned to look at her once. She wanted to mouth thank you, and she expected a thank you back, but the boy refused to look anywhere but at the blackboard. Frustrated with his lack of gratitude, she tore a small piece of paper and scribbled "Thank you" on it. She folded it once, twice, thrice, then made sure all the teachers were busy.

"Pssst!" She leaned forward, waving the note in front of Samuel's face. Susan, who sat between them, stared. "Hey," Betsie whispered. "Take it! Take it!"

"Take what, Miss Hershberger?"

Miss Diane Troyer, spectacles perched on her hooked nose, looked down at Betsie. She was the strictest teacher they had, her thin mouth never lifting into a smile. She was frowning now, her hand outstretched for the note.

"Hand it over," Miss Troyer said.

Betsie did so, her heart thundering against her ribs. First Isaac threatening to tell *Daed* about Sarah and Ben, and now getting caught passing notes by Miss Troyer; she was in big trouble.

MEN'S WORK

"And then she made me write a hundred lines during recess," Betsie huffed.

Her sister, Kathy, pumped water while Betsie cleaned her hands and face. She could still feel a thin residue of chalk dust all over her skin. Miriam, their other sister, was lying in the grass beside the hand pump, her hand behind her head. She was chewing on a straw of hay, her pale green eyes following the clouds.

"But that's not the worst part."

"What's the worst part?" Kathy asked. Her cheeks were flushed with the effort. She was sixteen, the most beautiful of all the sisters, with dark blue eyes in a pale heart-shaped face. She was also the most dramatic. She loved watching movies and had already watched six pictures in the first three months of her *Rumspringa*. Her *Englischer* friend, Julia, had a VCR at home, but Kathy had been too afraid to ask *Daed* for permission to go.

"Isaac Hilty said he'd tell *Daed* about Ben and Sarah," Betsie said.

Kathy gasped, her hand clutching her throat. Miriam only snorted.

"That Isaac Hilty is all bark and no bite," Miriam said. "He once said he'd tell *Daed* that I'd been picking plums from his family's gardens. I put such a fear of *Gott* in him, he was crying by the time I was done."

"But Miriam," Kathy lifted her *kapp* to scratch her sweaty scalp. "You're so brave and big. Betsie is only eleven."

"She'll be in her *Rumspringa* in another five years," Miriam shrugged. "She should learn how to hold her own ground."

Betsie thought about this as she finished scraping the last of the chalk from under her nails. Miriam was nineteen and fresh out of her *Rumspringa*. She had taken the most time out of anyone in the village before being baptized into the faith. Betsie knew it had worried *Daed,* but he had said nothing to Miriam. When it came to Miriam, *Daed* had a soft spot, and he showed lenience in most matters the others got in trouble for. Maybe it was because she had been the one who had found their mother the morning she had died.

Betsie had only been six at the time her mother had died, but she knew their mother had been ill for a long time, her health failing her day by day. Miriam had been up early that day, and she made breakfast for their mother.

Betsie could see it in her mind's eye: fourteen-year-old Miriam, tall and gangling, cooking porridge on the stove in her nightdress, her tongue sticking out of her mouth as she concentrated. She could also imagine the pride on her sister's face for finally being able to do something for their mother.

The house had woken to Miriam's wails. Their mother had passed away in the time it had taken Miriam to make porridge. Miriam hadn't cried since that day and the Hershbergers had grown an aversion to gloopy breakfast food.

"There," Kathy said, stepping back from the hand pump. "You're all clean and I'm late."

"Which movie are you going to see today?" Betsie asked.

"*The Empire Strikes Back*," Kathy said. "Julia says it is very Christian."

"Really?" Miriam chuckled in disbelief.

"Well, if you dismiss all the magic and the aliens, it's the Biblical story of overcoming evil." Kathy grinned. "Do you have five dollars?"

"Didn't you sell the eggs yesterday?" Miriam asked.

"*Ja*," Kathy said. "And I got ten dollars for them at the grocery store."

"That's enough for a movie and snacks, surely," Miriam said.

"Dolores said we might go for an early dinner afterwards at the diner," Kathy said.

"Dolores and her diner." Miriam rolled her eyes. "If she doesn't watch it, she'll be as big as her house soon."

Betsie giggled at the thought of Dolores Miller's legs sticking out of her front windows, her head pushing against the ceiling. Miriam took out her own fat wallet and handed Kathy ten dollars.

"Buy a few glazed doughnuts for Betsie," she said, winking.

"*Denke*," Kathy and Betsie said in unison.

Once Kathy left, Miriam made Betsie a few sandwiches to eat. Miriam refused to cook anything on the stove, and since Sarah was in town with *Daed* selling her quilts to a local merchant, sandwiches and fruit were all that was on offer. Betsie washed them down with a glass of milk, then stared across the table at Miriam.

"Do we have chores?" Betsie asked.

"I was supposed to mend *Daed's* socks," Miriam grimaced. "But I'd rather muck out the stalls."

Betsie made a face.

"It's not so bad," Miriam laughed. "The cows are friendly, it just the bull you have to beware of."

"It's stinky work," Betsie complained.

"At least it's proper work," Miriam said. "Come on," she urged, "We will spare *Daed* the extra chore and he'll be pleased we helped with the farm. He struggles on it alone."

Betsie bit her lip.

"But I'll ruin my dress," she said.

"Oh, I have just the thing for that," Miriam said, clapping her hands. She rushed out of the room and came back after a few minutes with a pair of old breeches and a small shirt. "These were *Daed's* when he was younger. Go on, put them on."

Betsie did as she was told. The pants felt comfortable, but she felt exposed. Miriam put on a pair of pants and a shirt as well, and they trudged out to the barn. The only time Betsie was allowed in the barn was early in the morning with Sarah to milk the cows. The bull frightened her a little with its snorting.

Daed was very strict about the chores. The girls were supposed to keep to the house and leave the fields and the barn to him. They could milk the cows, feed the hens, and collect the eggs, but the rest was a man's job, and they were not men.

Miriam handed her a small trowel and took the shovel herself. Betsie had to cover her face with a handkerchief to stop herself from gagging on the stink. They started from the back, far away from the bull, mucking out stall after stall, sweat trickling down their faces. Miriam was animated, singing songs and making jokes, and Betsie re-laxed as well. The bull grunted and pawed the ground, getting agitated by the minute as they ap-proached his stall.

Throwing caution to the wind, Betsie decided to show Miriam the trick she had learned the other day when she had been milking the cows. She walked up to the stall of Sadie, the most sweet-tempered of their cows, and dragged the milking stool by her side.

"Look, Miriam," Betsie said, climbing on top of the cow in the second-to-last stall. "I'm in the circus!"

"Be careful, Betsie," Miriam warned.

"I'm doing it! I'm doing it!" Betsie laughed, balancing herself on one leg. The cow shifted slightly and Betsie lost her balance. She swayed one way, then forward, and before she knew what was happening, she had tilted off the cow and into the next stall. Her face smacked against the sweaty hide of the bull, and she landed on her back in the vile muck on the floor.

Betsie screamed. The bull snorted and roared, its eyes rolling in its head. It backed up, ready to charge. Fear paralyzed Betsie, her eyes wide and staring, a scream lodged in her throat so she couldn't breathe.

"Betsie!" she heard Miriam scream from a great distance, but it was enough to snap her out of her trance. She ran towards the stall door. It was locked from the outside, but her adrenaline made her agile, and she jumped up till she hooked one foot over the top of the door. Scrambling with her hands and feet, she found purchase and lifted herself up just as the bull struck the door, jarring her entire body with its impact. Miriam grabbed her by the waist and pulled her down on the barn floor to safety.

"You're safe!" Miriam whispered, her voice hoarse. "You're safe!"

"What is going on here?"

Betsie's heart lurched. Leroy Hershberger, tall, blond, and frowning, stood with his arms akimbo in the barn door. His gaze took in Betsie's soiled clothes, his frown deepened, and he took a step forward. The bull slammed its horns against the stall door. Betsie screamed.

BEDTIME STORIES

"It's not her fault, *Daed*," Miriam said. "It was my idea to clean the stalls."

"She is not a child, Miriam!" Leroy said. "She should take responsibility for her own actions."

"What's wrong?" Sarah had arrived. She took one look at Betsie's soiled breeches and their father's thunderous expression and rushed forward. "Betsie, are you okay?"

"The bull is in a fit state!" Leroy thundered. "It will take ages to calm it down."

"She was only trying to help, *Daed*," Sarah said. "You work so hard and Betsie sees how much it's affecting your health. You can't blame her for trying to lighten your load."

Leroy frowned but said nothing. He turned

towards the bull's stall and began chucking hay inside. The bull snorted, but it had calmed greatly after hearing Leroy's voice. Sarah winked at Betsie, and Betsie felt a little better about the whole incident. Miriam pushed Betsie off her lap and gestured for her to follow her outside. Betsie all but ran out of the barn, her sisters by her side.

For the rest of the day, Betsie tried to avoid Leroy as much as she could. She took a long bath and allowed Sarah to scrub her till she was pink, but she could still detect a faint smell of manure from her skin. Leroy wasn't present at dinner, so Sarah left him a plate of food in the oven. This wasn't unusual because the farm kept Leroy out of the house most nights.

Kathy came back home just after dinner, a pink box of glazed doughnuts in her hands. Betsie's mouth watered, but she ignored the box and went directly to bed. After the events of the day, she didn't think she deserved sweet treats. A part of her blamed Miriam, but if she were honest, she blamed Leroy. For as long as she could remember Leroy had been busy with the farm, spending day and night on planting, harvesting, and caring for the barn animals. His parenting was distracted, and when he did focus on his daughters, it was a harsh comment here, a snide remark there, and nothing more. The girls weren't allowed to help, so they felt isolated from their father.

Betsie wished their mother was still alive.

"Betsie?"

Sarah slid under the covers, Miriam sat on the other side, and Kathy plopped down at the foot of the bed, the box of doughnuts in her lap. She lifted the cover to show Betsie the perfectly glazed doughnuts, twinkling in the candlelight.

"I'm not hungry," Betsie said.

"Betsie not hungry for sweets?" Kathy's mouth opened in surprise. "Are you running a fever?"

"Don't be upset about what happened in the barn," Sarah said, brushing the hair off Betsie's brow.

"It wasn't your fault," Miriam said, pinching her cheek. "*Daed* knows that. He just gets agitated because of the stress he's under."

"But I added to that stress," Betsie whined. "I wanted to help take some away."

"There's what we want and what *Gott* wills." Sarah shrugged. "You can't fight against *Gott's* will."

"Besides," Kathy said, pushing the box under Betsie's nose. "You've already been punished enough today, why punish yourself some more?

Eat the doughnuts before I do!" she threatened, her smile toothy and mischievous.

Betsie took a large bite, savoring the taste of fried dough and licking the sweet glaze off her lips.

"Why doesn't he let us help?" she asked, after she had devoured the first of her doughnuts. "It's not like girls don't help around the farm and on the field. Susan helps thresh during the harvest, and she makes fun of me for being lazy."

Sarah and Miriam exchanged looks.

"Why does he hate us?" Betsie cried, her doughnut dropping out of her hand and back in its box. Kathy put the box aside and hugged Betsie. Sarah and Miriam let her cry it out, then helped her under the covers. Betsie sniffled, looking up at the faces of her sisters.

"He doesn't hate us," Miriam said. "He fears overworking us."

"It's because of *Mamm*," Sarah said, laying a cool hand on Betsie's cheek. "She used to help him out in the field and the barn. She kept working even though she grew weaker and weaker."

"He thinks he could have stopped her dying if he hadn't made her do all that work," Kathy finished.

"But that's silly," Betsie said.

"*Ja.*" Miriam kissed her forehead. "But we all have silly ways of coping when our loved ones leave us." Her face looked paler in the dim light, her eyes hooded. "Don't think about it too much. I promise *Daed* will have forgotten about it by breakfast."

She waved and walked towards the bedroom door.

"Save some doughnuts for breakfast," Kathy said, getting up and following Miriam. "Don't eat them all up in the night."

Sarah tucked Betsie in and blew out the candle.

"Sarah," Betsie said, taking her sister's hand. "I have to tell you something."

Sarah sat back down, and Betsie's throat went dry. Breath felt like sandpaper rubbing against her throat.

"I did something bad today," she said, licking her lips. "I told a lie, and Isaac Hilty said he would tell *Daed* about Ben. He saw us at the edge of the woods."

Sarah sat still. Tears stung Betsie's eyes.

"It was naughty of me, and I shouldn't have," Betsie confessed, "but it was also Samuel King's fault! He shouldn't have said my lie was true. I think Isaac hated that more than anything. And then I was forced to defend Samuel, and that just made it worse!"

"Hold on," Sarah interrupted. "What lie? What are you talking about?"

Betsie told her from the beginning. Her heart raced, but she steeled herself for Sarah's cutting disappointment. She owed her sister the truth, even if it meant Sarah would hate her forever.

"It's all my fault, and I'm sorry," Betsie said in a small voice.

"Oh, Betsie," Sarah sighed. "What are we going to do with you?"

"I'll make it up to you, I promise," Betsie sobbed. "I'll go and apologize to Isaac and tell him to punish me, not you."

"You will do no such thing," Sarah said, and Betsie could make out a deep frown on her face in the moonlight. "Isaac Hilty is a bully, and Hershbergers don't give in to a bully's demands." She pinched the bridge of her nose, and Betsie knew her sister was thinking hard. "I'm not angry, and Isaac's threats don't bother me. What does bother me is that you think defending Samuel King was the wrong thing to do."

Betsie chewed the inside of her cheek.

"He's just so strange," Betsie said. "He doesn't

talk to anyone and keeps fiddling with junk. He wouldn't even take my note and that got me in trouble with the teachers!"

"Be that as it may," Sarah said, "he took your side in an argument he did not need to get into. It shows courage, and care for you, the perfect recipe for a friend."

"Like Ben?"

"Like Ben."

"Sarah?" Betsie bit her lip. "Why is Ben a secret?"

Sarah was quiet for so long, Betsie thought she would not answer.

"You remember Arthur Yoder?" Sarah asked.

"*Ja*," Betsie nodded. Arthur had been Sarah's friend. He had moved to another Amish town a few years ago. "But what does he have to do with Ben?"

"I'll explain," Sarah said. "Arthur had to move to another town because his *Daed* didn't get to inherit the farm, remember?"

"*Ja*," Betsie nodded. "Libby Yoder's *Daed* got the farm."

"Just like our *Daed* inherited this farm from *Grossdaed*." Sarah picked at a loose thread on Betsie's bedspread. "Most men only give the farm to one of their sons, the rest having to find land for themselves. The Lambright men are a bit strange like that. Ben's *Grossdaed* had five sons, and he divided his land among them. Ben's *Daed*, Obadiah, has done the same, and he has four sons of his own. That leaves Ben only a small parcel of land that he can't even erect a barn on."

"Oh," Betsie frowned. "Is that why *Daed* doesn't like him, because he doesn't have any land?"

"Partly," Sarah said. "What *Daed* dislikes is what he considers disloyalty on Ben's part. You see *Daed* in the fields, slaving away on the farm on his own. He thinks Ben should offer out his services to Amish men, on Amish farms, rather than help *Englischers* line their pockets with fat profits because they pay more."

Betsie considered this a moment and had to agree. They had been taught since they were young that community was what made the Amish way work. Everyone had to do their part or else the whole village would fail.

"*Daed* thinks he's a traitor," Betsie said.

Sarah chuckled. "*Nee*, he thinks Ben is unreliable," she shook her head, "but it's not like that at all. Ben is a proud man, he wants to be able to buy land for himself and build his own barn. The way the community works, they will provide him with funds, but Ben wants to do it on his own merit. I know that might sound arrogant, and not a trait worthy of an Amish man, but that is who Ben is, and I love him for having a purpose he's passionate about."

Betsie chewed on that information, her mind whirring over the two men and how different, yet alike, they were.

"I'll try to make *Daed* see the Ben we know, Sarah," Betsie promised. "I don't know how yet, but I'll think of something. Leave it to me."

Sarah chuckled.

"And Sarah…"

"*Ja*, beautiful Betsie?" Sarah kissed her little sister's forehead.

"Don't have more than one son, please," Betsie said. "You can have as many daughters as you want."

Sarah burst out laughing. She patted Betsie on the arm and wished her a good night. Betsie lay awake for a little while longer, a small smile playing across her lips as she thought of Sarah and Ben, and their children. She was drifting off to sleep when her mind turned to school the next day and Samuel King. Her mouth opened wide in a yawn and she snuggled deep in her pillow. She dreamed of yellow pinwheels.

A HERD OF COWS AND MILK

The wind was like a solid hand, slapping against her cheeks. Betsie could feel sweat trickle down her back, and she couldn't wait to get home and jump in a cool bath. Her satchel bounced against her hips as she sprinted across the Wittmar fields, but she didn't seem to notice. Her mind was on the foolish mistake she'd made during recess earlier in the day.

The entire school had been out in the yard, most of the children playing. Samuel hadn't been in school that day. Betsie had been sitting with her friends, talking about the new hymn they had learned. Isaac Hilty had been only a few feet away, talking to David Stoltzfus, a young boy Betsie's age. David was usually bright and friendly but he had looked nervous in Isaac's presence. Betsie had kept glancing in their direction, her ears pricked up when she heard them mention Samuel King.

"… you encourage him to sin," Betsie had heard Isaac saying. "You might think you're helping him, but you're only making things worse for him with *Gott*."

"It's harmless really," David had stammered. "What could a few handmade toys do?"

"It's not about what they can do," Isaac had snapped, "it's about what he will do next if this is allowed to go on."

"Why don't you worry about your own soul and leave the rest well enough alone?" Betsie had asked, her eyebrows raised archly. "I'm sure *Gott* will only judge you by your actions."

"You stay out of this if you know what's good for you," Isaac had warned.

She should have heeded the warning; she should have shut her mouth. But a deep anger had taken hold of her. She was quite sick and tired of Isaac telling everyone what to do.

"I think you're jealous," Betsie had said, rubbing her chin as if inspecting Isaac. "You're green with envy because you can't do half the things

Samuel can do. Are you saying *Gott* made a mistake giving Samuel talent?"

Isaac had taken a threatening step towards her, but the bell had rung and they had all filed inside the school. She had left quickly after the last bell had rung, dismissing the pupils for the day.

Now she was rushing home before Isaac Hilty caught up with her.

"There she is!" Mark Wittmar cried from across the field. "I told you she crosses our fields every day."

Betsie's throat constricted in panic. She ran. Heavy footsteps thundered after her. She found the dirt path and ran blindly, glancing over her shoulder to see Isaac Hilty, and the Marks, Wittmar and Graber, running after her. She faced front and put on a spurt of speed, only to smack into a cow. The collision forced her back; she lost her balance and landed on her bottom in the dirt path.

Cows lowed and came to a standstill around her. Betsie rubbed her bottom and got up. She stood amongst the herd and watched Isaac Hilty and his friends as they came cautiously forward. The village had a communal pasture near the woods, and it was common for farmers to herd their cows there according to a strict schedule. For Betsie, a herd meant an adult, and no matter how sure Isaac was of his judgment, Betsie knew he'd think twice before hitting a girl in front of adults.

"Betsie?"

A hat jammed on his auburn hair, his sleeves rolled up, Samuel King walked out of the herd and crouched down in front of Betsie. She saw him look from her to Isaac and the Marks, and understanding dawn in his hazel eyes. A calf from the herd tried to eat his hat, but he just waved its mouth away.

"*Gott* sure works in mysterious ways," Isaac tittered. "He has sent us the opportunity to chastise both culprits."

"What?" Samuel's eyes darted from the three boys to Betsie, who had come to stand beside him. The herd, deciding that the children weren't a stop for food, or remotely interesting, had moved on towards the pastures. Betsie could see Samuel's mind working behind his eyes. He was looking at the paths that led into the fields and sizing up the boys. Samuel was nothing if not resourceful.

"You can run along now, Betsie," Isaac warned.

"Let us deal with Samuel and you will be forgiven for your sins."

This was it. The choice was in front of her. Run and stay safe from the fists and ridicule of Isaac Hilty, or defend Samuel King and be condemned forever? In the end, it wasn't really a choice at all. Betsie took a step forward and stood her ground, her chin lifted in defiance.

"Don't say I didn't warn you," Isaac said, a nasty smile blooming on his lips.

He stepped forward, his eager fists coming up in front of him. Betsie tensed, her own hands going up in front of her face as both a defense and a weapon. Samuel placed a hand on her shoulder. Betsie glanced his way. He was smiling serenely.

"What's going on here?"

The growl was low and acerbic. It made Betsie's blood run cold. She whipped around so fast she cracked her neck. Melvin King was tall, his auburn beard riddled with gray strands that matched the steel gray of his eyes. He was the spitting image of Samuel, only he didn't radiate warmth like his son. Betsie had always felt skittish whenever Melvin's gaze landed on her during church services. It felt like being watched by a large, thin spider.

"I asked you a question!" Melvin barked and all the children flinched. Isaac's face drained of color, and Betsie's own teeth chattered. Melvin was not an adult you messed with under any circumstances. He had never raised his hand, nor punished anyone that Betsie knew of, but there was something forbidding about him that warned children off.

"They were just asking why I wasn't in school today," Samuel said. "They were concerned."

Samuel winked discreetly. His courage astounded Betsie. If Melvin had been frowning at her like that she wouldn't have been able to string two words together.

"They should concern themselves with their own business," Melvin spat. "My son has chores to attend to. He can't afford to go to school every day and gad about like the rest of you. Now get going!"

Isaac and his friends didn't have to be told twice. They turned and ran through the Wittmar fields. Betsie was still rooted to the ground. She wanted to run, but she was also afraid to leave Samuel alone. Her brain screamed that she was being stupid; why would Samuel be in danger alone with his own father? But a feeling at the back of her head persisted.

"And what do you need, miss?" Melvin growled, turning the force of his malevolent stare on Betsie. "A special invitation?"

"*Nee,* Mr. King," Betsie whispered, gave Samuel an apologetic look, and ran as fast as her feet could carry her. She glanced back from a safe distance. Samuel stood, his shoulders slumped, his head bent low while Melvin towered over him like a black crow superimposed upon the sun.

"OUCH!" Kathy hissed. "Miriam, your foot is digging in my back."

"Well, your hair is tickling my nose," Miriam sniffled.

"You're talking too loud!" Betsie warned. "*Daed* will wake up."

Kathy and Miriam settled back in Sarah's bed, Betsie between them. The moon was full tonight and bathed the floor silver. Sarah was bathed in moonlight as she looked out of the window for Ben's signal, a clutch of violets pinned to her apron. She was meeting Ben for a walk tonight and the sisters had agreed to stay up till she returned in case their father woke up and found her out of bed.

"He's late," Miriam yawned.

"Will you be back soon?" Kathy rubbed her tired eyes.

"I'll only be gone half an hour," Sarah said, distracted. "There he is!"

A wide smile bloomed across her face and it made Betsie's heart glad to see her sister so happy. Betsie wondered if she would ever find someone to love like that. She hoped so. Betsie watched Sarah go through the bedroom door and towards the kitchen, which had the only back door to the house. Sure that Sarah had gone, Betsie snuggled deep in bed. Miriam and Kathy whispered about Kathy's day in town, and Betsie felt waves of sleep stealing over her eyes.

CRASH!

Betsie sat bolt upright in bed. Miriam and Kathy had stopped breathing. They waited, not entirely sure what they were waiting for, and then the other shoe dropped. Leroy's bedroom door banged open. They heard his hurried footsteps rush to the sound of the crash.

Betsie panicked. If *Daed* caught Sarah, he would make sure Ben and Sarah never met again. She didn't think, she just jumped out of bed and tiptoed quietly towards the kitchen, where she could see a light. She peeked inside the kitchen.

Leroy, his hair disheveled, the side of his face crumpled and lined from his pillow, was looking blearily at Sarah and the stool that had fallen to the floor. Sarah was as white as a sheet, stammering incoherently.

"What are you doing in the kitchen this late at night?" Leroy asked.

"I... I... this..." Sarah stammered.

"Sarah!" Betsie wailed. She walked into the kitchen rubbing her eyes, pretending to have been disturbed in her sleep. "Is the milk ready yet?"

Leroy stared at her as if he didn't understand who she was for a minute. Sarah was just as wide-eyed and open-mouthed.

"I had a nightmare," Betsie whimpered. "I'm sorry."

Leroy frowned and looked from Sarah to Betsie.

"I was just making her some warm milk to help her fall asleep," Sarah said, finally cottoning on. "I accidentally bumped into the stool in the dark."

"Oh," Leroy said. He swayed slightly on the spot, then shook his head to regain consciousness. "Okay." He turned to get back to bed and Betsie breathed a sigh of relief. At the kitchen door Leroy stopped and turned around, a small frown on his face. He glanced at Sarah's face, then at her lapel. Betsie froze. Sarah swallowed and turned towards the stove, and Betsie hoped Leroy hadn't noticed the violets. "*Gut* night," he said, and left for bed.

"*Denke*," Sarah whispered.

Betsie put the stool upright and waved Sarah out of the house. Her heart hammered against her ribs and she hoped their father would sleep through the night and not get suspicious. She crawled back in bed and prayed for *Gott* to forgive her lie. It was well intentioned, and she hoped it counted for something.

When she woke up in the morning, it was in her own bed. Miriam must have moved her last night. Betsie scrambled out of the covers and looked for her shoes. Did Sarah make it back alright, or did *Daed* suspect something?

She found Sarah humming as she made breakfast in the kitchen. Kathy was holding a bowl in her hands, sleeping with her eyes wide open, and, sitting beside her at the table, Miriam was rubbing her face to wake it up. Leroy was the only one wide awake, his suspicious gaze fixed on Sarah.

DINNER FOR SIX

The house smelled of roasting chicken. Sarah mashed boiled potatoes with butter and chives while Miriam set the dinner table, Kathy made a pitcher of lemonade, and Betsie brought out the dinner rolls from the pantry.

Sarah wiped the fine sheen of sweat from her upper lip and glanced at the clock. It was nearly seven in the evening. *Daed* would bring in George Lengacher for dinner any minute. It had surprised Sarah when Leroy had instructed her to make a nice dinner tonight. Leroy hardly ever invited people over for a meal, especially during the summer. Sarah had pondered over who it could be all day and had been shocked to see their neighbor George Lengacher at their door.

"Why does he smell so bad?" Betsie asked, placing the rolls in a basket at the kitchen counter.

"Betsie!" Sarah admonished. "That's not a gracious thing to say."

"It's true though," Miriam said, popping a strawberry in her mouth.

"It's still not nice to say," Sarah said shortly. "And those are for dessert."

"I expect it's because he farms pigs," Kathy said, her face screwed up in deep thought. "That, and he doesn't shower much."

"Do you think the stench got to his late wife?" Miriam asked conversationally.

Sarah gaped at her sisters, horrified. Miriam had always been strange, but Kathy was becoming exactly the same. Their humor was so dry at times Sarah couldn't tell if they were joking or not. She knew it was highly inappropriate and she should put a stop to it, but she didn't have the heart to deny them the little pleasure they had in life.

After their mother had passed away Sarah was the closest thing to a maternal figure they had. Leroy's parenting was at best lenient, at worst negligent. He didn't have more than a fleeting impression of each of his daughters. He was so busy with the farm he hardly had time to be a parent.

"Can you die of bad smells?" Betsie asked. Sarah had to stop herself from laughing. There was no hint of horror in her youngest sister's eyes, just a bright curiosity. She loved Betsie dearly and took pride in her fearlessness.

"Hush, they're here!" Kathy whispered.

The front door opened and Leroy ushered George Lengacher inside. They had stepped outside to inspect the barley crop before the light faded. George sniffed and smiled at Sarah, his thin beard quivering with every twitch of his face.

"That smells delicious, Sarah," he said. His snaggletooth smile distracted from his wide nose. "I can't wait to dig in."

Sarah gave a weak smile and fetched the roasted chickens out of the oven. They said grace and dinner began. Sarah tried not to look directly across the table as she ate. Not that she disliked George Lengacher; he had been their neighbor for as long as she could remember and had been friendly and kind. It was Leroy's sudden change of heart.

Leroy wasn't a friendly neighbor. He liked to

keep himself to himself. So why the sudden warmth and the invitation to dinner? Why was he laughing at every weak joke George made and why did he keep looking at Sarah like that when George complimented her cooking or her house-keeping?

Dinner over, Sarah stacked the dishes up in the sink, ready to be washed. Water was boiling on the stove for *kaffe* and Sarah looked forward to the meal ending so she could go to bed. She was pouring *kaffe* in the mugs when Leroy walked into the kitchen, a large smile on his face.

"That was excellent, *dochder*," Leroy said, rubbing his hands in delight. "You did really well."

"I'm glad you're pleased, *Daed*," Sarah said, handing him a mug.

"I'm more than pleased," Leroy blew on the steaming liquid. "I'm thrilled and relieved. I have long worried about you and how you don't seem to attract any suitors, and after I saw you wearing flowers to bed, it broke my heart to see you slave away and not have any happiness of your own. But you don't have to worry about any of that anymore. George has agreed to marry you."

The mug Sarah was holding fell to the floor with a crash. Boiling *kaffe* splashed Sarah's shoes and soaked them. She didn't feel her skin scald; she was too worried about what her father had just said.

"What's the matter?" Leroy placed his mug on the counter and touched Sarah's arm. She could see the concern in his face but it only made her furious. How could a father be so blind to his children's desires?

"He's so old, *Daed*," Sarah said, trying hard to fight the trembling of her lips.

"*Ja*," Leroy said. "That's true. But I thought you wanted to get married. George is not the best choice but you will be next door, close to your sisters and me. He is also a kind man, which is what a woman should look for in a husband."

"But I don't want to marry for marriage's sake," Sarah protested. Tears threatened to fall, but she controlled them. "I want to marry someone I love."

The warmth left Leroy's eyes as if storm clouds had hidden the sun. His mouth pressed into a thin line.

"You're not still thinking about Ben Lambright, are you?"

Sarah pursed her lips, her gaze just as flinty as his.

"Take any thought you have of marrying Ben and put it out of your mind," Leroy said in clipped tones. "I won't give any of my daughters to a traitor like him."

"He is not a traitor."

"Isn't he? And what do you call working for *Englischer* farmers? The money he earns is tainted by *Englischer* profiteering."

"Oh, *Daed*, be realistic." Sarah tried to salvage the situation. "If taking wages from an *Englischer* is to be frowned upon than why do we sell them our eggs and milk?"

"That's different," Leroy said, his jaw jutting out.

"How is it different?" Sarah pressed on. "The *Englischer* uses the same profiteering money to buy our eggs and milk. Why is it okay for us to do this and not for Ben?"

"I will not have my *dochder* argue with me in my own home!" Leroy slapped his palm down on the counter. The mug of *kaffe* wobbled but didn't tip over. "You will not marry Ben Lambright, and that's the end of it."

"I won't marry George either," Sarah said with equal ferocity. "So you can tell him *nee*."

"Fine! Stay a spinster then, if you like," Leroy

said, turning his back to her. "I would rather see you an old maid than married to a man who will betray you for a higher profit."

Leroy stormed out of the kitchen, leaving Sarah the privacy she needed to let her tears fall.

BITTER DISAPPOINTMENT

It was here. She had seen it. Red, blue, and white, the main tent was larger than anything Betsie had ever seen. The Ferris wheel touched the belly of the sky and the smell of frying food hung in the air. Betsie skipped down the path leading to the river. She had spent her morning delivering eggs to town with Kathy. She had seen the circus, and now she couldn't wait to tell everyone.

It was a Saturday and school was off for the day. The children usually congregated near the river in the summer. Betsie hummed a song as she jumped over a stone in the path, already planning the rides she would take, and estimating how much money she had and if Miriam would loan her some from her considerable savings.

The woods thinned, but Betsie heard the children before she saw them. Some were fishing a little up the river; a few adults in their *Rumspringa* were enjoying a picnic under a large tree. Betsie's friends were sitting by the edge of the river, their feet dangling in the water.

"You have feathers in your hair."

Betsie startled so badly she nearly lost her footing. Samuel King was sitting in the twisted roots of a nearby tree. He was fiddling with what looked like tiny rubber tires and strange metal wheels.

"What are you doing?" Betsie asked.

"I'm trying to make a toy car," Samuel said, his tongue sticking out as he concentrated. "You still have feathers in your hair."

"What?" Betsie brushed her hair absently. "I was in the chicken coop this morning."

Samuel said nothing. Betsie watched him fiddle for a while. Watching him work was fascinating. It was like solving a puzzle, his deft fingers twisting, bending, and detaching each piece as he felt for their right place in the toy's scheme.

"Betsie!" Susan called from near the water. "Betsie, come on!"

Betsie turned away reluctantly. Samuel glanced up at her. He shook his head.

"What?" Betsie asked, curious about what he was thinking.

Samuel got up and brushed the seat of his pants. He walked forward, and before Betsie knew what he was doing, he plucked a feather from Betsie's hair.

"You missed one," he said, placing the feather in her hand.

"Betsie!"

"I'm coming!" Betsie called. She turned around to thank Samuel, but he was jogging up the path into the woods. It was typical of Samuel to come where the rest of the village was gathered and keep his distance, like he wanted to be a part of them but lacked the courage to walk the three feet it would take to join them. A little annoyed by his hasty retreat, Betsie shrugged and joined her friends.

"Where have you been all day?" Susan asked.

"I was in town," Betsie said, taking off her shoes and socks, dipping her toes in the warm water. "I saw the circus," she smiled like the cat who ate the cream. "It's finally here."

"Too bad none of us will get to see it," little

Dolly Yoder said, chewing on a strand of her dark hair.

"Isn't your *Daed* taking you?" Betsie asked, feeling sympathy for the little girl.

"*Nee*," Susan said, "you don't understand. None of our *Daeds* are taking us. The elders have forbidden it."

"What?" Betsie was shocked. The balloon of excitement that had been growing inside her popped, leaving a deflated husk in its place. "But why?"

"They said it was temptation," Dolly said.

Betsie looked around at the morose faces and a thought occurred to her. What if her friends were lying to her? Susan must have put them up to it to get back at Betsie for stealing her thunder the other day with the anaconda story.

"I'm going home," Betsie said, turning her nose up in the air. If this was how they were going to treat her, she would not play with them anymore. She ran all the way home till her lungs were on fire. She burst through the back door and bumped into Sarah.

"Where's the fire?" Sarah asked. Her eyes were puffy, and her face a little swollen. Betsie thought she might be ill.

"Did the elders forbid the circus?" Betsie

asked, gasping for breath as she clutched the stitch in her side. She searched for a smile, or a reassuring shake of the head, but Sarah's face was impassive.

"*Ja*, they did," Sarah said, folding a tea towel. "Miriam told me this morning."

"But why?" Betsie wailed. "Why would they do that?"

"They fear the circus will lead to temptation," Sarah said matter-of-factly, pulling out the risen dough from the cupboard nearest the oven.

"But that's ridiculous!"

"Not really," Sarah shrugged, stirring the contents of a saucepan on the stove. "We are forbidden to join in the town's Christmas celebrations. The principle is the same."

"That's different." Betsie stomped her foot.

"Is it really?" Sarah shouted, striking the spoon against the pan in anger. "Just because you want to go means we should change the rules?" Her eyes were blazing, her cheeks crimson. Betsie had never seen Sarah so angry. "Why does everything have to be about you, the way you want it? Life isn't fair, it's cruel and painful and the sooner you accept that the better for you."

Sarah burst into tears. She turned away so Betsie couldn't see her crying. Betsie rushed forward and hugged Sarah from behind. Her heart was hammering in her chest from the run and now from fright. Sarah, strong, wise Sarah, was crying like her heart was breaking and it was all Betsie's fault.

"I'm sorry, Sarah," Betsie sobbed. "I won't go to the circus. I won't even ask Ben to take us if he can't anymore."

Sarah cried harder at the mention of Ben. Footsteps came pattering into the kitchen from the living room. Miriam and Kathy separated the two sisters and set to drying tears.

"Sarah's just had a rough day," Kathy said, handing Betsie a glass of water. "Why don't you play outside with your friends for a few hours?"

Betsie didn't tell Kathy about leaving her friends, and she said nothing about the circus either, she was so guilt-ridden. But Betsie had seen how Sarah had reacted to Ben's name, and she had put two and two together. Something had gone wrong between Sarah and Ben. *Daed* must have found out because he had shouted at Sarah last night after dinner with George Lengacher.

Chewing her lip as she left the house to give Sarah the space she needed, Betsie formulated a plan. She was going to have to do it soon, and she would need help putting it into action. She thought of whom to confide in, running her hands through her hair. Something soft trailed her fingers. She stared at the small feather and Samuel King's pale face, screwed up in concentration over wheels, came to her mind.

It was time to pay Samuel King a visit.

DREAMS AND NIGHTMARES

The cracks in the ceiling looked like claws. Samuel blinked. The house groaned and whined, settling for the night. Samuel whispered a prayer, and forced his mind to think of other things, pleasant things.

He thought of his latest project hidden under a loose floorboard near his dresser. There were still a few parts missing to get it to work. He would have to pay the junkyard a visit again. Old Rider Ness, the caretaker of the junkyard, let him sift through the old refrigerators and broken television sets for parts in exchange for cookies made by Samuel's mother, Selma King. She had made a fresh batch of rock cakes this morning, so Rider

Ness should be happy to let Samuel have his way for a few hours.

The floorboards creaked and Samuel glanced at his bedroom door. It was slightly ajar. He wasn't allowed a closed door after the hummingbird. Samuel had been eight then, and he had worked on a small toy bird he had found in the junkyard. Lifelike, with soft feathers that caught the light like rainbows, the bird had fascinated Samuel. He had replaced a few parts, wound the bird up, blew on it to make the tiny feathers ripple and let it go.

Selma had been delighted; Melvin had crushed the bird under his boot.

Samuel got up in bed and tiptoed over to the loose floorboard. He checked to make sure the warped wood wasn't visible. He couldn't risk Melvin finding out about the toy car he was working on, or the other mechanical toys he had fixed over the years.

He got back in bed, his thoughts heavy with his father's hatred of him. Samuel had tried to please him, he had tried to not think of the junkyard and the treasures it held, but he couldn't help it if he was good at fixing machines. It was a gift. He could look at gears and spokes and know how to fix it to make it work. It was like a puzzle he was very good at. But that wasn't the kind of son Melvin wanted.

He winced as he settled on his side. It got lonely in the house with only his mother's worry and his father's hatred. He was the only one who didn't have any siblings. He wondered if that was one of the reasons his father was so hard on him. Maybe if they had had another son, one more willing to work on the farm, and devoid of a passion for junkyard scraps, maybe things wouldn't be so bad.

Samuel's eyes grew heavy. He thought of the hummingbird and its rainbow feathers. His tired mind jumped from feathers to rich brown hair and Betsie Hershberger. A smile crossed his dozing face.

A sharp knock on his window made him jump out of bed, his bleary eyes trying to focus. His heart was galloping a mile a minute; his hackles were raised. He peered at the window. It was as if his dream had manifested into reality. Betsie Hershberger stood outside his window wearing the deepest frown he had ever seen on her face.

The house groaned as if it sensed her there. Samuel shot out of bed and opened the window as noiselessly as possible.

"What are you doing here?" he asked.

"I'm here to ask you to return a favor," Betsie said, a hint of superiority in her voice.

"What?"

"I've been standing up for you in school when I didn't have to," Betsie whispered harshly. "It's got me in a lot of trouble with Isaac Hilty. The way I see it, you owe me a favor."

Samuel thought of the lie he told to legitimize her story but thought it best not to mention it. She looked as if she was worried about something and wouldn't appreciate being reminded of that.

"What do you need?"

"I need to go into town tomorrow morning," Betsie said. "I need you to take me because I don't know where Ben works."

"Ben?" Samuel frowned. "Ben Lambright? He works at the McCarthy farm."

"Do you know where it is?"

"*Ja.*" Samuel shrugged. "It's not too far from the junkyard. I'll take you."

"*Denke,*" Betsie sighed, her frown disappearing and a smile lifting her lips. It was as if she had been relieved of a very heavy load. "I knew I could count on you." She punched his arm in comradeship.

Samuel winced and clutched his arm gingerly.

"Hah," Betsie laughed. "I guess I don't know my own strength."

He grinned, his face flushing. The floorboards creaked and Melvin's wracking cough disrupted the peace of night like a flock of pigeons fleeing from the cat in their midst. Betsie and Samuel stared at each other, their eyes wide. Samuel waved her away. She didn't need to be told twice. Samuel waited a moment to watch her sprinting away in the moonlit night before jumping into bed, his eyes shut tight.

For the hundredth time, Samuel wondered if his father could hear his heart beating inside his chest. He tried to keep his face serene when his bedroom door creaked open like a long drawn-out scream. He balled his trembling hands into fists and fought the urge to bite on his knuckles to stifle his whimpers. A shadow blocked out the moonlight.

Samuel pretended to be asleep, praying that his father would believe the deception.

TRIP TO TOWN

"Doesn't the junkyard smell?" Betsie asked.

"It does." Samuel nodded. "But I don't go there for fresh air."

Betsie laughed. She hadn't known Samuel King, the quiet, serious boy, would be so funny. It was the middle of the afternoon, a time when most children would be inside their homes and out of the sweltering sun, but Betsie had a mission and Samuel was going to help her with it.

She hadn't been sure Samuel would come. She had waited by the river for twenty minutes, convinced that she would have to trek to town alone and ask for directions to the McCarthy farm. She had just decided to leave when Samuel emerged from the trees.

It was surprisingly pleasant to talk to him. He wasn't boring or dumb. Samuel was smart and funny.

They came out on the town side of the woods. A house edged with pear trees was the marker that town had started. Samuel and Betsie were helping themselves to some pears when the screen door opened and two boys a few years older than them came out. They were dressed in *Englischer* clothes, denim jeans and sleeveless shirts, and their red hair was clipped close to their scalps.

"Hey," the older boy called. "You can't pick those. They're ours!"

"They're outside your fence," Betsie said, pocketing two pears in her apron pocket.

"But it's still our property," the boy spat.

"Come on, Ronan," the younger boy whined. "Let them have the stupid pears. We're late. They must have already washed the bear."

"Bear?" Betsie asked, intrigued. "What bear?"

"Dad was right. You plain people really know nothing, do you?" the boy named Ronan said. "The circus bear. They wash it and feed it every day before the performance in the big tent."

"There's an alley behind the library where you

can see it all," the younger boy said. His cheeks dimpled when he smiled.

"That's where the freaks pitched up their sleeping tents," Ronan said. "Come on, Jack. Let these two have the pears. We'll buy candy apples."

Betsie watched the brothers go with longing in her heart. If things had been different, she would have told that Ronan a thing or two about the circus and plain people's intelligence. But as things stood, she wasn't allowed to go. She felt bitterness flood her mouth, and she threw a pear over the fence and into the garden, where it bounced twice before coming to rest in the grass.

"This is so stupid." Betsie ground her teeth. "We should go to the circus too."

"No point in crying over spilled milk." Samuel shrugged. Betsie stared at him as if he had gone insane. "That's what my *Mamm* always says."

"I don't remember my mother," Betsie mumbled, and stomped off towards the road that led to the town center. She was angry at the unfairness of it all. She loved her village and wouldn't dream of any life other than within the community. Yet sometimes, when she heard Kathy talk about the movies, or how Miriam had taken so long to be baptized, she wondered if her sisters didn't feel it too, a twang of discord at the back of their minds.

Samuel finally caught up with her when they reached the town courthouse.

"I'm sorry about your *Mamm*," he said. There was a muted sincerity about Samuel. He didn't feel the need to resort to big gestures, or earnestly prove his loyalty. He had come when Betsie had called. That was all the action needed to prove he was a good friend.

"It was a long time ago." Betsie shook her head. "Plus, I have sisters to make up for it. They care for me just as well."

"I don't have siblings," Samuel said, polishing a pear with his handkerchief. "So I guess we're even."

Betsie smiled and felt her mood lifting.

"How far is the junkyard?"

"Not far." Samuel took a large bite out of his pear. "Twenty-minute walk from the hospital."

They crossed the main square through the throng of people going about their day. There were flyers for the circus everywhere they looked, and Betsie felt an anxious need to at least peek in at the circus. Surely, looking at it from afar wouldn't be breaking the rules.

They were passing the library when Betsie stopped.

"Can we go into the alley for a minute?" Betsie asked, chewing on her lip. "The bear might still be there."

Samuel stared at her. Betsie felt bad for suggesting it. This hadn't been the plan. She had asked him to take her to Ben, and now she was being greedy and selfish. She wouldn't be surprised if Samuel said no.

"Okay." Samuel shrugged. "If that's what you want."

Betsie nearly jumped for joy.

"I feel so bad." Betsie giggled.

"I know." Samuel grinned.

"What are you two doing?"

The bellow made them both jump. George Lengacher was striding towards them across the street. His thin beard quivered as he looked from one guilty face to the other and put two and two together.

"How dare you two? Going to the circus when it was expressly forbidden!"

"*Nee*, we weren't," Betsie said. "We were going to meet Ben Lambright on the Englischer farm."

"Do not make your situation worse by lying, young lady," George said, holding up a hand.

"Come with me now. I'm taking you both home." He took Betsie's hand and tugged her along behind him. Samuel fell in step.

Betsie glanced at Samuel. They were in big trouble now, and it was all her fault.

PUNISHMENT

Gott *ott* was punishing her for being greedy. Betsie felt her insides burn with shame as she watched Samuel get out of the buggy behind George Lengacher. Melvin King was chopping wood across the yard, and Selma King was sitting in a chair on the porch with her mending basket. It was a large two-story house, and she wondered how three people lived in it without feeling dwarfed by its size. Melvin looked up from his stack of wood and wiped his forehead with a handkerchief. They were going to be very disappointed with Samuel, and Betsie was to blame.

Shame burned her throat, and hot tears threatened to fill her eyes. She had sinned, she had given into temptation, and *Gott* had struck her down before she could follow through with her wicked plan. She was willing to be punished for her sin, but she didn't want Samuel to suffer for her naughty behavior.

She hoped Melvin wasn't too hard on Samuel. He didn't have siblings like she did to protect her from their father's wrath, and so she hoped, him being an only child, he would have his parents' unconditional love. She wondered if Leroy would listen to the rest of his daughters this time or decide that this offence was too big to be swept under the rug without punishment.

Betsie absently watched Melvin come to meet George, as Selma got up from her chair. She was so lost in her own thoughts that when Melvin struck Samuel with his open hand, she thought she had imagined it. But then a second blow fell, and Samuel went down in the dirt.

"Stop!" Betsie screamed, scrambling out of the buggy. "Don't hurt him! It wasn't his fault."

George stopped Betsie mid-run. His skin was the color of whey and he was swallowing hard. Selma was holding back sobs on the porch. Melvin ran his hands through his disheveled hair, his face a forbidding mask of rage. Samuel got up and backed away a step, his head hanging low. Melvin took a threatening step forward.

"What were you thinking?" Melvin roared. "You've shamed me for the last time!"

Melvin raised his hand to strike.

"Melvin, wait," George bleated. "I, uh, I might have been mistaken."

"What?" Melvin asked, turning his sharp gaze on George, who trembled a little.

"I saw them near the library." George swallowed. "I, uh, I just assumed, I mean I thought they were going to the circus. But, er, the girl said they were going towards the McCarthy farm."

"Why were you going to the McCarthy farm?" Melvin jostled Samuel's shoulder. "Huh? Were you taking her to see that junkyard? Were you going to the junkyard, boy?"

"*Nee*, Melvin," George cried. "Let's hear the girl out."

"Please, Mr. King, sir," Betsie hiccoughed. "I wanted to see Ben Lambright because he made my sister cry. I didn't know the way, so I asked Samuel. We weren't going to see the circus, I promise!"

Melvin was breathing heavily, looking at Betsie with bulging, furious eyes. Betsie thought she would faint with fright if he didn't look away. Selma walked out into the yard and touched her husband's shoulder. He shrugged her off.

"Samuel is a good boy, Melvin," she whimpered. "He wouldn't go to the junkyard after you forbade it, would you, Samuel?"

"*Nee, Mamm*," Samuel shook his head. His cheeks were red from where Melvin had struck him. "I'm sorry for the trouble, *Daed*."

"There, see, the children are sorry." George tried to laugh it off, but it came across as a hoarse cough. "Let's forget this happened. It was a misunderstanding."

"Get out of my sight," Melvin snarled at Samuel, ignoring George. He picked up his axe and stalked to the back of the house. Samuel flinched but did as he was told. He walked towards his porch with Selma's arm around him. Melvin went back to chopping wood.

Betsie made to go to Samuel, but George pulled her back.

"I need to get you home," he said.

"But I have to apologize," Betsie said. "I have to tell Samuel I'm sorry."

"I'm sure he already knows," George said, dragging her to the buggy.

Betsie watched Selma wipe Samuel's face as the buggy pulled away. Samuel winced, but didn't cry. Betsie gasped, remembering punching him playfully on the arm the night before. She had thought she had hit him harder than she had intended, but what if he had a bruise on his arm? Looking at Melvin's forbidding figure at the chopping stump, and the blatant dislike he had for his son, she wouldn't be surprised if this wasn't the first time he had hit Samuel.

Betsie sobbed all the way home. She had never seen violence in her life. Leroy was often angry with her, but he had never lifted a finger to any of his daughters. But then again, none of his daughters had tried to go against the elders' express orders.

Would this be the straw that broke the camel's back? She knew Leroy thought her spoiled and coddled. He had been furious with her when she had agitated the bull. Would he consider this a mistake serious enough to be punished? Would he hit her like Samuel's father?

The thought made her blood run cold and her tears dried on her cheeks. She waited, in dread, till the buggy stopped in front of her home.

SHAME

The clip-clop of the horses' hooves was perfectly synced with Betsie's heart. The house came into view and she looked at it as if she were seeing it for the first time. It was a single-story house, sprawled a little haphazardly with the air of being incomplete. The screen door in the back opened and Sarah emerged with a bucket of chicken feed. Betsie watched her sister stare at the sky and the knife of guilt twisted horribly.

Betsie had gone to town to talk to Ben, she had gone to help Sarah, but she had failed because of her own selfish greed.

"There you go," George said, parking the

buggy by the house. "If it's all right by you, I won't tell Leroy."

He wouldn't meet her eye. Melvin's behavior had affected him. The community didn't condone violence, and it went against the peaceful Amish nature. George was a frail old man, and he had always been kind. He respected Melvin's right to discipline his own son, but that did not mean he had to like it. By choosing not to tell Leroy of Betsie's attempts to see the circus, he was trying to do his part in preventing another harsh punishment.

But this didn't bring any peace to Betsie. She stepped off the buggy and stood in the yard for a while, watching George Lengacher's buggy disappear behind the bend in the path. She felt more guilt twist around her gut and squeeze it. Samuel's father slapped him twice just for accompanying her to town, yet she was being given the chance of no punishment at all. No, she would not let this injustice happen. After all, wasn't she always crying about how unfair things were? She was going to do the right thing.

Betsie went to the fields first but couldn't find Leroy. Then she went to the vegetable garden and then the apple orchard. She finally turned to the barn. It would fit to get her punishment in there if she found Leroy.

He was tending to the goats. The herd was riddled with worms and Leroy had spent the past two days deworming them. Betsie stood in the doorway for a few minutes watching her father work. He was so intent on the task at hand that he did not notice her.

Screwing up her courage, Betsie walked inside. The bull snorted and paw the ground, and Betsie flinched. Leroy looked up, his brown eyes finding Betsie in the gloom, and she felt her breath catch in her throat.

"Tell your sister I'll have lunch later," Leroy said dismissively.

"Sarah didn't send me," Betsie said in a small voice.

"What? Speak up," Leroy snapped.

"I said, Sarah didn't send me," Betsie said a bit more clearly.

"Then what do you want?" Leroy said, still not looking at her.

"I wanted to talk to you."

"Look, if this is about the bull, I forgive you."

"It's not about the bull." Betsie sucked on her lower lip and burst into tears.

Leroy stood up, taken aback by her reaction.

He quickly washed his hands, his eyes darting towards the barn door, his expression deeply uncomfortable as if he was hoping for one of his daughters to come and save him from the situation.

"Er, don't cry," he said. "What's wrong?"

"I did a horrible thing," Betsie wailed. "You're going to hate me."

"How can I hate you when I don't even know what you did?" Leroy raised his hands. Betsie cried louder. "Okay, I promise I won't hate you, okay? What did you do?"

"I went to town with Samuel King," Betsie hiccoughed.

"To see the circus?" Leroy asked sharply.

"*Nee... ja...* I mean not at first," Betsie said. "I wanted to talk to Ben, but..."

"Ben!" Leroy thundered. "Why did you want to meet him?"

Betsie's face grew hot. She wanted to kick herself for being so stupid. She had come to confess her sin of temptation and leading Samuel astray, but all she had done is make things worse for Sarah and Ben.

"I...I...*Daed*, I wanted to ask why he made Sarah cry," Betsie said, deciding to stick to her decision to tell the truth. No more telling lies for Betsie. They got her in more trouble than they were worth. "She's been miserable, and I know she loves him, and I hadn't expected this kind of behavior from him."

Leroy's eyes flickered and Betsie thought she saw a hint of shame in them.

"You've met him?" Leroy asked, his tone offhand.

"*Ja*. They walked me to school a few times."

"And you think he's worthy of Sarah?"

"*Ja*," Betsie nodded, shaking a teardrop off her chin and onto her apron. "Of course. Because he's just like you."

"What?" Leroy was shocked.

"He is," Betsie insisted. "He's proud and takes his responsibilities very seriously. Just like you."

"Is that why he works on an *Englischer* farm?" Leroy jeered.

"I asked him about that," Betsie said, "and he told me he doesn't want to be beholden to anyone in the community for his success. He wants to buy the lands next to his small inheritance so he can make a barn worthy of Sarah."

"Not beholden to the community?" Leroy sniffed. "The entire community is about supporting each other and helping in their time of need. If he isn't willing to accept support, he will not be willing to give it."

"But isn't that what you do, *Daed*?" Betsie asked in a small voice. "Every year we ask to help bring in the harvest but you refuse. You refuse the help of the community and run this entire farm by yourself, for us, your *dochders*. Ben is doing just the same."

Leroy looked at Betsie for a long time, as if he was finally seeing her as an individual person and not a blabbering baby.

"And what were you doing in town that made you come crying home?" he asked suddenly, taking Betsie by surprise.

"We were going to peek into the circus," Betsie said. "But George Lengacher caught us before we could. I still shouldn't have done it. Samuel's *Daed* hit him because I made him go, and I now understand what the elders meant by temptation being a sin. I'm sorry, *Daed*."

She had expected him to stomp around, kick a bucket, scream, and throw her in the bull's pen. She hadn't expected him to chuckle, then roar with laughter. The bull found this turn of events very disconcerting because it lowed in remorse at losing a chance to gore her.

"It's all right," Leroy said. "I'm not mad. It's the

circus, of course you'd be tempted, you who have always gotten what you wanted. As long as no one came to harm, there's nothing to worry about."

"But Samuel did come to harm," Betsie cried. "Mr. King slapped him twice and shook him!"

Leroy ran a hand through his beard. He looked like the news didn't come as a surprise to him.

"Melvin has always struggled with his anger," Leroy sighed. "He had a very strict father as well. But I had no idea he was hitting Samuel. No wonder that boy is so quiet and aloof."

Betsie felt blazing anger towards his parents, Melvin for treating Samuel this way, and Selma for allowing it.

Leroy read her face and gently touched her arm.

"Don't worry about Samuel or Sarah," he said. "I'll take care of it."

She smiled weakly. For the first time in her life, she felt pride in her father that she had only heard in the voices of her friends. Looking at Leroy's kind smile, she knew she could trust him to keep his promise. She turned to go back to the house. She suddenly felt drained of all energy and just wanted to curl up in bed and go to sleep.

AMENDS

She didn't have a fever, nor was her throat sore. Sarah tucked Betsie in, collected the empty glass of milk, and left the room, wondering about Betsie's sudden lethargy and how puffy her eyes were. Had she been crying? But why?

"Sarah!" Kathy called from the front door. "I'm leaving. I won't be home till after dinner."

"Okay," Sarah called back.

She placed the dirty glass in the sink. Miriam was sitting at the kitchen table writing a letter.

Sarah loved all her sisters, especially Miriam. But there were times she felt she was being taken for granted. They had been too young when

Mamm died to really help her with any of the housework, then Miriam had developed an aversion to cooking, and Kathy had discovered the joys of *Rumspringa*. And Leroy let them all have their way. All except Sarah.

Sarah was expected to care for the house, no excuses. Even during her *Rumspringa* she was supposed to be at home during meal times to cook for the family. She hadn't had the luxury of a proper *Rumspringa* like her sisters. She had no time to spend on herself. The only thing she had found for herself, the one thing that gave her pleasure, was Ben, and even that had been snatched away from her.

Putting a few sandwiches on a plate, Sarah headed for the barn. If left to his own devices, Leroy would probably never eat lunch. It was her duty as a daughter to make sure he ate his meals. She found him sitting on a stool just inside the barn, a blade of grass in his mouth. He flashed her a big smile as she approached him.

"Lovely day," he said, but Sarah was in no mood to make conversation. She handed him his plate and turned to leave. "So when is his barn going to be ready?"

"Does it matter?" Sarah was sick and tired of

the baiting. Leroy had refused to have her married to Ben, so why drag this out?

"If you're going to marry this harvest season, it does," Leroy said matter-of-factly, biting into one of the sandwiches. "I won't have you sleeping under the stars."

"What?" Sarah was confused.

Leroy swallowed. He looked ashamed.

"I was wrong," he mumbled. "About Ben. I was looking at him from the aspect of a man who owns his own barn, his own fields. I didn't even try to understand the motive behind his actions. I judged him quickly and harshly, and I judged you for choosing him. I'm sorry."

Sarah stared, her mouth wide open. What miracle had taken place for her father to change his staunch beliefs in the space of thirty-six hours?

"Do you mean it?" Sarah asked. "You're okay with Ben and me getting married?"

"*Ja, dochder,*" Leroy said. "It's the least I can do after you helped me keep this family functioning after your *Mamm* passed away. I couldn't have done any of this without you."

Sarah burst into tears. She was so happy words failed her.

"Oh, *nee*," Leroy moaned. "Not another one. What is it with my *dochders* and crying? I just gave you joyful news."

"*Denke, Daed*," Sarah said, throwing herself in her father's arms and holding him tightly.

THE HEART OF INNOCENCE

Betsie was all alone. Kathy and Miriam had camped on her bed and told her a few stories before retiring to bed themselves. Betsie was finally alone with her thoughts, thoughts that twisted and turned over how her thoughtless actions had gotten Samuel in trouble.

A sudden knock on her window made her sit upright, holding her covers to her face. Had Melvin found out about Leroy's leniency and come to punish her instead?

It was Samuel, waving at her to open the sash. Betsie rushed over and lifted the window sash. The night air was fragrant and pleasant compared to the heat of the day.

"I'm sorry, Samuel."

"You don't have to be." He shrugged.

"You got hit because of me," she insisted.

"*Nee.*" He shook his head. "He would have done it anyway. He only needs a paltry excuse to get angry."

"Why does he do it? Doesn't he know it's wrong?"

"I'm not the son he wanted." Samuel shrugged. "I'm not athletic. I don't have any interest in farming or animal husbandry. I wish to learn about mechanics and build machines. I'm strange and nothing like he wanted." The notes of bitterness were distinct in his tone. "That's why he hates me." Fat tears pooled in Samuel's eyes. He brushed them away with fisted fingers.

"No one deserves this." Betsie held his hand. "And you're not strange. You're special. You have a gift from *Gott.* You just need to find a way to make it work in our Old Order community. You're kind and generous, you're loyal and a good friend. And if your father can't see that, then… you don't need him. You have me. I'll be your friend."

Samuel's smile turned into a wince. He chuckled, holding the side of his face that must still hurt from the slap he had gotten earlier.

"Then this was worth it," Samuel said, punching Betsie lightly on the arm.

She grinned like a fool.

"BETSIE! BREAKFAST!" Kathy called down the hall.

Betsie rubbed her tired eyes. She had spent half the night talking to Samuel. He had finally left a few hours before dawn, but Betsie had been too excited to go to sleep immediately. She had read a book till dawn and had only gotten two hours of sleep.

She sat at the table, her eyelids heavy with sleep. Sarah placed a large stack of pancakes smothered in butter and honey in front of her, then kissed her forehead. Betsie stared.

"What was that for?" she asked.

Leroy laughed from across the table.

"I told you I'd fix it," he said.

Sarah hummed as she went about the kitchen. It was a sight for sore eyes. Betsie bit into her pancakes, the sweet honey coating the roof of her mouth. Things were finally falling back into place, and she vowed never to disrupt them again with her selfishness.

"More pancakes?" Sarah asked.

"Yes, please," Betsie cried.

Life was good again.

EPILOGUE

The barn was too small to accommodate everyone, so half the tables had to be set outside. Betsie didn't mind. She served casseroles and bread with Miriam, Kathy, and half the community that had come to help.

The Lambright family was large and very close. They had prepared all the food to help out. Betsie thought they were very tactful to take up the job without making Miriam feel like a horrible sister for not being able to cook for her sister's wedding feast.

"She looks lovely," Kathy sniffed.

"And happy," Miriam agreed.

Sarah, dressed in her wedding gown of deep purple, looked radiant. Ben looked very handsome. He couldn't take his eyes off his bride. Betsie watched with the rest as the food was cleared and the dancing began. They glided gracefully across the floor, the picture of the fairytales Miriam used to read to her when she was younger.

"Beautiful Betsie," Ben approached her after a while. "Care to dance?"

"My feet are killing me," Sarah complained, taking a seat at one of the tables.

Betsie danced with Ben, then laughed when Leroy cut in.

"You've already taken Sarah," he joked. "You're not taking Betsie."

"Somebody will," Ben laughed.

"Not anytime soon," Betsie cried and ran to meet her friends.

Samuel was keeping his distance from the rest of the children, as usual. Betsie made a beeline for him with a large plate of cookies.

"Meet me in the green room!" she whispered, "And bring milk!"

She ran off without waiting for him, her high spirits thrilling at the joy of the day. Her eldest sister was marrying the man she loved, Miriam was being courted by Nathan Zook, and Kathy was being courted by no less than three young men, so popular was she in the village. Leroy had gone back to being the absent father, but now his daughters knew they could rely on him when they needed him.

Betsie ran into the edge of the woods where a patch of ivy had gone wild. Left unattended in the woods, it had covered an entire tree. The children of the village liked to call it the green room and often went there to play hide and seek.

Betsie sat down and waited patiently for Samuel to show up. He arrived five minutes later with two tall glasses of milk in his hands. He walked carefully so he wouldn't drop any. They settled on the dry leaves and tucked into the cookies and milk.

"I can't wait to be married," Betsie said. "I'll have many children, and they will get cookies and milk every day!"

"I will have my own room for my toys and machines." Samuel looked wistfully up in the canopy of drying leaves.

"And pancakes for breakfast."

"And books, lots of books."

"And roast chicken, and cheese toast!"

"Your children will have horrible tummy aches." Samuel laughed.

"And your children will have headaches!" Betsie giggled.

They broke the last cookie in half and shared it. When the crumbs had been swept away and the last of the milk drained, they settled against the trunk of the tree, their hands resting on their stomachs, content.

"Betsie."

"Hmm?"

"I wanted to thank you."

"I'll get you more cookies from the pantry."

"*Nee*, it wasn't for the cookies. One of the elders came to our house a few weeks ago. Saul Yoder. He talked to my *Daed* about the hitting. He told him it was against the community. My *Daed* was angry. He told Mr. Yoder that what he did with his family was none of the elders' business, but Mr. Yoder insisted that if *Daed* didn't stop, they'd have to consider taking action. Someone comes and checks on me twice a month now. *Daed* doesn't like it, but there isn't anything he can do about it."

Betsie hadn't known that the day would have gotten better somehow, but it had. Everything had fallen in place, and the niggling worry that she had had about Samuel's well-being was also satisfied.

"But why are you thanking me?" Betsie asked. "I did nothing."

"*Daed* is convinced that it was George Lengacher who told the elders." Samuel grinned. "But I didn't think Mr. Lengacher had it in him. So I asked Mr. Yoder how he found out, and he told me it was your *Daed.* He had talked to them about it after you told him. So thank you."

"You're my friend." Betsie punched Samuel in the arm, delighted when he didn't wince. "That's what friends do."

"I'm still new to the friendship thing." Samuel chuckled.

"You won't be for long," Betsie said. "Tag!" She punched him again and ran.

Samuel sat bewildered for a moment till he caught on to what was happening. Betsie shrieked with delight as she ran back to the party, her friend racing after her. The sun sank below the horizon, but the wedding party went on late into the night.

~

THE HEART OF
LONGING

BOOK DESCRIPTION

Torn between the choice of stepping out with her best friend or the handsome new man in the village, Betsie Hershberger must come to terms with her desires, and the nature of her own wild heart.

Betsie Hershberger's Rumspringa is full of surprises. Kathy is getting married, Sarah is having her third child, and Miriam is thinking of leaving the nest but not in the conventional way. And no sooner does Betsie start her *Rumspringa* than Samuel King, her childhood friend, asks her to walk out with him. But a new man in the village has caught her eye, and she is sure she has caught his.

Must she sacrifice her heart's desire to keep her childhood friendship, or will she follow her heart and find happiness?

"For you have need of endurance, so that when you have done the will of God you may receive what is promised."
~ Hebrews 10:36

A WEDDING

It was the last warm day of the year before fall took hold. The rust-colored leaves were still clinging to their branches, loath to let go. Under the canopy of dying leaves, a new life was being celebrated.

The freshly painted barn still smelled of varnish mingled with the scent of sweet hay. Mouthwatering food made the trestle tables groan, while the air was thick with music and the laughter of children.

"Careful!" Betsie Hershberger dodged in time. Eli, her four-year-old nephew, went whizzing past her skirts, closely followed by Amos, his younger brother. Betsie watched their flaxen heads weave through legs and disappear behind one of the tables. She adjusted the tray of hot *kaffe* mugs in her hands and continued to serve.

"Kathy looks so happy," Anna Lambright cooed. "I don't think I've ever seen such a beautiful bride."

Betsie glanced at the table across the yard. Kathy Fisher née Hershberger was dressed in a simple dress of inky blue that brought out the color of her eyes. Betsie recalled the long nights spent gossiping and teasing Kathy as she lovingly stitched her wedding dress. Kathy was the undisputed beauty of the Hershberger girls. Her natural good looks were reminiscent of Audrey Hepburn. Sitting next to her husband, Ivan Fisher, she looked fairly radiant.

"None for you." Betsie pulled the tray back when Sarah Lambright, the eldest Hershberger girl, tried to take a mug.

"Oh, I can't wait to have this baby," Sarah grumbled, folding her arms on top of her burgeoning belly.

"May *Gott* grant you a girl this time." Anna, her sister-in-law, giggled. "My brothers are just as much fools for sons as our father was. Granted, Ben has done better than the rest."

Sarah blushed with pleasure. The Lambright men were notorious for having sons and lacking the fortitude needed to leave their lands to only one. The generosity of spirit and abundance of sons had dwindled the vast Lambright holdings into small Lambright pockets across the village, forcing many Lambright men to sell and seek their fortune in other Amish villages. Ben Lambright, Sarah's husband, had been left a plot no bigger than a vegetable garden. He had worked with *Englischer* farmers till he could buy the adjoining fields and land for a barn, effectively making his the largest Lambright farm in the village. Sarah was very proud of her Ben.

"I wouldn't mind a little girl." Sarah patted her belly. "Eli and Amos are a handful. *Gott* have mercy on me if it's another boy."

The women laughed. The mugs all gone, Betsie headed back to the kitchens to fetch more *kaffe*.

"It's going well?" Eva Fisher, mother of the groom, asked, taking out another leek casserole from the oven. A tiny woman, she had grown wider instead of inching taller. Wide-lined face, with a wide-lined nose, she reminded Betsie of rocks piled on top of each other: harsh, jagged, sloping. There was nothing soft about her body. Yet, when Eva took you in her arms, her flesh radiated warmth, like stones left out in the sun, because the softness lived inside her: in her eyes, her smiles, and her loving heart.

"*Ja,* Mrs. Fisher." Betsie wiped the sweat off her brow. "We need more *kaffe.*"

"*Kaffe,*" Eva sighed. "The Amish and their *kaffe.* If you don't put a stop to it, that's all they'll be drinking."

"You love it too." Betsie giggled.

"*Ja,* I do." Eva laughed. "Go on then."

Betsie filled a pan with water and placed it on the stove. Fisher women and Lambright girls kept going in and out of the kitchen, lending a hand, tossing salads, and mixing sauces. Eva supervised it all like a mother hen. Not having known her mother, Betsie found Eva's nurturing nature endearing, and again thought how lucky Kathy was to be her daughter-in-law.

She was pouring the *kaffe* in mugs when Nancy Schwartz sidled up beside her.

"So." Nancy wiggled her eyebrows. "I hear you're walking out with Samuel King."

Betsie swallowed the tirade of explanations that always threatened to burst out of her mouth whenever anyone asked her about Samuel. She didn't understand why she felt the need to provide explanations for her choice to say yes to him. He was kind, sweet and had been her friend for five years. Of course, she had said yes when he had asked her to go for a buggy ride. Why would she say no?

She immediately silenced the voices in her head, giving the answers to that question.

"*Ja*," she said shortly, busying herself with her task.

"I must admit, I never pictured you with someone like him." Nancy swiped an apple off a fruit bowl and bit into it. The ripping of the fruit's flesh grated on Betsie's nerves. "He's just so…" Nancy waved her apple around, searching for a word. "It's like his head is in another place, do you know what I mean?"

"Probably meditating on the glory of *Gott*." Betsie shrugged, trying to hide her annoyance.

Nancy snorted.

"Thinking of another crazy invention, more like." Nancy laughed. "Are you really walking out with him?"

Betsie nodded tightly. She picked up the tray, signaling that the conversation was over.

"Well, at least you are walking out, and only a month into your *Rumspringa*." Nancy sighed, her florid cheeks deflating a little. "It's been a whole year of *Rumspringa* and I haven't walked out with anyone."

If Nancy had been a little kinder, Betsie might have felt sorry for her. As things were, she felt a mean satisfaction, but shame was fast on its heels. Betsie put the tray down and placed a comforting hand on Nancy's shoulder.

"You're only seventeen," she said. "Things will get better."

"You think so?" Nancy tilted her head; the desire to believe Betsie was bright in her mud-colored eyes. "Or will I turn out to be like Miriam, teaching other people's children and running after my nephews at my sister's wedding? Is it true she can't cook to save her life?"

By sheer force of will, Betsie stopped herself from digging her fingernails into Nancy's fleshy shoulder. Fuming, she picked up the tray and marched out before the urge to throw boiling *kaffe* in Nancy's bloated face won out over her restraint.

Making fun of Samuel was one thing, but Nancy had crossed a line talking about her sister Miriam that way. People in the village didn't understand things that were different from them. And Miriam and Samuel were different.

Miriam refused to cook, not because she couldn't but because she didn't want to. Approached to walk out a few times, Miriam had refused each suitor, not having any desire to marry. She loved to teach, and could have spent all day at the school if the pupils didn't have to go home.

Samuel loved machinery, an unheard-of thing in an Old Order community. He could fix the rudimentary pulley systems across the village in seconds and had a collection of gadgets he had made from scraps from the junkyard under his bedroom floorboards.

They were both considered odd, and Betsie guessed it was this oddity in Samuel that she liked best because it reminded her of Miriam.

Yet...

Betsie weaved through the crowd, offering *kaffe* to everyone, her mind deep in thoughts of Samuel and why she had agreed to walk out with him when she hadn't really wanted to. She hadn't ever thought of Samuel romantically, so when he had asked her to go for a buggy ride she had thought nothing of it, thinking it would be a platonic ride to town. When Samuel had shown up with a bunch of freshly picked flowers, her mistake in understanding him finally hit her. But by then it was too late.

"Would you like to dance?" Ben Lambright

asked as she passed by the barn floor. "You have had no opportunity for fun all day."

"Just have to serve this last batch of *kaffe*." Betsie grinned. She turned to walk to the men seated at the far side of the barn but stopped. "Ben. Why don't you ask Nancy to dance?"

"Nancy Schwartz?"

"*Ja*. She looks like she'd like to dance if someone were to ask her. Go on," she urged. "It will make her day. And I want everyone to be happy on Kathy's big day."

Ben scouted for Nancy and found her on the far side, leaning against the wall, watching the dancing couples. He nodded to Betsie and maneuvered his way towards Nancy. Betsie served *kaffe* but her attention was on Nancy and Ben dancing, so she didn't hear the pattering feet or the tiny running figures coming in her path.

"Coming through!"

Eli ran past Betsie again, his giggles high-pitched. Betsie managed to steady herself.

"Coma thoo!"

Amos, always one step behind Eli, charged for her legs.

"Amos, *nee*!" Betsie cried.

"Careful!" someone else said.

Betsie braced herself for impact, her eyes shut

tight in anticipation of the crash and tinkle of mugs. But there was no collision. The tray was firmly in her hands. Betsie opened her eyes to find Amos lifted up in the air, his shrieks of delight bringing a smile on every face. The man holding him up had his back to Betsie, but she could see his powerful arms and broad shoulders.

"You nearly did the pretty miss an injury," the man said. He had a pleasant voice, laced with warmth.

"I sorry, *Ant* Besthie," Amos lisped.

"It's okay," Betsie said, distracted by the man who had turned around. She had never seen him before in the village. He was remarkably handsome. His smile was striking, showing even white teeth. "*Denke.*"

"It was my pleasure," the man said. He looked to be in his mid-twenties, his strawberry blond hair just reaching the nape of his neck. He had a frank gaze that made Betsie's cheeks blaze involuntarily. "I'm Caleb; Caleb Nolt. I'm new around here. Ivan was kind enough to invite me to his wedding."

"Are you a friend of Ivan's?" Betsie asked, casually.

"Neighbor," Caleb said. "But I hope to be a

friend soon. I might be wrong, but you look remarkably like Ivan's bride, Kathy."

"She's my sister. I'm Betsie. Betsie Hershberger."

"Pleased to make your acquaintance, Betsie."

She had the strangest tingling sensation in her belly hearing her name on his lips.

"Are you staying in Jamesport long?"

"I was hoping to make a home here." His smile was infectious. Betsie's stomach was full of butterflies. "My village in Indiana was moving away from the Old Order, and since I wasn't ready to move with them, I moved away."

"That must have been hard for you."

"*Ja.*" Caleb nodded. "But I have found this village, and I hope I can serve it well."

"Welcome to our village," Betsie said. "I hope you find the peace you are looking for."

"I'm confident that I will," he said with a meaningful nod, and Betsie's heart began to beat a step faster.

She made to turn, but Caleb shot his hand out. Betsie gasped, thinking he was trying to grab her arm to make her stop. When he picked up a mug of *kaffe* instead, chuckling knowingly, her entire face flushed crimson, and she felt waves of embarrassment radiate off of her like heat.

Flustered, Betsie made it back to the kitchen, half the *kaffe* cups still on her tray.

"They've had enough of *kaffe* then?" Eva asked.

"Huh? Oh, *ja.*"

"Are you all right?" Eva asked, placing a cool hand on Betsie's forehead. "You look feverish."

"I'm fine." Betsie shook her head and tried to smile reassuringly. "Just feeling a little lightheaded."

"You haven't had a bite since dawn." Eva tut-tutted. "Here, eat this."

She thrust a plate of roasted chicken and mashed potatoes in Betsie's hands. But Betsie had no appetite. She kept picturing that knowing smile, and her own mouth responded. She realized she must look foolish, food in her hands, smiling at nothing, her eyes glazed, her cheeks pink. She shook her head and forced herself to eat a little while her mind whirled about with possibilities.

Had she read that smile right? Caleb had shown clearly that he found her charming, worthy of his interest. And she had to admit she felt the same way. She didn't know him like Samuel, but she felt a keen desire to find out everything about him. He was Ivan's neighbor, that much she knew; he had moved to Jamesport because it was conservative like he wanted it. But this wasn't enough information.

She wanted to know where he had come from, what family he came from, his favorite food, his favorite color, the hymn he liked to sing while working in the field, and the passage of the Bible he related to most. She wanted to know all this and more.

Chewing on her chicken, the thought struck her that she knew none of these things about Samuel, and worse still, that she didn't care to know.

Betsie swallowed with difficulty, her throat suddenly parched.

DEEP DESIRES

Blood rushed to his head till the pounding of his heart was all he could hear. Caught in the tide of his desire, Samuel King's mind was focused on the building in front of him. A large gray stone monolith, the public library was a trove of information. His mind's eye conjured up the sight of endless rows of books, the slanting rays of the sun providing enough light to read by.

It wasn't unusual to find Samuel on a Thursday afternoon sitting on a bench under a tree, across the street from the library. He had been doing it for a few months now. The librarian, a bespectacled man in his forties, had often waved at him across the street. The first time he had done that Samuel had run away, afraid that the man must see his desire naked on his face, and judge him for it. Now, it was a weekly ritual they performed.

Samuel watched the young and old climb the short flight of stairs and go inside. He wondered if they realized how lucky they were to be able to walk through rows and aisles of books and pick up whatever they liked and read it. It was a reckless amount of freedom. One could get drunk on it.

A young woman in a leather jacket dragged a small child towards the library. The boy was kicking and screaming. Samuel felt a tinge of resentment. If he had been that little boy he would have gone inside the library skipping. As it was, the people who had such blessings always took them for granted.

He was watching the boy so intently he didn't notice the librarian till the man sat beside him on the bench. Up close, Samuel saw that the man's face was heavily lined, and that one of his eyes was heavily lidded. It gave his face a lopsided appearance.

"Are you hungry, son?" the man asked. "The Mrs. packed a heavy lunch and I could sure use your help to finish it off."

Samuel's throat was dry and his lips had

grown numb. He couldn't trust himself to speak. He took the offered sandwich silently and waited for the man to start eating before he took a bite. It was tuna and pickle, with a lot of mayonnaise.

"May I know your name, son?" the man asked. "Mine's Hector if it makes the exchange any easier."

"Sam," he cleared his throat. "Samuel King."

"That's a mighty fine name," Hector nodded. "I had a teacher by that name when I was younger. He would give a peppermint after every pop quiz. 'To dispel the bitter taste,' he used to say. Are you fond of peppermint?"

"*Ja, nee,* I mean I like it, but I'm not fond of it," Samuel said.

"Ah," Hector grinned. "A man conscious of the true meaning of words. It's refreshing to see from a generation that uses strong words like 'hate' and 'love' so excessively."

Not sure how to respond, Samuel took another bite of his sandwich.

"So," Hector said, wiping his hands on a napkin. "Are you ever going to come in?"

Samuel swallowed audibly. Hector stared at him, mildly detached but keenly interested.

"I would very much like to," Samuel said. "But I'm afraid."

"I didn't think the Amish had anything against book learning," Hector said.

"It's not the books. It's the kind of books."

"And what might you be interested in?"

"Machines," Samuel whispered.

"Well, you're in luck," Hector laughed. "We have tons of books on machines. Big machines, tiny machines, how to work them, how to build them... we have books on them all. Would you like to come in and see?"

Samuel nodded.

"Come on then," Hector stood up and threw his paper bag in a trash can nearby.

Samuel hesitated for a minute, blinking rapidly to muster his strength, his brain sending signals of distress that required immediate action. He couldn't spend his entire *Rumspringa* on a bench outside the public library. It would be a waste of his *Rumspringa* if he didn't seek the knowledge he so craved. Building tiny pulleys and gears around the farm had come naturally to him, but he wanted to know more. He wanted to give his natural talent the shine of expert knowledge.

He got up and followed Hector, his heart in his throat the entire time. His feet climbed the first of the five steps and a bubble of excitement burst in his belly, filling him with joy. He was finally going to do it. He was going to overcome his fears and do what he had always wanted.

"Hey, Sam!"

The joy turned to bile. David Stoltzfus and Henry Helmuth were standing across the street by the bench Samuel had just vacated. Isaac Hilty was coming up the street with his friends, the two Marks, Graber and Wittmar, following close behind. They were all Amish boys his age, but Isaac Hilty and his friends had no liking for him. They would see him going into the library and they would tell his father. Samuel flinched at the thought of his father's anger.

"Come to the movies with us," Henry said. "They're showing *Commando.*"

"Johnny Mayhew said it was worth a watch," David grinned. "You'll like it, Samuel. It has that new action hero in it, the guy who played that robot from the future you loved so much."

"The Terminator," Henry said in a deep Austrian accent. "The show starts in ten minutes," He waved Samuel over.

"It is such a pity when young men stray from the path of *Gott*," Isaac said loudly in his preacher voice. "They forget that *Gott* granted them this youth to do His good work, not squander it in some dark theater of sin."

"Give it a rest, Isaac." Henry rolled his eyes. "It is perfectly acceptable for us to see a movie. The *Ordnung* allows for it in *Rumspringa*."

"Just because the *Ordnung* says it is okay to delve in *Englischer* ways in the *Rumspringa* doesn't mean you have to," Wittmar shot back, sneering.

"You're very right, Wittmar," Isaac said, nodding his head in approval. "Why, look at us." He spread his hands to include his two friends. "We're spending our *Rumspringa* spreading the good word of *Gott* to the *Englischer* populace. It is our duty to spread the good message."

"And that's your choice," David said amicably. "We choose to do something different. Come on, Samuel. We're running late."

"Looks like Samuel is more interested in books," Graber said. Wittmar laughed.

Samuel felt himself sweating profusely even though the day wasn't hot, the cool of winter finally in the air.

"Samuel?"

He looked from his friends to Isaac and the Marks. What could he say to dispel their suspicion about his wanting to go into the library?

"Thanks for helping me cross the street, son,"

Hector blurted, loud enough for everyone to hear. "You go on and have fun with your friends now."

"I... uh... yeah," Samuel stammered. "Don't mention it, sir."

"You've waited this long," Hector said in an undertone, winking at Samuel. "What's another week?"

Samuel smiled at him gratefully and watched him climb the library steps.

"Samuel! We're running late."

"Sorry." Samuel turned and rushed to his friends. He glanced back at Isaac and his heart skipped a beat. There was naked suspicion on his face. He glanced from the library to Samuel, the wheels in his head turning. Samuel faced forward again, hoping against hope that Isaac would let sleeping dogs lie. But knowing Isaac, he would chew on this bone till the marrow was sucked through.

THE LETTER

The parchment was rough and heavy. Miriam closed her eyes, inhaled the scent of ink on paper and sighed, a lazy smile dancing on her wide lips. She opened her eyes to find Betsie staring at her across the kitchen, her hand still stirring the soup on the stove.

"Er..."

"You like smelling letters." Betsie shrugged. "I'm not judging you."

Miriam laughed and pocketed the letter. She pulled the tray of biscuits from out of the oven and placed it on a wire rack to cool. Grabbing a broom, she kissed Betsie on the back of her head and began cleaning, the only chores she would do around the house.

Miriam knew she should feel guilty for not helping out with the kitchen, but she had her reasons and was lucky enough to have a family that understood them without making her say them. The last time she had stood at that stove, she had been a girl in her nightdress making breakfast for her ill mother. The last time she had cooked anything, someone she loved had died. She couldn't risk that kind of loss again.

Humming to herself, Miriam made the beds and dusted the living room. She watered the plants and fed the chickens; all the while her letter lay snug and heavy in her apron pocket, a ray of sunshine to open at the end of the day.

She hoped it was good news.

Stopping by the barn, she saw her father's balding head bobbing up and down as he forked muck into a wheelbarrow. She knew what they said about Leroy Hershberger in the village. It wasn't easy being the father of four daughters, with not a son to ease the burden. Now, two were married which meant fewer mouths to feed, but it still didn't grant him extra hands to work the farm.

Though most of this was true, Miriam also knew that it was only one view of the picture. Yes, she wasn't keen to help in the kitchen, but she had always been willing to help with the farm. Her arms were skinny but strong enough to help harvest, to plow, to shovel and swing a scythe. If Leroy had wanted, all four of his daughters would have been better than men when it came to helping around the farm. But Leroy deemed it man's work and ignored the willing hands in his own home.

"Miriam?" Betsie called from the kitchen.

"Coming," Miriam walked the short way to the screen door at the back of the house that led into the kitchen. Betsie was cleaning the counters with a wet tea towel, her thick eyelashes hooding her brown eyes. "*Ja?*"

"The soup's cooked and I've put the roast in the oven," Betsie said. "It should be ready by dinnertime."

"Is Samuel picking you up?" Miriam asked, lifting the lid off the tomato soup. It smelled delicious.

"*Nee,*" Betsie said, placing the tea towel flat on the counter to dry. "I'm walking across the woods to meet him on the other side. His father has him chopping wood there. We thought we could have a soda, and then I'll help him bring the wood to his farm."

"Romantic walks while completing chores," Miriam teased. "How economic."

Betsie's face fell.

"Oh, I'm only teasing," Miriam said. "I'm sorry. Don't let me ruin your walk. I'm sure it will be a lot of fun."

Betsie looked like she was going to say something. She bit her lip and stared at Miriam as if sizing her up for the thing she was going to tell her.

The screen door screeched on rusty hinges and slammed shut.

"When's dinner?" Leroy asked, patting his balding pate with a handkerchief.

"In a few minutes, *Daed*," Betsie blurted, the moment gone. Miriam tried to show her concern, but Betsie wouldn't meet her eye. "I'm going for a walk with Samuel and will come home later."

"Hmm." Leroy lifted the lid off the soup, his attention on the food.

"Right." Betsie shook her head. "Goodbye."

"I'll walk you to the door," Miriam said.

"*Nee*, why don't you serve *Daed* some soup to tide him over till the roast is ready," Betsie said, rushing down the hall to the front door.

Miriam stared after Betsie, puzzled. What had gotten into her little sister? She was usually very talkative and told Miriam everything. Had Samuel said anything to her? Or was it something else? Trusting that Betsie would eventually tell her what was on her mind, Miriam ladled a bowl full of soup for Leroy and served it to him with a few biscuits.

Leaving her father slurping his soup, Miriam sat in the rocking chair in the living room. Her maternal grandfather had been an accomplished carpenter and had made this rocking chair for his only daughter's wedding. The cushions, though lumpy, still held the lemony scent of their mother.

Miriam made herself comfortable before pulling out the letter from her apron pocket. She ran her finger once over the return address:

Dorothy Lantz
165 – Gasthof Village
Montgomery
Indiana

Miriam circled "165" with a fingernail. There were seventy-eight farmsteads in Jamesport, and though the number was growing steadily, it was nowhere near the two hundred and thirty-two of Gasthof village. Her friend Dorothy's account of

the village had fascinated her in the first few letters she had sent after her marriage, fascination
growing into an obsession that Miriam guarded
like a secret.

With her thumb and forefinger, Miriam broke
the wax seal and extracted the letter inside. In the
fading light of the day, she unfolded the single
page. It was a brief letter, to the point and exact,
but Miriam read it thrice nonetheless, heart racing, and sweat pooling under her arms.

"Where's Betsie?"

Leroy stood in the kitchen door. Miriam saw
the dark circles under his eyes, the biscuit crumbs
in his beard, and the blooming red stain of soup
on his trousers.

"She went for a walk with Samuel," Miriam
said, licking her lips. She folded the letter and
tried to stuff it back in its envelope.

"Miriam, are you all right?"

She looked up, and in the last sharp burst of
sunlight before it sunk under the horizon, she
saw tremendous concern in her father's eyes.

Maybe it was this rare sign of paternal attention, or the thundering of her madly beating
heart, that softened her resolve. Or maybe she
hoped to finally be rid of her secret, to no
longer live a lie and speak her mind. Whatever

the reason, she stood up from the chair and faced her father, the letter extended for him to take.

"I've just received word from Dorothy."

"Hooley?"

"Lantz now," Miriam said, clicking her tongue in impatience. "She's written about a permanent teaching position in her village. It's a sizeable village and they offer housing close by the school for easy access."

"What's wrong with teaching here?" Leroy asked. "It's close to home, and no one is stopping you."

Miriam chewed her lips. She couldn't tell him about the well-meant questions about her single status, or the subtle suggestions of things she could do to be more attractive. As much as she found these mortifying they weren't the only reason she wanted to leave. Gasthof was much more progressive than Jamesport and was initiating teacher training programs that Miriam was eager to take. She had always felt the eighth standard education wasn't enough. She wanted to know more.

"I just think it's a great opportunity," Miriam mumbled.

"Is this about Betsie walking out with that

King boy?" Leroy said, a knowing smile on his lips.

She hadn't been this humiliated by anything the women in the village had said than she was by her father's sly smile.

"Don't worry, Miriam," Leroy said, puffing out his chest. "Your *Daed* is on the case now. I'll find you a suitable husband. No daughter of mine will have to leave this village to hide her spinsterhood if I can help it. You will be married in no time. You'll see!"

"The roast must be ready," Miriam managed to say in a voice more steady than she felt. She stood up and walked towards the kitchen, the sound of wood knocking on wood filling the room. For a minute she thought it was her shaking knees, knocking into each other in rage for the world to hear.

Then she saw her mother's rocking chair, vacant and keening to be filled. Miriam could empathize.

THE WALK

He smelled of resin, his chestnut hair drizzled with sawdust. It was early evening when Samuel finally finished chopping wood. Betsie stifled a yawn and helped him pile the blocks up in the handcart he had parked at the edge of the clearing.

"I don't know about you," Samuel said, mopping his brow with a handkerchief. "But I could sure use a cold drink right about now."

"I won't say no to some French fries." Betsie grinned.

"Smothered in ketchup." Samuel laughed.

Betsie had discovered the tangy, sweet condiment in her *Rumspringa* and couldn't get enough of it. She had gained a few pounds in the summer by consuming sleeves of fast food fried potatoes drowning in ketchup.

They walked the short way to the town talking about Kathy's wedding, the movies they had seen so far and the ones they were looking forward to. Betsie made Samuel stop by the bookshop for a minute to buy the latest issue of *Archie* comics. They met Henry Helmut in there, engrossed in a *Spider-Man* comic.

Full on French fries and a chocolate milkshake, Betsie was content walking down Main Street hearing the dead leaves crunch under her feet. She stopped at an antique store to look at the things on display, the pretty jewels twinkling under artificial lights, the gems taking in the dull glow and giving back rainbows.

"See anything you like?"

The proprietress, a tall woman with a strong jaw, stood at the shop door, her hands on her hips. Her stature was menacing, but her expression was friendly enough. Betsie swallowed and backed away a step.

"We were just looking," Samuel said, touching Betsie's shoulder. She appreciated the gesture of solidarity.

"Sorry," Betsie mumbled.

"This one here," the woman pointed towards a small brooch in the display, "belonged to a princess." Her eyes were too far apart, but aglow with excitement. "Would you like to hear her story?"

Always interested in a story, Betsie would have jumped at the chance if a group of Amish girls weren't crossing the street at that very moment. She heard their sniggering first, and then her name.

Nancy Schwartz and a host of *Rumspringa* girls her age were talking behind their hands and throwing dirty looks towards Samuel. They then glanced at her and burst out laughing. Betsie noticed what they were looking at, and she saw Samuel's hand on her shoulder.

Roiling with shame she didn't know she felt, Betsie shrugged Samuel's hand off and put some distance between them.

"No, thank you," Betsie said, jutting her chin out. "I should get on home."

"It's still early," Samuel said, falling in step with her as she marched down Main Street towards the woods. "We could go to the arcade and play a few games."

"Don't you have wood to take home?" Betsie snapped.

"*Daed* doesn't expect me home anytime soon." Samuel shrugged.

"Well, your *Daed* might not care where you go, but mine sure does," Betsie sniffed.

She started jogging away from him, trying to leave him behind, but like a desperate puppy dog he kept up with her. She knew in her heart that it was unkind to think of Samuel like that, but the giggling and nasty looks of Nancy and her friends had annoyed her to the point of fury.

They came to the clearing where the handcart had been left, but Betsie didn't stop. It was all Samuel's fault that she was being treated this way, and she couldn't forgive him. Why did he have to ask her to walk with him? Why did he mistake her kindness for love?

"Betsie, wait," Samuel called, but Betsie only hastened her pace. "Betsie!"

But she had already broken into a run.

MAMA'S BOY

"About time," Melvin snarled. "I asked you to get the wood hours ago."

He was sitting in a spindly rocking chair on the front porch drinking iced tea, Selma sat on the porch swing beside him.

"It's his *Rumspringa*, Melvin," Selma cooed. "Let the boy have some fun. He did as you asked, didn't he? Why don't I get you another glass of iced tea?"

Samuel tried not to watch his mother inch her hand forward, her eyes darting between her husband's stony face and his still hands, trying to measure the extent of his displeasure in case the glass went flying across the porch.

Samuel let go of the breath he didn't know he

had been holding when Selma extracted the glass from Melvin's hand without incident.

"I'll get some for you as well, Samuel," Selma said in her sing-song voice. "Why don't you put that wood in the shed and join us on the porch?"

Samuel pulled the handcart towards the back of the house and piled wood the way his father had taught him. The sickle moon was fading and soon there would be no light to see by. He wondered if Betsie had made it home alright. He also wondered if he should have followed her to make sure.

He frowned as he thought of Betsie and her behavior this evening. She had been merry and talkative till they had come to the antique shop. Then it was as if someone had turned a switch and she hadn't wanted to look at him, let alone talk to him.

Had he been wrong to ask Betsie to walk with him, knowing she was too kind to refuse? There was no other girl he liked as much as Betsie. He also knew that Betsie only thought of him as a friend. He had stolen Betsie's chance of finding someone by asking her to walk with him, and it didn't surprise him that deep down Betsie must resent that.

Brushing the sawdust off his hands, Samuel

decided that it was best to give Betsie her space at the moment. There were obviously things she was struggling with in her heart, but he knew she would tell him when she was ready. He just hoped he was strong enough to accept her decision.

"Here you are," Selma handed him a tall glass of iced tea as soon as he climbed the front porch steps. She patted the seat beside her on the porch swing for him to sit down.

Samuel sipped the bittersweet drink and looked out across the darkness where the tree-tops burned black against the indigo sky. It always fascinated him how many shades of darkness could be found in nature.

"I hear you're walking out with the Hershberger girl," Melvin's low growl cut through the evening. "The one you went to that circus with."

Samuel's shoulders hunched up, his fingers tight around his glass.

"She's a lovely girl," Selma twittered. "Very pretty, and she can cook unlike her older sister..."

"No one cares about your opinion." Melvin's voice was dangerously low. "Now shut up."

Selma flashed Samuel a bright smile, blinking the tears out of her eyes. Samuel felt his chest tighten with rage, his hands bunching into ineffectual fists.

"That girl is spoiled rotten, and willful to boot. She will make a terrible wife." Melvin sipped his tea. "Don't make the same mistake I did. Tell her you won't be walking with her anymore."

The silence was prickly and suffocating.

"Did you hear me, boy?"

Selma nudged Samuel with her knee. He saw fear in her large hazel eyes. Samuel gulped down his iced tea and smacked his lips.

"Thank you for the tea, *Mamm*," Samuel said. "It was delicious."

The glass crashed against the wall.

"I said," Melvin snarled, "did you hear me?"

Samuel considered the situation and how best to handle it but his split second to think was enough to tip Melvin over the edge of rage into the full fury of the storm.

"Stupid, idiot boy," Melvin roared. He stood up abruptly, the chair rocking like a madman crouched in the corner of an insane asylum. Melvin picked up the rocking chair and sent it flying against the wall. The arm of the chair caught Samuel in the face, scraping the side of his cheek up to his temple and hitting him in the eye.

Samuel sunk to the floor in agonizing pain.

Melvin hadn't laid a hand on him since he was a boy and the elders had warned him against it. Now Melvin was picking up pieces of wood and throwing them willy-nilly as he cursed Samuel.

"Worthless mama's boy!" Melvin screamed. "Thinks his father's an idiot. I will not be disrespected in my own home!"

Samuel held the side of his face, his one good eye staring at his father with malevolent hate.

"He didn't mean it!" Selma squeaked, her hands clutching at Melvin's sleeves in an effort to calm him down.

THWACK.

Selma's head snapped back from the impact of the slap. For a moment, time froze. Samuel stared at his mother's shocked face. Even Melvin looked shocked at his own actions, but he was recovering quickly, a look of belligerent defensiveness coming over his face. Samuel felt sick to his stomach.

"You useless woman! This is all your fault," Melvin accused her, backing away from Selma and his injured son. His eyes roved over the two, as if he were seeing them for the first time. "Only gave me one son and then unmanned him! You call this a son? A daughter would be better than this!"

Samuel stared back with his one good eye. He got up to his full height. He was a couple of inches taller than Melvin, and he knew his father despised that. Samuel came to stand by his mother, taking her into the protection of his arms.

"Mama's boy," Melvin growled and stalked off inside the house.

"*Mamm?*" Samuel tipped Selma's chin up to examine her face.

"I'm fine. Oh, Samuel," she moaned, "your poor face!"

"I'll be fine, *Mamm*," Samuel said.

"Let's clean you up at least," she fussed. Samuel let her. He knew it was a way for her to cope, to immerse herself in her child and her home so not to think about her husband too much.

Samuel often wondered what Selma had ever seen in Melvin, and if Melvin was right and he was making a mistake by walking out with Betsie. But he shook his aching head and decided that Melvin was wrong.

Some people thought of Betsie as spoiled and selfish, but he knew the big heart she hid from most. She had been the only friend he had ever had, and she had stood up for him against the likes of Isaac Hilty, and saved him from the wrath of Melvin when most people had turned a blind eye.

Nee, Betsie wasn't the wrong choice. Listening to his father would be.

THE RUMOR

It started as simple speculation amongst the *Rumspringa* crowd. Isaac's influence was far-reaching and if he thought Samuel King was dabbling in questionable book learning at the town library, then it was more likely true than not. Yet some were doubtful. Some still held the belief that Samuel was one of them and his interest in mechanics was a passing phase.

It was Samuel's black-and-blue face that gave truth to the speculators' claims in the village. "Why would Melvin beat his only son so badly if he hadn't had cause?" the villagers wondered. Melvin didn't have a history of beating his child. Something must have forced his hand. He must have discovered the borrowed books lying around the house.

Over the next few days, the rumors spread like wildfire through the Amish community. Sarah and Kathy bent their heads over *kaffe* and wondered if they should intervene. Miriam kept a sharp eye on Betsie to catch that look of doubt she had seen a week ago. This time she would offer help instead of teasing.

But Betsie was blissfully unaware of any rumors. She had spent the past few days at home and not received any visitors. She had taken her anger and frustration, and she turned it into action. For two days she had polished every surface and piece of furniture in the house, then turned her hand to silverware and cutlery. The pots were sanded and scrubbed till they looked brand new and the sheets laundered twice with dolly blue and lavender.

Miriam had confided in her married sisters how Betsie's behavior alarmed her, but she would have been even more concerned had she learned of Betsie's own confusion. The truth was that there was a worm in Betsie's brain, a small wiggling thought that would only stay still when Betsie drowned it out with work. She didn't know why she was afraid of the thought, but she knew it would be her undoing, so she buried it under urgent thoughts of work, tamping down pebbles of worry as well. Therefore, the worm-thought had to struggle longer to come to the surface of her mind.

"I'm off to the woods," Betsie called across the hall, carrying a large basket on her arms.

"Are you meeting Samuel for a picnic?" Miriam asked from the living room. She was writing a letter. Her fingers were inky, and some of it had smudged on her forehead.

"*Nee.*" Betsie laughed at the sight. She walked over and rubbed the smudge. "I'm going to pick apples before all the good ones are gone. I was thinking of making a pie tonight."

"That sounds delicious," Miriam nodded. "We could invite Sarah and Kathy."

"*Ja*! Eli and Amos love apple pie. I'll even whip up some ice cream."

Betsie was content as she walked down the path towards the woods. She had a whole evening of her family to look forward to. Her mind went over all the ingredients she would need for the ice cream and how many apples she'd have to pick to make two large pies, and whether there was enough ice or if she would need to get more from town.

The wind picked up suddenly as she entered the woods, and clouds scudded in front of the sun. Birds sang and fought over morsels of food in the treetops, and squirrels ran through the foliage, collecting as much food as they could before winter hibernation.

In the center of the woods was a copse of apple trees. A few years ago this natural orchard had come under scrutiny. The Wittmar farm was closest to the woods, but the Stoltzfus homestead was right beside the path that led to the orchard. The Wittmars had laid claim to the copse, but the Stoltzfuses had campaigned for the woods to be a freehold of the community, not just one family. The Stoltzfuses had won, and apple picking in fall had become a tradition.

Betsie joined the throng of women and children who had come early like her, hoping to get the orchard to themselves. She greeted Kathy and Sarah, who were also there; Eli and Amos did most of the picking while the sisters gossiped.

"I won't hear a word," Betsie said, polishing an apple and placing it in her basket. "Miriam and I expect you for dinner. It's been so long since we all sat together for a meal."

"We can't expect you to cook for all of us!" Kathy protested.

"We'll help with the meal," Sarah said. "I'll bring the meatloaf I'd prepared for dinner."

"And I'll bring the chicken I've put in for roasting." Kathy clapped her hands.

"Excellent!" Betsie laughed.

"Escalent!" Amos garbled, pumping his tiny fists in the air.

"I'd better get started on the pastry." Betsie picked up her basket, considerably heavy now with a bounty of apples. "I'll see you tonight!" She waved goodbye.

Nodding her head in greeting to acquaintances, stopping here and there to enquire after the health of loved ones, it took Betsie longer to leave the orchard than it had to come in. She was enquiring after the health of Mildred Hilty, the old matriarch of the family, when she heard baleful sniggering. She glanced behind her to see Nancy Schwartz and her group of friends munching on apples and staring at her, their eyes narrowed with cruel resentment. Betsie ignored them, even though the thought-worm wriggled faster in her head.

"*Gott* willing, she will get better soon." Betsie pressed Patience Hilty's warm hand and took her leave. She hadn't gone far beyond the orchard when Nancy and her friends encircled her. Nancy's chin was slick with apple juice, her smile feral in her face.

"Have you decided where you'll be living, Betsie?" Nancy asked. "The town would be too small for the likes of you."

"What are you talking about?" Betsie frowned.

"Acting like she doesn't know." Rhoda Miller rolled her eyes.

"She's clever, our Betsie." Tessa Beiler sneered. "Pretending to be pious in the village while looking for wedding rings in town."

"Will you be wearing a lace dress at your wedding?" Nancy asked, "Which church will you be a part of, the church of science?"

"If you're not going to talk sense, there is no need to talk to me." Betsie dismissed Nancy with a wave of her hand.

"Your Samuel has been learning about machines and electricity in the town library," Nancy said, triumph in her voice. "He will not be baptized, we all know that. So just who do you think you're fooling?"

"Samuel would do no such thing," Betsie said.

"He has," Tessa said. "Or hasn't he told you? Oh, *Gott*, Betsie, does your Samuel not share his secrets with you?"

"Or are you lying because you would rather

leave the Amish ways to join the sinful world of *Englischer*?" Rhoda asked.

"I'm just glad to see perfect Miss Betsie Hershberger brought down a notch by *Gott's* great design." Nancy preened. "That's what you get for going around putting on airs, thinking you're better than the rest of us. Now *Gott* has made it so only the likes of Samuel King will walk out with you."

Their high-pitched laughter struck her like physical blows, and she felt her face go crimson. How dare they pity her! The worm-thought wiggled and burrowed deeper in her skull till she thought she would go insane with rage. Holding her head up high, she walked down the path at a steady pace so they wouldn't think their taunts had affected her in the slightest.

All the way to the dirt road she thought of how thoughtless Samuel was, how he hadn't considered once what his actions would do to her reputation. If this was the way he was going to be, then he shouldn't be surprised if she no longer wanted to be seen with him. Never in her life had anyone looked down on her like this. Nancy and her friends had never dared sneer at her. Now Betsie was ridiculed, and it was all Samuel's fault.

"Whoa there!"

A buggy came to a stop beside her. Betsie looked up to see the handsome face of Caleb Nolt looking down at her. He had rolled up his sleeves, and his hat was missing, allowing the wind to play havoc with his hair.

"What are you doing out in such horrendous weather?"

"I was picking apples in the orchard," Betsie pointed towards the woods.

"Is that right? Planning on baking a pie?"

"Indeed." Betsie grinned. "Two of them and ice cream, if I can manage."

"Sounds like an absolute treat." Caleb smiled. "Hop on and I'll give you a ride home."

"Oh, it's really no trouble." Betsie flushed. "I can walk. It's not far."

"Now what kind of person would I be if I let a pretty lady, like yourself, walk with a heavy basket in weather that's turning foul before our very eyes?"

Betsie couldn't meet his expressive blue eyes, she was so overcome with nervousness.

"I suppose," Betsie said. She gave him her basket to stow in the back. She placed a foot on the wheel spoke to lift herself up only to stumble. She would have landed in the dirt if Caleb hadn't caught her and pulled her in.

The wind howled in the trees and brushed Caleb's hair across her face. But for Betsie, time stood still. She was inches away from his face, and could feel his heart beating under her palm. His eyes darted from her eyes to her lips and she felt her mouth go dry. With great strength of will, she pulled herself away from Caleb, her nervous fingers clutching each other on her lap. She stared directly ahead, trying not to give away the depths of her feelings for this stranger sitting beside her.

"Heya!" Caleb cracked the reins on his roans' backs and they moved forward.

The silence was heavy and awkward. Betsie chewed on her lip, wondering how to break the ice.

"So." Caleb cleared his throat. "Your sister Kathy has been awfully kind to me."

"Is that so?"

"She's been sending over meals almost every day," Caleb said. "I never asked her to, but the entire community has been very nice. Kathy, Nancy, all the women have made me feel very welcome."

"Nancy? Nancy Schwartz?"

"*Ja.* You know her? The kindest girl, Nancy. She has often come to clean the house while I work in the field and cook up a meal. I guess she knows I don't have any women in the house to do it for me."

"Hmmm, that's sweet." Betsie's mouth twisted into a semblance of a smile. "Why don't you join us for dinner tonight?"

"Oh, I wouldn't want to impose."

"*Nee*, it would be our pleasure." Betsie grinned. "Give us a chance to do our neighborly duty."

"If it's not too much trouble."

"Not at all. Ivan and Kathy are also coming to dinner, so there will be two familiar faces."

"This is very kind of you," Caleb said. "I look forward to the evening."

"My sister Sarah will be coming as well," Betsie said, shielding her eyes from the wind. She saw a figure walking ahead of them on the path. "She has small children, so be mentally prepared for that."

"I shall be on hand to rescue you from any mishaps," Caleb laughed. Betsie giggled as the buggy stopped beside the man in the path. "Can I offer you a ride?"

Betsie, still laughing, looked down and her smile fell off her lips. Samuel's left eye was nearly closed from the swelling. His jaw was bruised, but healing. Yet none of this shocked her as much as the look of betrayal in his one good eye. She felt her insides fold up to become tiny.

"*Nee, denke.*" Samuel shook his head, his voice quiet with dignity. "I'm headed the other way and wouldn't want to inconvenience you."

"All right, safe travels." Caleb nodded and cracked the reins again. The buggy moved and Betsie felt jostled, not only by the motion of the carriage but by the shock and pinching guilt of her own heart.

Who had done that to Samuel?

Part of her wanted to jump off the buggy and run after Samuel, ask him what had happened and help her friend. The other half was crippled by guilt at the way she had been treating him recently.

"That's the King boy, isn't he? I heard he's delving into electricity and some such book learning. What his father has done may seem excessive, but I can understand it. I know, I know." He held his hand up when Betsie startled. "It's the boy's *Rumspringa,* and he's free to explore whatever he likes, but even *Rumspringa* should have limits. It was exactly because of this that I left my community. The Amish way wasn't sacred anymore. If I had children, I wouldn't want to see them leaving the Amish fold, and I'll bet Melvin

King loves his son too much to allow him to stray away from *Gott's* path."

Betsie gave this some thought. She believed Caleb when he said his concern for his children would be paramount. She had often felt a similar protective instinct towards her nephews.

But did that justify hitting the people you loved for their own good?

Very few people knew of the incident five years ago that led the elders to inspect Melvin's home and warn him against any form of violence. Betsie was one of them; she had seen the act first hand and reported it to her father. It was that incident that had cemented their friendship.

A keen emotion of nostalgia took hold of her and she wished they were children again, eating cookies in the green shade of a tree, with no romantic feelings tainting it. She felt the need to explain the buggy ride to Samuel. He had looked so hurt.

She shook her head to dispel the feelings of guilt. She wasn't doing anything wrong. She had just taken the help of a man who had offered it. It was just like Samuel to impose his feelings on Betsie, whether or not she wanted them. Well, she'd had enough of it. If he was going to do whatever he liked and didn't care about how Betsie felt, then neither would she.

Betsie guided Caleb to her home and skipped out nimbly when the buggy came to a stop beside her front porch. Miriam came out of the front door at that moment, and Betsie avoided her sister's gaze by turning to retrieve her basket of apples.

"*Gut* morning." Caleb waved.

"*Ja*, same to you," Miriam responded.

"This is Caleb, Miriam," Betsie said.

"Ah, Kathy's neighbor." Miriam smiled. "We've heard wonderful things about you."

"Your sister is too kind."

"He'll be joining us for dinner," Betsie said.

"Oh?" Miriam looked at Betsie, her eyes narrowed with concern, seeking answers in her little sister's nervous twitching. "That's wonderful. We'll see you tonight then."

Caleb waved goodbye and drove off. Betsie didn't wait to see him off. She rushed into the house and through to the kitchen. Soon her hands were busy washing apples and measuring flour for pastry.

"Betsie?"

"Hmm?" She didn't look up from her task, but

she knew Miriam must be leaning against the door frame, her hands folded as she assessed her.

"Is everything all right?"

"Of course." Betsie smiled brightly. "Miriam, would you be a dear and get some leeks and potatoes from the vegetable garden? I think I'll make a casserole."

Miriam stayed leaning against the doorframe a little longer, long enough to make Betsie break into a nervous sweat, but then thankfully she left, not asking any more questions. Betsie wiped the sweat off her brow and buried herself in her work just as she buried the thought-worm deeper in her head.

THE STRUGGLE

It ached to breathe, but Samuel did it anyway. It was the only form of rebellion he knew.

The ditch wasn't deep enough, and the wind was working against him, blowing dust around, filling up the bottom of the canal he was trying to make. But Samuel was stubborn, if he was anything. He continued to work, even as the light failed.

They had lost five chickens last year when the fall rains had fallen because the chicken coop was built on a lower incline, and it had been prone to flooding. Melvin's solution had been letting them run wild in the barn, but they agitated the rest of the livestock and were difficult to catch after the rains had gone.

Samuel had started constructing a new coop inside the barn, but Melvin had destroyed it in a fit of rage. So digging a ditch and a canal to divert the water was the only solution. Temporary, but needed, unless they wanted to lose more chicken.

With his one good eye, Samuel surveyed the work and was confident it would do. Lightning forked the sky near the horizon, and he estimated that rain would hit the village in another few hours.

He ushered the chickens into the barn, just in case.

It was only after he was finished with his work, and cleaning his hands at the water barrel outside the barn, that he allowed himself to think on what was really hurting his insides. Betsie Hershberger, laughing in the buggy of a stranger. And not just any stranger: a man the villagers had taken to, who was more accepted in Jamesport than Samuel was.

He should have known things with Betsie were too good to be true, and if he were honest, he knew she had never felt for him the way he felt for her. In a way, it was inevitable. But that didn't mean it didn't hurt the way it did, to see her happy with someone else.

The least she could have done was be honest with him.

He washed his face and let the water spill on his shirtfront as he decided to go over to her house that night to confront her. If she wanted to see someone else that was her prerogative, but she should have told him before making a fool of him in front of the rest of the villagers.

Breathing in and out to calm his mounting rage, he let himself inside through the backdoor of the house to await the evening.

APPLE PIE WITH A SCOOP OF RESENTMENT

"So what does this mean exactly?" Sarah settled into a chair.

"Nothing." Betsie shrugged.

"It has to mean something, Betsie," Kathy rolled her eyes, her grin infectious.

"Does Samuel know?" Miriam asked.

"There is nothing to know." Betsie slammed the casserole on the tabletop. "I just invited Caleb to dinner because he mentioned he liked pie and missed home cooking."

"I've been serving him meals." Kathy's tone implied that she didn't believe a word Betsie was saying. "And so has Nancy Schwartz."

"As if anything Nancy cooks is edible." Betsie made a face.

"Aha!" Sarah clapped her hands in delight. "I sense jealousy."

"I'm not jealous of Nancy Schwartz!"

"But you do like Caleb." Miriam smiled knowingly.

Betsie blushed but said nothing. Miriam helped set the table and Kathy asked the men to come in for dinner. Leroy was especially animated during the evening meal. He laughed at everything Caleb said and clapped him on the back several times. Betsie was secretly pleased because Leroy had never had such a positive response to anyone before.

"It's very difficult running a farm alone," Leroy said, flecks of pie crust in his beard. "You should look to marry soon and start a family."

Caleb caught Betsie's eye, and she blushed.

"I'm surprised you aren't already married," Sarah said, rocking Amos, who had fallen asleep in her arms, his tiny fist still clutching a crust of pie.

"Just never met anyone I liked enough." Caleb shrugged.

"I'm sure there must have been someone in your village," Kathy teased.

"Where are you from again?" Miriam asked, sipping on water. "Somewhere in Indiana, right?"

"Gasthof, Montgomery," Caleb said, scooping up melted ice cream and hot pie in his spoon.

"What a coincidence!" Miriam was delighted. "My friend Dorothy married a man from your village."

"Well…" Caleb chewed on his apple pie, his eyes on his plate. "I won't say that is my village anymore. I left it because of how progressive it was becoming. Why, I'm sure your friend has told you how they no longer follow the Amish ways, and have strayed so far in modernity that one can't tell if they were ever Amish to begin with."

Miriam looked confused. Betsie saw Caleb smile at her kindly.

"*Nee*," Miriam finally said. "Dorothy didn't mention that. She told me they are very strongly Amish, but they are introducing changes to their school system."

"Aha!" Caleb waved his spoon triumphantly. "There you have it. They are making school longer, teaching children more when all they need to know is how to run a farm and be able to read the Bible. What is all this book learning for if not to help their youth forget their roots?"

"I disagree." Miriam's jaw was set. Betsie laid a hand on her sister's arm, silently pleading with her to not make their guest uncomfortable, but

Miriam shrugged her hand off. "I think teaching should be advanced and a child should be taught for as long as they want, about whatever they want. Our children don't necessarily need to compete in education with the *Englischer* children, but I don't believe in stifling curiosity just because some might think it risks losing our children in *Rumspringa*."

"I can understand how you feel," Caleb said. "I also agree that knowledge is *Gott's* gift to man. But our youth won't know restraint unless it is taught. How many young children will be baptized into the faith once they are allowed to feast on every sin in the *Englischer* world? The number of Amish children who leave the fold is on the rise. Faced with this crisis, it is imperative to curb their curiosity, not fan the flames."

"I never did like the sound of this village, Gasthof." Leroy frowned. "And I always thought Dorothy was a shifty girl. She has been lying to you, Miriam. Misguiding you about that village and making you hope for a future that goes against our Amish ways."

"Oh, now," Caleb spread his hands towards Miriam, trying to make amends, "I have met Dorothy, and she is a lovely woman. She is a dutiful wife, but it is unfortunate that her husband has strayed from the Amish path. He must have told her to lie to you. Please don't hold it against her."

Miriam didn't respond. She refused *kaffe* and made patterns in her melted ice cream for the rest of the meal.

The men got up to go to the living room while the women cleaned up. Kathy collected silverware while Betsie collected the dirty dishes to hand to Miriam at the kitchen sink. Sarah shifted uncomfortably under Amos' weight.

"Here." Caleb walked back and gently took Amos from Sarah. "I'll keep him for a while, if you don't mind."

"*Denke*," Sarah said. "My back was killing me."

"It's a man's duty to provide every comfort for a young mother," Caleb said, rocking Amos in his large arms. "If you need anything else, let me know."

Caleb left for the living room, humming a hymn in Amos' ear. Sarah raised her eyebrows, but Betsie refused to meet her eye.

Rain had held off throughout the evening, but the wind had gotten colder by the time Caleb took his leave. Sarah and Kathy had already left with their families, while Leroy had made Caleb linger over *kaffe* with inane questions about farming in Indiana.

Betsie walked him out, her heart aglow in her chest. Other than the minor confrontation between Miriam and Caleb, the evening had gone well. Leroy had been happy and laughing, the children had been on their best behavior, and Caleb had been making eyes at her every time someone mentioned marriage.

Was she dreaming? This was too good to be true.

"Betsie."

"Hmm."

"I hope you won't think it forward of me, but would you like to go on a buggy ride with me sometime?"

Suddenly there was no air in her lungs. She felt lightheaded with joy.

"Betsie?"

"*Ja.*"

"Is that a yes to walking out with me or are you just responding to your name?"

His grin was mischievous, and it made her blush.

"Both," she whispered, but Caleb heard her before the wind snatched her answer away.

"*Gut*," he said and grinned. "Friday?"

Betsie nodded.

"Then I shall take leave of you before the heavens pour their blessings on us." He laughed.

She stood on the porch and waved him off, her belly full of butterflies. Was there anyone as lucky as her in the entire village? Nancy Schwartz would be green with envy at the sight of them riding along in the buggy.

"When were you planning on telling me?"

Betsie jumped, her hand clasping her mouth at the sudden interruption of her triumphant moment. Samuel stood in the shadows of the porch, leaning against the wall, his hands stuffed in his pockets like the *Englischer* delinquents they saw in the movies.

"You startled me," she said.

"No more than you did me." Samuel shrugged. He came forward, his eyes aglow with a strange light Betsie had never seen before. "I never thought you'd be the one to hurt me this way, Betsie."

Her cheeks burned as if he had smacked her. Thunder boomed, mirroring her own anger. How dare he say these things to her, turn the tables as if he were the victim in this relationship?

"And I never thought you'd hurt me, Samuel, but here we are." She spread her hands. Lightning streaked across the indigo sky. "Don't act innocent. You know what you've done. I had to hear from the likes of Nancy Schwartz that you've been studying books on machines from the library."

She held her hand up when Samuel opened his mouth to protest.

"Now, I know that you care little about your own reputation, but didn't you think about me and how your actions will reflect on me?"

Samuel looked as if he would argue. His cheeks were blotchy and his bruises were as indigo as the sky. He balled his fists and thumped them against his thighs so brutally that Betsie took a step back in alarm. She had never seen him do anything remotely violent; the anger in his face frightened her.

"Samuel!"

"I apologize for any stain I might have put on your perfect reputation," Samuel said through gritted teeth. "I wish you happiness."

He turned on his heels and vanished into the night as rain fell in earnest. Betsie stared after him, not sure what she was ashamed of more — hurting the feelings of her friend, or the immense relief she felt at being rid of him.

CRUMBS

Rain battered the roof like the tiny pattering feet of mischievous children, soaking the world, stripping it of its dead leaves before plunging it into winter. Inside the Hershberger house, candlelight still glowed against the encroaching darkness.

Miriam hummed to herself as she cleaned the dishes. Betsie had claimed a headache and gone to bed, so the task of cleaning up after the big dinner fell on Miriam. She didn't mind; it was the least she could do after Betsie had spent all day cooking.

Like a top spinning on its axis, her mind kept coming back to the same conversation, again and again. She went over Caleb's words and his actions. Something didn't ring true. He was very handsome and charming to boot. He was well respected and liked in the community, even though he hadn't been with them very long. Yet Miriam felt uneasy when she thought about him and the things he had said about Dorothy.

"That went well." Leroy came into the kitchen, his thumbs tucked into his suspenders. "I think our guest went home happy."

"Hmm," Miriam murmured.

"I have a feeling he'll be back here soon." Leroy smirked, looking sideways at Miriam. "In fact, I'm sure of it."

"Huh?" Miriam hadn't been listening. She turned her attention to Leroy, who was grinning openly. "What's happened? Why are you so happy?"

"I told you things would turn around, didn't I? I told you *Daed* was on the case."

"Huh?"

"You're very smart, Miriam, but *Gott* help me, sometimes you can be very slow. I'm talking about Caleb! How will he do for a husband, eh?"

She was so shocked at her father's declaration, she nearly dropped the plate she had been cleaning. Mistaking her surprise for stunned pleasure, Leroy laughed and clapped his hands.

"Oh, I am so glad *Gott* sent Caleb to deliver us! And straight from that village you wanted to move to no less. *Gott* works in mysterious ways, bringing the best of that village to your doorstep so you don't have to leave and go so far away."

"I don't want to be married." Miriam slammed the plate into the sink, two pinpoints of pink blooming in her pale cheeks. "How many times do I have to say this?"

"This is the first I'm hearing of it." Leroy's brow furrowed, his expression darkening. He wasn't used to being rebuked or chastised by his daughters. He expected to be thanked and praised when he brought them some sweet token or good news, not having his offering spat on. "What young girl doesn't want to marry? Isn't Caleb good-looking enough for you?"

"It's not that." Miriam sighed. She rubbed her temples with soapy hands. "All I want to do is teach. That is all I want from my life."

"No one's stopping you from teaching. I'm sure if I talk to Caleb he will allow you to teach as well after marriage, granted all the housework is cared for. And you're going to have to learn to cook. No more nonsense about being afraid. I will not be able to convince anyone to marry you if you refuse to cook."

"Am I speaking in tongues? I said I don't want to be married! And as far as Caleb Nolt is concerned, you're mistaken about his affections. Yes, he will come back to this house but not to court me. He was making eyes at Betsie the entire evening. You would know that if you ever paid attention in your own home!"

The silence was suffocating, pricking their skins with sharp knives that cut to the quick with every breath. Miriam knew she had taken things too far. Leroy deserved her respect by virtue of being her father, but he had pushed her to the edge where she had no choice but to push back or fall over the edge.

"He wouldn't have made eyes at our Betsie if you had let things alone," Leroy growled. "But no, you had to question him, argue with him, and make him feel unwelcome. No man likes a disrespectful wife, and you're hacking my efforts at the knees by being unsociable. Your mother would have been disappointed."

He shook his head, his mouth a thin line, his eyes accusing her of forcing him to say the hurtful things neither of them had wanted to say. Miriam offered no argument, no solace or reproach, so Leroy left her in the kitchen with the single candle burning bright to keep the dark away.

Finished with the dishes, she dusted the crumbs off the table. All she was asking for was crumbs of affection from the world, because that was all she could hold in her palms. Too much love made her panic about losing it. It always had. It was a fact about her she could not change, just as she could not cook to save her life.

Sighing, she made a mound of the crumbs on the windowsill for the ants, then blew out the candle and took herself to bed. Just before drifting off to sleep she decided to write to Dorothy and accept the job. She needed to get far away from Jamesport for the sake of her own sanity.

NEWTON

The sun hadn't come out since the storm broke three days ago. Clouds scudded across the sky and the wind had grown extra teeth to bite through sweaters and jackets. People didn't linger long on the street, preferring to be indoors where warmth could be shared over mugs of *kaffe*. They scurried on the sidewalks looking for shelter.

All but one.

Garbed in a thick winter coat, his straw hat resting low to hide the yellowing stains on his face, Samuel stood across from the public library. He looked at the gray stone building quizzically, cocking his head to the side, and wondered why he had been so afraid to go in.

His steps were confident as he climbed the short steps. The door was heavier than he had imagined; the hinges needed oiling, and the wood looked like it would warp in the bitter cold. His breath crystallized in front of him as he shoved the door open.

The inside was mercifully warm and overly bright. The fluorescent light pinched his eyes and for a moment Samuel stood blinded. Rubbing his eyes with his cold knuckles, Samuel stimulated them enough to open.

It was just like he had imagined. Rows upon rows, aisles upon aisles of books; short books, tall books, small, large, thick, thin, brand new and falling apart. Samuel inhaled the smell unique to a library and felt his lungs fortified with their magic.

"I see you've finally mustered the courage."

Hector walked around the desk at the front of the library, his hand outstretched in greeting. Samuel took the proffered hand.

"What made you decide?"

"I realized I have nothing to lose." Samuel shrugged. "That was liberating."

"That's great!" Hector slapped Samuel on the back. "Now, let's get you started. I've already taken out a few books I thought you might like. Now where did I… ah! Here they are."

From under a pile of paper, Hector extracted three books and handed them to Samuel.

"You placed these aside for me?" Samuel looked at the covers of the books with wonder. "How did you know I was going to come?"

"I knew you'd get the courage one day, so I set aside the basics of engineering and physics for you after we talked a few weeks ago," Hector grinned. "I even made you a library card."

He held out a small card. Samuel took it and examined it. It was pink, and it had his name on it, with a date of issue and expiration.

"*Denke*," Samuel whispered. "This has been the best thing to happen to me in a while."

"I'm glad," Hector said, his concerned eyes roaming over the fading bruises on Samuel's face. Samuel knew the harsh light must put his injuries in greater relief, yet in this moment he didn't care to hide them. "You're welcome to stay and read and learn for as long as you want, and I'll check these books out for you to take home at the end of the day."

"*Denke*," Samuel said again. "*Denke*."

Hector guided him to a secluded spot, furnished him with pen and paper, and let him dive into the world he had only ever dreamed about.

BOOKS TUCKED UNDER HIS ARMS, Samuel walked towards the edge of the town that met the woods. He passed a few familiar faces that stopped and ogled at the books he made no move to hide. Some gasped, some prayed for *Gott* to forgive him his trespasses, yet none of that stung or hurt anymore.

He was past the point of caring about the opinions of people that had always been quick to judge him, but never offer him or his mother a helping hand. The elders had stopped checking on Melvin when Samuel had turned fourteen. As time had passed Melvin's anger had gotten worse, and he felt no need to control his rages anymore. All of that had resulted in Melvin's raging on the porch that had injured Samuel and hurt his mother.

And now the village judged him for being different, for being curious about a world beyond the Amish village. Samuel had decided he would no longer restrain his pursuit of happiness to please these people.

Samuel considered what he had said to Hector about not having anything to lose, and he realized it was true. There had been only two things holding him back from getting into the library — the thought of what Melvin would do if he found out, and what Betsie would think or have to face because of him. Yet none of his restraint had done much good. Melvin had still lost his temper, and Betsie had trusted the gossip more than Samuel, moving on to a more suitable suitor as quick as blinking, before she had even informed Samuel of the fact.

The thought of Betsie's betrayal made him feel rage he didn't think he was capable of. The night he had visited her to ask her about Caleb and seen her making plans for buggy rides on the porch, he had tasted a little of the violent venom that ran in Melvin's blood. He had been so blinded by anger he had felt his hands twitch to strike out for all the hurt and humiliation. The urge had been so strong he had turned his fist on his own thighs, rather than betray his mother's upbringing and prove he was, after all, his father's son.

"Every object in a state of uniform motion tends to remain in that state of motion unless we apply an external force to it," he recited as he walked through the darkening woods towards home. Reading the books had brought him peace. He was curious to know more, but the hunger for knowledge wasn't as urgent as it had been before, because now he knew that frequent meals of information would be coming.

Though it was early evening, the King house was dark. Melvin hated waste, and he deemed twilight enough light to see by. Candles were only permitted after proper dark had fallen. Samuel took two steps at a time and went directly to his room to deposit the books under his floorboard. He didn't care if Melvin found his books or his mechanical toys, but he cared about Selma, so for the time being he'd pretend to be following Melvin's rules.

"What have you got there?"

Samuel froze, the loose floorboard in his hand. Heavy footsteps came into the room, the soft patter of female feet behind them. Melvin glowered down at his son, while Selma whimpered behind his back.

"I asked what you've got there." Melvin's voice was dangerously low but Samuel didn't feel his bowels tighten, or his hackles rise as they used to. Instead, he felt a weightlessness that was new, yet empowering.

"These are the books I borrowed from the town library," Samuel said, straightening up to his full height. "And the rest are toys and machines I made from scraps I found at the junkyard over the years."

Melvin was breathing so hard he sounded like a locomotive Samuel had seen in one of those Western movies David Stoltzfus loved so much. The thought of Melvin the angry locomotive was so ridiculous, yet accurate, it made Samuel chuckle.

"What are you laughing at, you worthless maggot? I'll give you something to laugh about!"

Melvin pulled back his hand, accidentally hitting Selma in the nose with his elbow, and swung it towards Samuel's face. But Samuel was too quick for him. He caught Melvin's wrist in his hand and held it firm. Melvin jerked and grunted to get his hand free, but Samuel wouldn't let go.

"Are you okay, *Mamm?*" he asked.

"Let go of me this instant," Melvin snarled, "or it will be terrible for you!"

"Worse than what you've done till now?" Samuel asked, increasing pressure on his hold, twisting Melvin's arm ever so slightly enough that it would bring the older man pain. He saw the twinkle of fear in his father's eyes, but it brought him no pleasure. "Worse than hitting *Mamm?*"

Twist.

"Worse than your taunts, your constant disappointment?"

Twist.

"Samuel! You're hurting him!" Selma screamed.

He looked at her then, the cowering shape of his mother, her arms up around her face in case she needed to protect it, her eyes full of terror; yet she wasn't looking at Melvin, the sole bringer of misery in her life so far. She was looking at him.

Samuel let go of Melvin's arm as if he had been burned. He took a step back from his father, who was rubbing his wrist and starting at him as if he had seen a ghost. Shame scalded Samuel's stomach and lined his intestines like lead.

"Let me take a look," Selma whispered, trying to touch Melvin's hand.

"Don't touch me!" Melvin roared. "You put him up to this!" He raised his other hand to strike Selma.

"*Daed.*" Samuel didn't raise his voice, but the warning in it was plain.

Melvin stared between mother and son, his large eyes bugging out of his skull.

"*Gott* have mercy on your damned souls." He spat and left, rubbing his aching wrist. "I'm done with the lot of you!"

He had done it. Samuel had finally conquered his fear and stood up to his father. Yet there was no triumph in his victory, only burning shame at the knowledge that at the heart of it he was no better than his father. Selma edged up to him and touched his hanging head.

"I'm sorry," he murmured. "I was only trying to protect you."

"You've grown so big," Selma said quietly. "I know you'll soon grow out of your father's shadow."

She kissed his forehead and squeezed his hand. After Selma left, Samuel gazed down at the treasure trove under his floorboard. There was no point in hiding it to collect dust anymore. He fished out all of his models and toys and placed them on the windowsill and the desk in his room. He put the books in the place of honor and, to calm his shaking hands, opened one of them to distract himself.

Rule III - For every action there is an equal and opposite reaction.

Samuel couldn't help but laugh at how true it was, his mind marveling at the wonder of science and how people couldn't see the hand of *Gott* in it.

EYE OF THE BEHOLDER

Betsie sat with her back straight. The rug on her lap was warm, but she didn't feel the need for it. She was flushing hot and cold sitting in such close proximity to Caleb. It was their third buggy ride together and already she had seen that his eyes became a darker shade of blue when he was thinking and a periwinkle blue when he was happy, that there was a small dimple in his chin, and that he had a small mole under his left eyebrow.

Caleb had asked her to decide where they would go. She had taken him for *kaffe* at a small café in the center of town, and then to an ice skating rink because it was still too early in the winter to skate on the frozen lake. Slipping and sliding, they had laughed on the ice as they got their bearings, hands clutching, warm breath on their faces. Betsie couldn't remember the last time she had felt so excited to be alive.

Now they were just riding around town, prolonging the time when the ride would have to end. They passed a gaggle of *Rumspringa* girls in front of a diner, and Betsie saw Nancy Schwartz amongst them. Betsie looked away. There would have been a time she would have looked Nancy straight in the eye and relished the other girl's pain, but she wasn't that girl anymore. Samuel had helped her see how mean-spirited that was.

There was a collective gasp, and Betsie knew they had spotted her. She tried to look impassive as they passed the girls, but a thrill of delight had gone through her, imagining Nancy watching Caleb talking animatedly with Betsie in his buggy beside him. Betsie had changed much over the years, but Samuel's influence hadn't changed her basic nature. A large grin widened across her face.

As if he had manifested out of her thoughts, she saw Samuel crossing the road. He was preoccupied, and she could tell he wasn't aware of his surroundings because he hadn't turned towards the gasping, screaming girls, or the clip-clop of the buggy. She noticed he was smiling and murmuring to himself, a stack of books in his hands. So it was true. He had been taking books out of the library.

"That boy will be the death of his mother," Caleb said, his tone somber. "Getting into scrapes with local boys and delving in mechanics and such. I pity his parents."

"Samuel doesn't get in scrapes," Betsie said.

"That's what Nancy told me." Caleb shrugged. "She says he is deeply unsociable and frequently gets in fights for minor reason. She told me," Caleb whispered as if he were about to say something vile, "Samuel hits his own mother."

"That's not true," Betsie said in clipped tones. "I am much better acquainted with the King family than Nancy, and I can tell you that Samuel wouldn't hurt a fly."

Caleb shrugged.

"Either way," he said. "If he were my son, I'd teach him a thing or two about his duty to his family and community. All this book learning is rotting his brain, making him selfish."

"What do you mean?" Betsie asked, a vague sense of panic scratching at the back of her head.

"You have to start early. You can't spoil them when they're young and expect them to follow rules when they're older. It requires a good father figure, a role model boys can look up to."

Betsie smiled and let out a breath she hadn't known she was holding. They were entering the village now and as they passed homesteads Betsie saw men and women look at them with obvious delight in their eyes. Children waved and men doffed their hats at Caleb in greeting, nodding at Betsie in approval of her choice.

No one laughed at her, no one gave her superior looks or sneered. She was finally getting the respect she deserved, and it was all thanks to Caleb Nolt.

THE LETTER

"This just arrived for you."

Leroy placed the letter on the table beside the basket in which Miriam was shelling peas. Instead of leaving to tend to his work on the farm, he pulled out a chair and sat down. Miriam glanced up once at his gaunt face and turned her attention to the letter.

Dorothy's reply had finally arrived!

Miriam patted her fingers dry on her apron and made to open the letter, but Leroy placed his hand on hers, stopping her. His hand was warm and worn, like old leather, grown wrinkled and scabbed over years of toil.

"Is this really what you want?"

They hadn't been on speaking terms for over a

week now. After the hurtful things they had said to each other, casting them like stones, it wasn't easy to get back into the glass house of illusion they had lived in before.

Now Miriam saw that Leroy looked thinner and older than he had the previous week. All his bravado had evaporated and in front of her sat a father who couldn't understand why his daughter would want to leave.

"*Ja*," Miriam nodded.

"May I ask why?"

"I told you, *Daed*." Miriam sighed. "I wish to travel, to know more. Dorothy's village offers more opportunities, they offer learning courses for teachers, they offer much more than I can achieve here."

"Marriage..." Leroy spread his hands. "Is marriage completely off the table?"

"I don't know." Miriam shrugged. "All I know is that I don't feel any desire to marry. If we were Catholic, and not Amish, I probably would have entered a nunnery."

"Then I thank *Gott* that you are Amish. At least this way we'll get to see you," Leroy smiled weakly. "Your mother was like you. Fiercely independent and she knew her mind. Once she'd made it up, it was impossible to change it. She was a *gut* woman and I miss her every day."

Miriam squeezed his calloused hand.

"May I ask one favor of you?"

Miriam nodded.

"May I go with you to see this village first before you move there? Caleb's description has me worried and I want to see it for myself."

"Of course you may accompany me," Miriam said. "It will comfort me that you know in which circumstances I will live in. But please, don't take Caleb's word over Dorothy's. We have known Caleb only a few weeks, but we have known Dorothy our entire lives. Her grandfather was one of the elders."

"You're right, but we can't dismiss what Caleb says lightly either. Why don't you like Caleb?"

"There's just something about him I don't trust," she said, opening the letter. "I can't place my finger on it. Oh!" She bit her lip as she unfolded the letter. "I hope my reply was in time and the position hasn't been filled."

She skimmed the letter, her face breaking into a large grin that faded quickly as her eyes went further down the page. She flipped pages, reading quickly, her hands clutching the papers.

"What is it? You didn't get the job?" Leroy asked. Miriam ignored the hopeful tone.

"I got the job but," Miriam sighed, "I mentioned Caleb Nolt in passing in my letter."

"And?"

Miriam didn't know what to say, or how to say it, so she handed the letter to Leroy to read. She had found mention of Caleb in the second paragraph, and a host of details that made her stomach tighten into a knot of fear. It was as she had suspected, but worse. Much worse.

ACCUSATIONS

As they drove up to the Hershberger house the sun finally broke through the clouds, throwing its rays on the land of fading colors. The dull greens and the fading yellows thrilled for a while in the weak sunshine, the dead leaves swayed and danced, rejoicing in the warmth.

It temporarily blinded Betsie, and she had to shield her eyes to see the movement she had glimpsed on the porch. She recognized Miriam's tall figure, silhouetted against the open front door. Betsie wondered if everything was okay. Her first thought was Sarah and her baby. But Sarah wasn't due for another month. Still, what if the baby had come early? It wasn't unheard of.

"Everything all right, I hope," Caleb said.

"I think it might be Sarah," Betsie said, wringing her hands. As soon as the buggy stopped Caleb jumped out and helped Betsie get off. "What is it? What's happened?"

"Betsie, I need you to come with me," Miriam said. Her mouth was a thin line, and her eyes were stony. She hadn't greeted Caleb as was her custom, and she wasn't looking at him at all.

"But what's happened?" Betsie asked, not moving away from Caleb.

"Betsie, come inside, please!"

"Miriam," Caleb said, extending a hand. "You're scaring Betsie. Just tell her what's happened, I'm sure she can handle it."

Miriam gave Caleb a scathing look and walked down the porch steps till she was standing in front of them. She was nearly as tall as Caleb and towered over Betsie.

"Here." She thrust a letter in Betsie's hand. "Read it."

While Betsie read the letter Miriam maneuvered her away from the buggy and closer towards the porch. Betsie wasn't aware of anything being done to her. She was engrossed in the letter as it landed one blow after another.

"... niece in Rumspringa... wore jeans in town... at-

tacked... arrested for assault... charges dropped... shunned..."

"We'd like for you to leave, Mr. Nolt," Miriam said. "Our father isn't at home at the moment, and it wouldn't be appropriate."

"I want to help," Caleb said. "Is it Sarah? I can get you to her house in my buggy."

"*Nee, denke,*" Miriam said. "We'll manage on our own."

"You know, you must really start accepting people's help when they offer it, Miriam. Pretty soon you'll need someone and no one will be there to help you."

"We don't need your help."

"May I ask why?"

"Is this true?" Betsie asked breathlessly, finally surfacing from the depths of her shock. She handed Caleb the letter. "Is this true?"

Caleb scanned the letter, his mouth an irreverent grimace. He scoffed as he read and finally handed it to Miriam, a scornful smile on his face.

"It's from Dorothy, no doubt," he said.

"Is it true?" Miriam asked coolly.

"*Ja,* and *nee,*" Caleb said. "*Ja,* I stopped my niece from going down a sinful path when my brother couldn't control his offspring. *Nee,* I did

211

nothing wrong as my old village insists on painting it."

"Nothing wrong?" Miriam was outraged. "They hospitalized the girl."

"And I'll bet you she never sins with jeans and those vulgar tops again." Caleb shrugged.

"It was her *Rumspringa*," Betsie said. "She was within her rights to dress as she wanted."

"*Gott* allows for finding a fit spouse in *Rumspringa*. He does not allow for vulgarity," Caleb growled. "Vulgar behavior, vulgar dress. They are never okay to use."

"So you beat her," Miriam said. "You beat her in the town square to make an example of her."

"She was asking for it." Caleb slashed his hand in annoyance. "And you're asking for it as well, if you don't stop pestering me. I've seen countless mean-spirited busybodies like you, turning the minds of young girls against their men just because you can't have one. Bitter spinsters like you make me sick."

He took a threatening step forward but Betsie launched herself in between, her heart thumping, mad with terror. She had visions of a young boy being beaten by his father while she screamed for him to stop. The terror she had felt then came back, but twofold, as she faced the abuser head on, instead of standing on the sidelines.

"Tell your sister to behave while she talks to me," Caleb warned. "Your father might tolerate her headstrong ways, but I won't."

"Leave!" Betsie cried.

Caleb smirked, then laughed.

"Who's going to make me?" he asked, looking around the yard. "You?"

"Ben!" Miriam cried and waved. The buggy passing by the yard stopped and Ben waved back. Miriam waved at him to come over. "Ben, I need to send a pattern Sarah asked for!"

The buggy turned into the drive and Caleb backed away a few steps. He doffed his hat at Ben, made a show of saying goodbye to Miriam and Betsie, then got into his buggy and left.

"Are you two okay?" Ben asked. "You're as white as a sheet."

"The flu." Miriam coughed. "It's been going around so we won't ask you to stay long."

"I'll just wait outside." Ben rushed back to his buggy.

"Come on." Miriam dragged Betsie inside the house. "Are you okay?" She held Betsie's face in her hands. "I didn't know what to do. *Daed* had gone off to see Mr. Hooley, Dorothy's father, and I wasn't expecting to see *him* so soon after."

"It's okay." Betsie patted Miriam's arm absently. "We're all right now."

"Should we go to the elders?" Miriam asked. "I think we should go to the elders but *Daed* thinks everyone deserves another chance."

"*Daed's* right." Betsie nodded, only half listening, her mind fixed on that boy in the yard five years ago: a boy without a friend. "Everyone deserves a second chance."

"Really?" Miriam looked at Betsie as if she were seeing her for the first time. "Are you so determined to be married that you're willing to see past a man who has a record of abusive behavior and who just threatened you and your sister?"

"Miriam." Betsie stroked Miriam's arm. "I have to go."

"Betsie!"

She ran down the front porch, ignoring Ben's calls to her as she ran across the yard and into the dirt path. She ran to catch up with a mistake she had made before it became unforgivable.

FRIENDLY VISITS

It was dusk, night hadn't truly fallen, but a candle shone in Samuel's room. He pored over open books, murmuring the long tough words aloud to feel them roll on his tongue. Every word felt like he was unraveling a parcel of possibilities. The smell of printed paper, dust, and candle wax was intoxicating and heady. He jotted down notes, names he needed to look up, definitions and experiments he needed to familiarize himself with. A whole world had opened up for him, and Samuel wondered if he dared take the leap.

Making sure his door was firmly closed, Samuel kneeled under his bed and took out the one thing he still felt uncomfortable leaving out in the open.

The glossy cover was as inviting as the smile of the woman on it. Samuel ran a finger across the title and felt his throat tighten with unbridled desire.

Hector had given it to him on his last visit to the library. He said Samuel didn't have to bring this one back. It was for him to keep, whether or not he used it. Samuel sighed and opened the prospectus of Missouri State University and read the letter of the Dean of Admissions.

His heart thumped madly against his chest and sweat broke out on his forehead. Opting for college meant that Samuel would have to sit for a high school examination, take the SATs, and then look for scholarship programs because he couldn't afford the tuition fee. It would also mean leaving the community, and as things stood there wasn't much to keep him here.

Opening up the prospectus to the end, Samuel poised his pen to enter his name when there was a knock on his window. He jumped two feet into the air, his pen went flying and rolled under the bed, his prospectus smacked on the floor.

Betsie Hershberger was at his window, moving from foot to foot, looking at him anxiously. He opened the window, surprised to see her. He had thought she would never want to see him again after their last meeting. Yet here she was, climbing inside his window as if they were children again, and she had come to blackmail him into taking her to town to see Ben.

"I need to say two things to you," she said in hushed, harried whispers. "One: I'm sorry. I was wrong and selfish and you deserved better than that because you have always been honest with me except about the books..."

She halted, her eyes taking in the books, the toys, all his hidden secrets out in the open.

"Are you crazy, Samuel?" she whispered harshly, punching him on the arm. "Your *Daed* will kill you."

"He tried." Samuel shrugged. "He's not very good at it."

"What are you saying?" Betsie looked confused.

"A lot has happened since you and I stopped talking." Samuel casually kicked the prospectus under the bed and sat down at his desk. He pretended to be reading so she couldn't see his perspiring face.

"Samuel," Betsie said, "I'm really sorry. It was a rotten thing that I did. You were right. I betrayed you. I was so hung up on what people thought, on what I thought of myself, that I forgot about what's important."

Samuel licked his lips. He turned around.

"I shouldn't have lost my temper," he said. "I also shouldn't have asked you to walk with me when I knew you didn't have feelings for me. I understand how you must have felt trapped."

"I didn't feel trapped. I felt like our friendship was fading because of it. I need your friendship because it has always been a guiding force for me, and I need a lot of guidance right now."

"Tell me," Samuel said, placing a slip of paper in his book and closing it.

"It's about Caleb." Betsie bit her lip. "He isn't the man we think he is. He is an abuser, and he's not ashamed of it. In fact, he threatened Miriam and me, if we dared say anything or disrespect him."

Samuel felt pain radiate up from his palms. He looked down to see he had been digging his nails into them so hard he had left crescent impressions in his palm.

"*Daed* thinks we should stay quiet about it and let him have his second chance at an Amish life," Betsie said, too lost in her own narrative to notice the effect it was having on Samuel. "But Caleb feels like there was nothing he should be ashamed of and is threatening the same violence. He doesn't want a second chance; he wants to continue where he left off."

"You should tell the elders," Samuel said. "Men like him shouldn't be allowed near our community. We already have more than enough amongst us."

"You think so?"

"*Ja*," Samuel nodded.

"But what about your *Daed*?" she whispered, avoiding looking into his eyes. "Did you report him? Is that why you can..." She waved at the forbidden things around her.

"The elders stopped checking on *Daed* a few years ago, which is why this happened." Samuel pointed at the fading bruise on his face. "But the elders stopped *Daed* from doing more harm than he is capable of. They would want to know about a man like Caleb. He wants to discipline more than his own family, and that won't sit well with the elders. Now is your chance to cut him out of the village."

"But then how... how can you get away with this?"

"I realized I'm a few inches taller than my father, and while he grows weak, I grow stronger."

Samuel smiled an ironic smile. "He realized these things too."

"So it's stopped?" Betsie asked, her hand touching Samuel's arm. He could see the bright delight in her eyes and he suddenly knew that he could never walk away from this village because his heart belonged to Betsie Hershberger, and Betsie belonged to the village. He decided to hand the prospectus back to Hector. He could only do with so much temptation in his life.

"Yes, it's stopped." Samuel smiled up at her. Her laughter was infectious, but she stopped suddenly, no doubt thinking of the task that lay ahead of her.

"*Denke* for your help, Samuel," she said. "I'll go talk to the elders right now. This thing can't wait till morning."

"If you need anything else, just let me know. I'm still your friend. I never stopped being that."

He was surprised for a second time when Betsie leaped forward and engulfed him in a hug.

THE VERDICT

She held Betsie's hand, giving as much comfort as she was receiving. Miriam stood in the yard of Caleb Nolt's house with the rest of the neighbors, waiting for the men inside to decide the fate of their newest member.

"Is it true?" a woman asked.

"Why would Miriam lie?"

"She's a spinster. All her other sisters are married and now the youngest one is catching the most handsome man to walk the village."

"You're right. She's bound to be jealous."

"He's too charming to be abusive."

"He helped me plant my runner beans the other day."

"He helped me carry the pails of water. I can't manage with my back."

"Such a nice boy."

Miriam tried to drown out the vapid drone of the women and concentrate on the shape of Betsie's hand, the ridges, the bone structure, the smoothness of the wrist to the rough patches of her palms.

"We believe you," Kathy said, rubbing her back. "Don't listen to the old crone brigade."

Miriam gave her sister a small smile. She would never show it, but Caleb's threats had unnerved her. She had never faced such violence in her life. It had shocked her and made her appreciate how kind Leroy was as a father, even if he was a little neglectful.

She had heard of Melvin King and his angry outbursts from Betsie, but she had been so far removed from it that she thought it could never affect her. How wrong she had been. To allow abuse to happen at all was to make yourself vulnerable to it.

"I can't believe she's brought him food," Kathy groaned.

Nancy Schwartz walked into the yard with a tray full of food. She was sashaying about, a secretive smile on her face. She was darting triumphant looks towards Betsie.

"I can't allow the poor man to starve," Nancy shouted. "It's bad enough that *gut* men like him are being accused of such vile acts, must we also starve him to death?"

She hadn't made it to the porch when the front door opened and the elders filed out. Caleb wasn't among them, but Miriam could see Leroy and Arthur Hooley, Dorothy's father.

Joseph Miller, the eldest of the elders, came forward on the porch.

"I would request that no one disturb Mr. Nolt from this moment on," Joseph said in a carrying voice. Nancy shot a ferocious grin at Betsie. "He has lied by omission about his past. If we had known of his shunned status in Gasthof, we would not have allowed him to live amongst us. This community has hereby shunned him for threatening two of our own. Now, please. Head home. No one lives here."

"*Nee!*" Nancy cried. "*Nee*, you lie."

"Nancy." Her father, a big beefy man, strode forward and grabbed her by the arms. "Come home this instant!"

"But she's lying. She's just being spiteful!"

Nancy Schwartz screamed. She threw a dish full of potato salad at Betsie's head. Betsie ducked, but the woman behind her didn't. The dish struck Eva Fisher, splattering her dress with potatoes. "This is enough madness," Joseph Miller shouted. "Martin, control your *dochder*. Someone take Mrs. Fisher inside and check her for injuries. This man has been worse than the devil to divide our community, and it reinforces the elders' decision to shun him forthwith!"

"You did it." Miriam hugged Betsie.

"*Nee.*" Betsie grinned. "We did it. He won't bother our women anymore."

"Well, at least now you'll have one less thing to worry about before you leave," Kathy said.

Miriam looked confused.

"*Daed* told us," Kathy said. "He talked to Mr. Hooley and has been reassured about Dorothy's village. He's finally coming to terms with your leaving."

"Really?" Miriam looked across the yard at her father. Leroy was frowning at the house, his brow dark and his mouth twisted down in a scowl. Miriam felt a love for her father she had never known before.

He was forgetful and distracted at best, neglectful at worst, but his heart had always been in the right place. Leroy loved all his daughters, and anyone threatening them was enough to make that person his enemy. She could finally see what their mother must have seen in him.

EPILOGUE

"I might not write often, but you write to me every week," Leroy said.

"You'd better do as he asks," Ivan said, "because if you miss a week, he'll catch a train to see if you're okay."

"And haven't been murdered by an axe-wielding lunatic," Ben joked. Leroy went visibly pale.

"Ben!" the Hershberger girls protested, slapping him on the arm as a reprimand.

"I'll be fine, *Daed.*" Miriam said. "And I will write every week. You have my promise."

"Is all your luggage in the carriage? Do you have the money I gave you? Did you pack her lunch, Betsie?"

"Yes, *Daed!*" the Hershberger girls cried in unison.

The whistle blew, and passengers headed inside the train.

"I love you, *Daed*," Miriam hugged her father. "And *denke*, for letting me do this."

"*Gott* be with you, my *dochder*." Leroy tried hard to keep from crying, but failed. "Now go. You'll miss the train."

Betsie waved with the rest and watched the train pull away from the platform, Miriam's smiling face becoming blurry as she got further and further, or maybe her tears made Betsie's vision blurry, she couldn't be sure.

On the way back to the village, Betsie asked to be dropped off at the King house. She had been thinking about it for a while and she had some questions she needed to ask.

She had discovered a few truths about herself this past month. Truths that weren't pretty. She had realized that she had a high opinion of herself, and that she thought she was better than most. But her biggest crime was to think she was better than Samuel, and that she was aiming beneath her when she said yes to walking out with him. It shamed her to admit it, but now that she had it was easier to work on these problems.

Coming upon the King house, she hid in the bushes and aimed pebbles at Samuel's window, not sure if he would be in his room or not. After the second pebble, she saw his face peering out. She waved at him to come out. He joined her in the bushes and they walked towards the woods, their shadows going before them.

"If I were to ask you to quit your book learning for me, would you?" she asked, bending to pick up a smooth pebble.

"I know you want me to say yes, and *Gott* knows I'm tempted to say yes," Samuel said slowly, as if he were measuring every word. "But that would mislead you and I can't lie to you. I have spent most of my life lying to myself, trying to be something that I'm not to please others. I have finally found the courage to be myself. So the answer is no."

Betsie pursed her lips.

"Now I have a question for you, Betsie. Would you want to marry someone who lived under others' shadows, who was so easily swayed by what others wanted he couldn't stand up for what he believed in – himself, and his family?"

"*Nee*," Betsie said.

"Then why would you ask me to be someone like that?"

She looked at him and saw what she hadn't noticed before. He was taller, broader in the shoulders, and he held his head higher than he had before. His eyes were still kind and generous in their compassion, but they were also guarded now.

Betsie Hershberger saw a man she could grow to love. And for now, that was good enough.

They walked back out of the woods, their shadows holding hands.

Before turning the page and reading the next book in the series, you might be interested in **clicking here to get notification when the next book is available,** and to hear about other good things I give my readers (or copy and paste this link into your browser: *bit.ly/Grace-FreeBook*). **You will also receive a free copy of *Secret Love* and *River Blessings*, exclusive spinoffs from the Amish Hearts and the Amish Sisters series** for members of my Readers' Group. These stories are NOT available anywhere else.

FREE DOWNLOAD

EXCLUSIVE and FREE
for subscribers of
my Readers' Group

CLICK HERE!

amazon kindle

THE HEART OF PERSEVERANCE

BOOK DESCRIPTION

After three years of courtship, Betsie Hershberger wants to get married, but it doesn't look like Samuel King is going to propose anytime soon. Frustrated with his lack of commitment, Betsie is thinking of finding someone else. But when her father expresses the same wish and presents her with two suitors, Betsie is conflicted about what to do.

Samuel wants to marry Betsie, but he has problems at home that need his attention. His mother is very ill and needs treatment that his father refuses to let her get. His earnings in the village aren't enough, and the job in town goes against the Amish way.

With one thing going wrong after another, will Samuel and Betsie ever be able to reconcile their love and get married?

"Blessed is the man who remains steadfast under trial, for when he has stood the test he will receive the crown of life, which God has promised to those who love him."

~ James 1:12

GREAT EXPECTATIONS

The sun had yet to peek over the horizon, but the sky was bright with the light of dawn. While the *Englischer* town of Jamesport still slept, the Amish village had been up for hours already, going about their day. The birds hopped from branch to branch as they sang in ecstasy, greeting the sun, before swooping down to fish for worms in the grass.

Betsie Hershberger slept on through the surrounding activity. Drool had made a large wet patch on the pillow, and the sheets were scrunched around her legs. Her copy of *Misery* lay on the bed beside her hand, inching closer to the edge as Betsie shifted in her sleep.

THUD!

The book fell and it startled Betsie out of her sleep. The first rays of the sun hit her in the face and she cried out. She had been dreaming of Annie Wilkes stalking through the village, carving knife in hand, looking for Betsie. It took her a moment to grasp the reality of the day and where she was.

"Oh, *nee*," Betsie moaned. *"Och, Daed* will kill me!"

Bolting out of bed, she ran to her dresser only to double back to check if her candle was still burning. She had been so hooked by the book last night that she had fallen asleep while reading it, completely neglecting to snuff the candle flame. She breathed a sigh of relief when she saw it had guttered out. A chill of horror ran down her spine. She knew what an untended candle could do. All the houses in the village were made from wood, and it took only a small flame to start an enormous fire.

She sent a hasty prayer of thanks up to *Gott* and got dressed.

There was no one in the kitchen, but the remains of a lonely breakfast were on the table. The dish of butter, crumbs from the loaf of bread, and a dirty glass next to the milk jug sat there. Betsie sighed, disappointed with herself. She had been responsible for the kitchen since her sisters, Sarah and Kathy, had married and left for their own homes. Miriam, her other sister, had also been helpful around the house, but she had left to teach at another Amish village in Indiana three years ago. It had been only Betsie and her father, Leroy, in this house since then.

Betsie silently cursed Stephen King and his addictive horror novels as she cleaned the dishes and set the kitchen to rights. She knew she shouldn't be reading *Englischer* novels, but it was a *Rumspringa* habit she found hard to quit. It didn't help that Samuel frequently borrowed novels from the town library on her behalf.

Shaking her head to rid herself of the disappointing start to her day, Betsie went to work on making it better.

THE TV WAS ON TOO loud. The lights were too bright and bounced off the obsessively cleaned Formica tables. Mike Tyson's lisping voice blared throughout the diner. Larry Holmes, though taller, was dwarfed in comparison. It was all anyone could talk about, the new kid taking on the legend that was Larry Holmes. The fight was scheduled in another fortnight and the whole *En-glischer* town was looking forward to the live broadcast. Betsie wished they would shut the TV off. Her head ached, and that was just the cherry on top of her terrible day.

The bread had burned to a crisp. She had trod on three eggs in the chicken coop. Not to mention she had mistakenly put salt in the cookies, sugar in the stew, and the cow had kicked the pail as soon as Betsie finished milking. By the time Samuel had ridden up in his buggy to take her for a ride, she had been close to frustrated tears.

She knew she shouldn't focus on the bad, but on the blessings *Gott* had given her. Like the use of all her limbs and senses, the love of her sisters and father, and the love of a good, honest man who sat in front of her.

Samuel King took a few sips of his milkshake, his gaze roving around the diner. He looked distracted and a little nervous. A spark of hope bloomed in Betsie's heart. She had been waiting for a proposal for some time now. She was nineteen, and most of the girls her age were either married or going to be married soon. Samuel hadn't asked her yet, but she wished he would do it soon.

Marriage to Samuel was only a matter of time,

Betsie knew, but recently she had an urgency to see herself wed that she couldn't explain. Maybe it had to do with the fact that she craved a home of her own, children of her own. She was tired of waiting and wanted to start on a new phase of her life. Or maybe it had to do with Nancy Hilty née Schwartz giving her pitying looks at every church gathering while she roped in congratulations and well-wishes on her second pregnancy within months of giving birth to her first *boppli*, a boy.

"Here you go, dear." The waitress, an elderly woman with iron gray hair and "Sandy" stitched in red on the lapel of her shirt, placed a steaming plate of French fries in front of Betsie. "Are you sure you won't have anything else?" she asked Samuel.

"No, thank you," Samuel said.

"I'd like another soda, please," Betsie said.

"Coming right up."

The French fries were piping hot. Betsie Hershberger could see the granules of salt on them, and her mouth watered at the sight. She was feeling much better already. Dousing the potatoes in ketchup, she devoured half the plate before she thought of offering some to Samuel.

He had his head bent over a paper napkin, a

toothpick in one hand while the other held his long chestnut hair out of his eyes. He was drawing something on the napkin with ketchup. They looked like words from where Betsie was sitting.

Excitement took hold of her suddenly, and her throat felt tight. She quickly cleaned her greasy fingers with napkins so she wouldn't look like a fool when Samuel finally proposed. It would be just like him, thoughtful, romantic Samuel, holding up a proposal written in her favorite condiment.

Samuel stroked his chin, as if deep in thought. Betsie giggled. He looked adorable when he was nervous. She could still remember the day she had fallen in love with him. It had been gradual, her affection growing from friendship to dependence and eventually a love so deep she hadn't known she could feel that way about anyone.

They had been walking by the river on a summer day two years ago, and she had slipped in the mud. The children playing nearby had started to laugh and make fun of her. Samuel had simply taken off his hat, handed it to Betsie and dived into the mud. She had watched aghast as he had rolled around in it, the children's hysterical laughter turning to squeals of joy and excitement when Samuel ran after them, giving them muddy hugs and kisses. She knew in that moment that she wanted Samuel to be the father of her children.

Now, sitting opposite him, she felt a keen love for him that she knew must be plain to see on her face if he would only look up. He would get strength from it to ask her the question she had been burning to hear. But Samuel continued to stroke his chin and ponder over the napkin. He slashed out a few of the ketchup blobs and dipped the toothpick in more ketchup to jot a few more things down.

Frowning, Betsie leaned forward to get a peek at what he was writing. It was a list of numbers next to the figure of a rudimentary machine. Blood flooded into her face. She should have known Samuel would be working on formulas and machines. This was the last straw to her horrible day. She didn't wait for him to finish. In fact, she didn't think she'd want to see his face without clawing his eyes out for a few days. She pushed her plate away, slid out of the booth, and walked out the door.

"Betsie?"

She didn't turn or respond. Margery Miller ran a haberdashery store in town and would be more than willing to give her a ride back home. This would give her enough time and distance to cool off and think about her future with Samuel.

If there was going to be one.

She slowed her pace in case Samuel ran after her, but when he didn't arrive by her side after three minutes had passed, Betsie set her jaw and hurried forward. Tightening her hands into fists, she decided that if Samuel didn't propose to her by the time Mike Tyson met Larry Holmes in the boxing ring, she would find someone else to marry.

FORTUNATE FORTUNE

Samuel got up to chase after Betsie, but the waitress stood in his way, barring his exit.

"You still have to pay your bill!" she screeched.

Samuel watched Betsie's frowning profile from the diner window, stalking past the storefront and rushing away. He knew from experience that when Betsie Hershberger was having one of her rages, it was best to steer clear of her till she cooled down.

Samuel sat back down in his booth. He signaled for the check and went back to his calculations, his head buzzing with what could have gotten Betsie so angry. He saw that she had only finished half of her French fries and soda. He ate a few of the fries. They were nice and salty and liberally doused with ketchup, just the way she liked it, so it couldn't have been the food.

Yet in his heart, he knew he was only fooling himself by thinking it was the food, or his choice of diner, just like he knew the real reason he hadn't gone after her. He was acting like a coward because he didn't want to acknowledge that Betsie expected a proposal from him, and he wasn't ready to propose yet. It was a conversation he would avoid.

He finished the fries and her soda. He didn't see the point of wasting a perfectly good plate of food. The check came and Samuel grudgingly paid the bill. He rather begrudged Betsie her second glass of soda, but how was she to know of Samuel's financial problems?

The waitress cleared the table and Samuel went back to his calculations. He worked on the farm with his father during the day, and the second half he worked on the Yoder farm. He earned nothing from his father Melvin, but only earned three dollars a day from William Yoder. By his calculations, he would need another two years to save half the amount he needed.

He balled up the napkin in frustration and threw it in a nearby wastebasket. He rubbed his temples in frustration. Staring at nothing, Samuel went over his imminent need for money, a need he hadn't even discussed with Betsie.

His mother was ill. Selma King had been ill for a long time, but it was now getting out of hand. For as long as Samuel could remember, his mother had suffered from abdominal pains and had a very poor appetite. She would feel dizzy and lethargic during the day, and Samuel would have to help her complete the household tasks lest Melvin find any undone. Now, it was as if she were wasting away before his very eyes.

He had gone to see his *Englischer* friend, Hector, a few months ago, and he had introduced him to an *Englischer* doctor, Dr. Banner. They had discussed Selma's condition and a week later Dr. Banner had found the cause of her condition, Superior Mesenteric Artery Syndrome. The final portion of the duodenum was compressed between the abdominal aorta and the overlying superior mesenteric artery. Treatable, but costly.

When Dr. Banner had explained Selma's illness, Samuel had been struck by the minute detailing of *Gott's* design. Humans were just like machines. One millimeter off in the design or calculations, and the machine wouldn't function properly. It was the same case with humans. A small fraction of Selma's abdomen was compressed, but it was enough to eventually kill her.

Samuel rubbed his tired eyes, thinking of ways to earn more cash as fast as he could.

"Third time this week, Dom! How can you expect me to keep my shop open if he won't show up for work?"

"He's a little punk. Don't worry, Jason. I'll have him in the shop today."

"I've got three cars that need servicing, Dom, three! I'm not made of money, you know. You tell Cody that I'm cutting his pay to minimum wage."

Samuel turned around. A tall man with a hive of curls was leaning against the kitchen counter talking to the cook through the small window. The cook's bulbous nose and blotchy complexion dominated his face.

"Come now, Jason. That's a bit harsh," the cook said.

"I was only doing you a favor by hiring him in the first place." The man named Jason shrugged. Samuel couldn't see his face, but he saw a *Gott*-sent opportunity when he saw one. Minimum wage was $3.25 per hour. That was more than Mr. Yoder gave him for four hours' work around his barn. Samuel's mind whirred as he calculated how much money that was per week. "He mopes about the garage, he's lazy, and he hardly shows up to work on time. I'm not paying him $6 per hour."

"Excuse me, sir." Samuel got up hastily and approached the man named Jason. He turned around. His skin was the color of caramel, his cheeks pockmarked. "I think you're paying him too much."

"And what do you know about my business?" He had a set of yellowing teeth.

"Not much, sir." Samuel shrugged. "But I know cars, engines, and machines. And I would do it for $2 per hour."

"Hey!" the cook bellowed. "You stay out of this, you opportunistic troll! That's my son's job."

"No, Dom," Jason snapped. "That's my job. Mine to give and your son's to keep. Looks like your son couldn't keep it." He turned his attention back to Samuel. "What can you do?"

"I could show you," Samuel said.

"All right." Jason nodded. "Follow me."

Samuel followed Jason out of the diner. They walked down Main Street and away from the commercial district. Someone was building a new mall and had cut down trees to make way for the foundations. Little Jamesport was growing every year till it became almost unrecognizable as the town Samuel remembered from childhood.

"So, how does an Amish boy know so much about cars?" Jason asked, falling in step with Samuel.

"I just like knowing about machines." Samuel shrugged. "A car's a machine, so I found out everything about it."

"Well, let's see if you're any good with them."

He guided Samuel into a garage behind the 24/7 pharmacy. It was a large space and smelled of gasoline and grease. There were tires stacked in one corner, tools on hooks on one wall, and three cars in various phases of disrepair parked side by side.

"Tell me what's wrong with this one." Jason pointed towards the car nearest to them.

Samuel went to work. He opened the hood and checked the engine. He looked under the car and inside it. Straightening up, Samuel rubbed his hands clean on a towel Jason handed to him, and he grinned.

"It's got two flat tires."

"One," Jason said.

"No, two." Samuel kicked the tire in the back. "This one's losing air as we speak. It's punctured deceptively and will need work as well."

Jason raised his brows. He looked impressed.

"Can you name the make and model?"

"Pontiac 6000STE, 1985."

"You're hired," Jason said. "$2 you said?"

"Yes." Samuel nodded.

"I'll make it $5. But I want you on time! I keep strict hours, so shop opens at 11 a.m., sharp!"

"Yes, sir. I promise, sir!" Samuel shook Jason's hand.

"All right, all right! I'll see you tomorrow."

Samuel ran all the way back to the wagon he had parked in front of the diner. He felt so happy he thought he could fly if he tried hard enough. His financial problems were over!

"Hey! You!"

Samuel looked up in time to dodge the glass bottle aimed at his head. He backed away with the horse's reins in his hands. Dom, the cook, a large man with beefy arms, stalked towards him.

"You just cost my son his job."

"I need the money," Samuel tried to explain. "My mother…"

"I don't care about your mother! I care about my worthless, lazy bum of a son. Do you have any idea how hard it was to get him the job in the first place?"

"I'm sorry." Samuel climbed inside the buggy. "But I need the money."

"Get out of here!" Dom roared. "And don't ever come back!"

Samuel cracked the reins, and the horse started trotting back home. He was so excited by the prospect of getting treatment for his mother that he was soon smiling. The incident with the diner's cook faded out of his memory.

THE KING FARM WAS LONELY. The closest neighbor was a fifteen-minute walk away. It was a two-story house, meant for a large family. But Melvin and Selma had only had one child. Samuel remembered the resentment, the unspoken accusation Melvin directed at Selma for not giving him more children. At first, Selma's sisters had visited with their offspring, but when Melvin had been rude to them on more than one occasion, they had stopped visiting.

Now, armed with the diagnosis of his mother's condition, Samuel knew why Selma hadn't had more children, how his own birth was a miracle that Selma must have borne with great pain and discomfort.

Samuel unhitched the buggy and walked the horse into the stables. He couldn't wait to tell Selma the good news.

The smell of food made his stomach rumble, and he realized how hungry he was. He had suppressed his hunger at the diner so he wouldn't have to spend too much, but now he was looking forward to dinner.

"Back so soon?" Selma asked. She placed a large pot of stew on the table set for dinner. A pained expression crossed her face as she straightened up. Her skin was stretched thin across the bones on her face. Her hair had grown brittle and gray under her *kapp*. But her smiles were still sweet, and the love she had for Samuel still shone through her eyes.

"I couldn't stay away knowing you'd made beef stew." Samuel grinned. He kissed Selma's dry cheek. "I have good news."

"You've finally asked Betsie to marry you." Selma clapped her hands.

"*Nee*," Samuel sighed.

"*Och*, why not?" Selma looked disappointed. She stepped away from Samuel to retrieve the buns from the oven. "I would like to see my grandchildren before I die, you know."

"Don't talk like that, *Mamm*." Samuel took the

tray from her. "You'll be fine. In fact, that's the good news."

He put the tray down on the counter and held his mother's hands. The skin was papery thin and felt delicate and dry as dust to the touch. He squeezed gently.

"I've found an *Englischer* doctor who says he can help you. I will have the money soon and then we can start treatment. Imagine that, *Mamm*," Samuel grinned. "No more pain, no more hurting. You'll be fine!"

"What nonsense is this?"

Samuel jumped. Selma startled.

"I'll have no such blasphemy in this house." Melvin shuffled into the kitchen. His face was scrunched up in its perpetual frown. Where Selma's eyes had nothing but love for Samuel, Melvin had nothing but disdain. "You can do whatever you want with your books and crazy ideas, but you are not dragging my wife into it."

"She's my mother," Samuel said. Selma shook her head, warning him to stop, but Samuel ignored her. "And you might be able to see her in pain but I can't."

"If its *Gott's* will, then she will suffer through it." Melvin sat down and poured himself some water from the jug. "*Gott* knows I've done my share of suffering. If I can take it without complaint, so can she."

"And what have you suffered from?" Samuel knew the answer to that question, knew what Melvin was going to say. Selma held his hand, caressed his face to look at her, to persuade him to leave well enough alone, but he wanted to confront his father. It was a need he could not explain. "What pains has *Gott* bestowed upon you?"

"Aren't you enough of a pain?" Melvin roared. "You, with your devil's insistence on doing everything in your power to thwart and disappoint me? Your mother, with her barren womb and her weak body, what has she given me but mewling complaints and a disappointing child?"

"And this is why you'd rather see her waste away before your eyes, then allow me to get her the help she needs?" Samuel slammed his fist on the table. The stew in the pot rippled. "You're nothing but a heartless, petty man, and *Gott* will not think highly of your lack of generosity."

Melvin was breathing hard through his nose. Plain hate was in his face.

"Now, you listen to me, and you listen well," he said. "As long as you two live under my roof, you have to follow my rules. If you want your *Mamm* to get that fancy treatment you can get out right now and live under the stars for all I care because you're not getting this house. I'm going to give the farm to the church to sell when I die, because I won't have you parading your abnormal machines and books in here when I'm gone! So what's it going to be? Selma?"

Selma jumped. Her fingers trembled and her lower lip quivered. She looked pleadingly at her son as she sat down at the table. Samuel swallowed hard. Melvin looked triumphant, and he couldn't stomach that look on his father's face.

"Pass the salt," Melvin growled. Selma did so.

Samuel walked out of the kitchen, his hunger drowned under the bile of hate.

There was only one thing to do now. He'd have to save for a house and Selma's treatment. There was no way he would give up on giving his mother the little comfort that she deserved in her life.

He didn't mind not getting the farm or the house. He had never wanted anything from Melvin, especially not his begrudging inheritance, so in a way it was better that Melvin had denied it to him. But he knew it would disappoint Betsie. He knew she was looking forward to a proposal, and now he'd have to postpone it until after he could afford his own farm and barn. He hoped she would wait. He was sure she would once he explained it all to her.

With that determination, Samuel tamped down on his anger and looked forward to the future.

THE RAVAGES OF TIME

The air was frigid. It slapped his face as the buggy made its way through the town. Leroy Hershberger could see his breath as it came out. He smiled at an ancient memory from his childhood, holding twigs between his fingers, huddling close to the fire in the woods, pretending to smoke like they did in the movies. He laughed at his own shenanigans.

Those carefree days were long gone. Leroy was a responsible grandfather now, five in total, three boys and two girls. He winced as he shifted his weight from one hip to the other. The aches and pains had grown from infrequent twinges to constant companions. His neck ached in the mornings, his feet by midday, and he could no longer rely on his hands to grip things without his mind concentrating on holding an object. As he had matured, his limbs had regressed into mischievous, misbehaving childhood.

Old age had crept up on him when he wasn't looking.

Leroy grinned. His thoughts often sounded like the rambling books he used to read in his *Rumspringa*. He supposed when one had over six decades under their belt, thoughts crowded into one's head like a room overstuffed with furniture, overlapping each other so the eye couldn't distinguish where one began and where it all unraveled.

Leroy supposed he never found the time to think after Mabel died. She had been so frail by the end that she weighed next to nothing when they finally put her in the ground. He could still remember the day he had seen her at his sister's wedding. She had been singing with the rest of the *Rumspringa* girls, her voice clear and cheerful like the river full of melting snow. Mabel had been ten years his junior, but she had been smarter than most women his age. Although he had to wait till she turned nineteen to finally marry her, Leroy knew it would be worth it.

Too soon, he thought. *She was taken away too soon.*

Their first few years of marriage had been a whirlwind of children and chores. Hardly a day went by when they wouldn't be disturbed in their bedroom by either one girl crying over a nightmare, or another needing milk or cookies.

When Betsie had finally turned five, Mabel had asked for a promise: that they would now take at least one evening from the week and spend it in each other's company. Maybe she had known by then that she wouldn't have many evenings left in this world.

The tear felt warm against his cold skin. He brushed it away. He wondered if she had felt the same need to tidy her affairs as he did when the warning of her demise had come on tiptoe. Every morning when he opened his eyes to the darkness of dawn, he felt an itch at the back of his neck. It was like a noose tightening in panic, telling him he had to set his affairs in order before it was too late.

On one score, he was confident. Two of his daughters, Sarah and Kathy, were happily married with children of their own to care for. Children were a great boon in times of loss. He remembered the funeral of his own father. Sarah and his other daughter, Miriam, had been little girls then. Mabel had been expecting Kathy. Leroy's mother had derived patience and joy from the sight of her granddaughters, and Leroy, himself, had been hopeful throughout his despair.

It was then he had realized how *Gott's* mercy was all-encompassing. He gave with the same hand He took away with, and it was all to lighten the burden and sorrow of the human heart.

It was for this reason he worried so much about Miriam and Betsie. He needed for them to have someone to give them hope when he was gone.

Reaching the post office, Leroy hitched the horse's reins to a parking meter. He had never understood much about the *Englischer* ways but he understood parking meters. Parking meters, to his mind, were the embodiment of life on *Gott's* green earth. You paid for your time with kindness and hard work, and praise for *Gott*, and when your time was up, you had to remove yourself, or you got penalized for it. It was comforting to know you would not live forever.

He hoisted the box packed with jam jars full of preserves and boxes of home-made cookies. Once a month he was charged with the responsibility of taking the goodies his daughters had made to town to ship them to Miriam in Indiana with their letters. Miriam, for her part, wrote to them once a month, elaborating on her life as a senior teacher in the large school in Gasthof village. She lived in the teachers' quarters, made especially for teachers who hadn't married, and had even begun to cook a little, as long as it didn't involve standing at the stove.

Leroy still remembered her visit on Christmas a few weeks ago, when she had surprised him by baking pies. They were good pies, and they reminded him of the Christmas pies Mabel used to make. His hand trembled a little as he addressed the box. He hoped Mabel would understand that he had tried his best to see Miriam married off, but the girl was headstrong and willful.

Betsie, on the other hand, had found a good match in Samuel King. He was a quiet young man, and a little strange, but Leroy supposed anyone would be quiet and introspective with a father like Melvin King. He still remembered the day his youngest girl had come crying to him about Samuel King, her face tear streaked and her heart aching over the treatment that boy got at the hands of his own father. Leroy had seen to it that the elders found out. None in the community had much patience for people who used their hands for anything but working *Gott's* given land, providing for their families, and raising their children in the glory of *Gott's* grace.

And yet, Samuel stood to inherit his father's farm and barn. That was a great prospect for Betsie, who would have a home of her own to go to right after marriage. That only left Miriam. Leroy couldn't leave the barn to her; custom dictated that only a son could inherit. Maybe if he could persuade some of the second sons of the community to marry Miriam and inherit his barn? But that was impossible. Miriam refused to marry, repeating her disdain for marriage on her Christmas visit.

Once the package was sealed and signed, Leroy got back into his buggy and tipped his hat in greeting at a few *Englischer* men passing by. They looked at him strangely, but one of them nodded his head. Leroy made it a point to be on his best behavior in town. He knew he represented the entire community on such visits, and he aimed to do his best.

Humming a hymn under his breath, he guided the horse down the street, making its way back home. He had just turned into the side street that led to the town square when he saw Samuel King crossing the street. Leroy raised his hand in greeting, but Samuel was too far away and too preoccupied to notice. He disappeared in one of the shops.

Leroy urged the horse forward, hoping to surprise Samuel and maybe offer him a ride back to the village. If he remembered of what Betsie had told him, Samuel would be running late for his job on the Yoder farm. A few feet closer to the shop, Leroy saw that it was in fact a garage. Two men in pale blue overalls were working on one of the cars. One of them was a black stranger Leroy had never seen before and the other was Samuel King, his head bent over an engine.

As if his hands had acquired a mind of their own, they struck the reins hard to urge the horse to speed up. The buggy sped down the street and into the main square, just as fast as Leroy's mind sped from one thought to the other.

Samuel was working at a garage. Did Betsie know? If so, had she lied to him about the Yoder farm? Leroy couldn't conceive why Samuel would go out of his way to work for an *Englischer* in the first place, let alone at a garage, a job the *Ordnung* would never approve of. Didn't he have a farm to care for in the village? Didn't he have a barn full of animals to tend? Why would he shame his community by working for an *Englischer* stranger in town?

The revelation of the day shook Samuel. His hands trembled worse than they had earlier. He had been wrong about Samuel. A man so steeped in his own obsession was no fit husband for his daughter, and if Betsie had lied to him to save Samuel's reputation then he had failed in his duties as a father.

Hoping against the latter, Leroy made his way home.

SISTERLY ADVICE

Two days.

It had been two days since she stormed off from the diner in town and Samuel hadn't followed her. In fact, he had not tried to contact her since then. Betsie wondered at his absence as she fried more doughnuts.

The sound of children at play drifted into the kitchen from the window. Betsie glanced out to check on them. Eli and Amos, Sarah's sons, were the eldest and were organizing the games. Sarah's daughter Joy and Kathy's eldest Michael, only a year apart, were rebelling against their authority while little Charity, Kathy's eighteen-month-old daughter, tottered behind the chickens in the yard, clapping her hands in glee.

"Are they playing nice?"

Sarah and Kathy sat at either end of the kitchen table, their feet propped up on stools. They were the mirror image of each other, tired eyes in pale faces, bellies protruding in their sixth month of pregnancy, one blond and one raven-haired.

"They're fine," Betsie said. "Would you like more cake?"

"*Och, nee*," Kathy moaned, rubbing her swollen belly. "I couldn't eat another crumb."

"I could eat a horse," Sarah said, accepting another slice of carrot cake.

They had arrived earlier in the day with the supplies they wanted to send to Miriam. It was a monthly ritual they had attended to without fail since Miriam left for Indiana. Not only did it serve as a chance to meet and catch up on their busy lives, but to give their father something to do to feel involved with his daughters. They knew how lonely he must feel.

"My *boppli* is the wrong way up," Kathy complained. "He keeps kicking me, and it hurts."

Sarah laughed. "Mine won't stop squirming."

Betsie tuned out her sister's *boppli* talk. There was only so much she could stand of their married chatter. She knew she was being uncharitable, that it wasn't their fault she wasn't married and expecting children, but she felt resentful nonetheless.

Why hadn't Samuel come by?

They had misunderstandings and arguments in the past, but they had never stayed angry for this long before. Samuel was always the first one to make amends, so where was he? Something was different now. Betsie had been feeling it for a few months, but she couldn't point out exactly what had changed. Samuel had grown distant from her, erecting a curtain between them that she couldn't seem to cross. His mind, usually open to her to read like a book, was closed and well-guarded. Betsie couldn't recall the last time she had looked in his eyes, and panic gripped her chest.

"Soon Betsie will sit around while we make cake and tea for her," Kathy laughed, bringing Betsie out of her reverie.

"What?" Betsie asked.

"I said it won't be long till you're heavy with your own *boppli*," Kathy smiled. "Then you'll make us wait on you, hand and foot."

Betsie looked at the surety in her sister's eyes, the utter conviction that their prediction of the future was true when Betsie herself wasn't sure.

Her panic bubbled up her throat till she couldn't breathe and she burst into tears.

"Betsie!"

Wood scraped against the floor as both sisters stood up in their haste to get to Betsie's side. They helped her to a chair. Sarah held her hand and Kathy brought a glass of water for her to sip on once she calmed down.

"What's wrong, Betsie?" Sarah asked, caressing her arm like she used to when she was a child.

"Is everything okay between you and Samuel?" Kathy asked.

Betsie sniffed and dabbed her eyes with her handkerchief.

"I don't know," she said, her face morose. "We've been walking out for three years now and still nothing. He hasn't even hinted at when I can expect a proposal."

"Samuel is a bit shy," Kathy said. "Do you think he might need encouragement?"

"He isn't shy with me." Betsie wiped her eyes. "He might come across as aloof and distant but with me he is open and—" Her voice hitched in her throat like a hook catches in a fish's mouth, because he hadn't been open and frank with her recently. He had been a closed book. She began to cry again.

"*Ant* Bee! *Ant* Bee! Are the doughnuts ready?"

"Shush," Kathy scolded the children teeming at the backdoor that led to the backyard. "Your *Ant* isn't feeling well. Go play!"

"Is she dying?" Michael asked. "Because *Grossdaed* wasn't feeling well, and then he died."

"Is it true?"

"Are you dying, *Ant* Bee?"

"Please don't die!"

"Could I have your lovely lace *kapp* after you die?"

"*Nee*, I wanted that *kapp*!"

"You can have it when I die."

"No one is dying!" Kathy snapped. The children's faces crumpled. Their lips trembled and their eyes became moist with tears. Kathy pinched the bridge of her nose, audibly praying to *Gott* for patience. "If I promise to bring you the doughnuts out in the yard, will you go outside and play?"

Considerably cheered, the children agreed and went back to bickering about games and rules and chasing chickens.

"Maybe he's preoccupied with something," Sarah said as soon as the children had left. "Is there anything going on in his life which might keep him distracted?"

"He started working at the Yoder farm in the evening a few months ago," Betsie said.

"That's odd, don't you think?" Kathy asked, glazing the doughnuts at the stove. "He's going to inherit a farm, so why work on anyone else's?"

Now that Betsie thought about it, what Kathy said made sense. Why was Samuel working on another farm when he had his own to tend? What was he hiding from her?

"Look," Sarah said, "that's neither here nor there. The point is, Samuel is an honest man, and he wouldn't string you along. I'm sure he is in it for the long run, so just be patient."

"Or better yet, take the lead," Kathy said. "Don't look at me like that. I took the lead in our relationship and I'm happily married, aren't I?"

"You did not!" Betsie exclaimed.

"*Ja*, I did. All the boys that kept asking me to walk out with them intimidated Ivan. He wasn't sure if I'd be interested in him, so he avoided asking me. I had to ask him to walk with me for him to finally get my hints. He blushed as red as a watermelon."

Betsie laughed. She couldn't help it. The thought of Ivan Fischer, tall and handsome, blushing and simpering like a bashful girl was just too much.

"My girls having fun?"

Leroy walked in from the backyard door. He looked paler than usual, and Betsie saw in a moment of clarity that her father was getting on in years. His hair was more silver than blond, and there were more lines on his tanned face than before. His eyes darted towards Betsie and there was deep concern in his eyes that piqued her curiosity.

"The children mentioned someone was dying."

The Hershberger girls burst out laughing.

"Come, *Daed*." Betsie got up and guided her father towards the table. "Join us for cake and doughnuts and we'll tell you all about it."

She felt much better about Samuel and vowed to drop hints the next time she saw him.

FIRST RIGHT

S amuel was tired, but pleased. His work at the garage was demanding, but he was learning something new every day. He loved being around the cars and the tools, and Jason was a generous employer. It was a shame that all of this was fleeting, yet that's what made it all the sweeter.

The sun was sinking when he finally made it back to the village. Dinner would already be over, but that didn't matter. Selma left food for Samuel in his room now that he and Melvin were barely on speaking terms. Samuel would get up at dawn and finish all of his chores by ten a.m., then he had a quick lunch, and left for town. He had told no one about the *Englischer* job. It wasn't *Rum-springa* anymore, and his indulgence in machinery wouldn't be taken as a passing phase. He could be punished or shunned for his choice, but at the moment he was beyond caring. He needed that money for Selma's treatment.

As he walked home, he could see candlelight illuminating homes. Families must be gathered around dinner tables, exchanging news of the day and preparing for tomorrow. They looked like happy homes, warm and comforting. He turned a corner and saw his own house at the end of the lane. A single candle gave the kitchen a weak glow. The rest of the house was dark.

"Samuel? I was hoping to find you here."

Samuel started. Joseph Miller, the head of the elders, was standing behind a birch tree. His hat was in his hands and he looked abashed.

"Mr. Miller, is everything okay? Are you here to see *Daed*?"

"*Nee*." He passed the hat from hand to hand. "I came to see you. I was hoping to catch you before you got home. Can we walk in the woods while we talk?"

Samuel thought this very curious. What could Joseph Miller have to say to him he couldn't say inside the house? They walked in the gloom of the woods, the night bringing an extra chill in the air. Samuel thought of his warm bed and hoped

Joseph Miller would get on with whatever he had to say and not beat about the bush.

"Your *Daed* came to me the other day." Joseph Miller cleared his throat, opened his mouth to continue, then closed it again. "Look, there's no easy way to say this, but your *Daed* wants to sell the farm."

Samuel said nothing. In fact, he didn't react at all. This was old news as far as he was concerned.

"I can see by your reaction that you already knew. I guess the fault lies with the community. We did our best to keep Melvin's physical wrath from you but we forgot to do the most important thing, nurture love between you two."

"You have done more than enough. I am grateful for your involvement. If things aren't better, at least they're not worse either."

"Indeed." Joseph nodded, his silver head bent low. "The elders have decided that we can't stop Melvin from selling the farm if he wishes to. But we have also decided that you have the first right to make a bid on it. We will not put it up for sale unless you refuse to buy."

The gesture oddly touched Samuel. The elders had always tried their best to look out for him over the years, and they were doing so even now. The knowledge that someone cared that much made Samuel feel loved, as if he was briefly part of that warm circle of light he saw in other homes.

"I can't," Samuel said with great regret. "I can't afford it."

"But I thought Yoder paid you wages."

"*Ja*, but they aren't enough to cover the cost."

"You can put up the amount you have and the church can finance the rest. You can pay it back with time."

"That is very kind of you, Mr. Miller, and I appreciate it, but I'm saving that money for a special purpose."

"Surely to buy a farm for Betsie Hershberger. We all know you will want to marry soon."

"*Nee*, I mean *ja*." Samuel floundered. "The truth is, I want *Mamm* to get treatment for a disease she has."

Joseph Miller looked alarmed.

"It's been eating at her from the inside for years. I want her to get it treated before it's too late."

"*Englischer* treatment?"

"*Ja*. Is that against the *Ordnung*?"

"*Nee*." Joseph rubbed his chin. "It isn't forbidden, but it's still best to avoid it."

"This is my *Mamm* I'm talking about." Samuel felt his face flush with anger.

"I can understand your concern, and I will never stop you from buying her treatment. But I am much older than she is and I know that if I were that sick I wouldn't want a treatment to prolong my life when *Gott* had meant it to end. I think Selma doesn't want that either. She would much rather see you in your own home with your wife and children."

Samuel didn't have an answer to that. He felt like Joseph had shown him a door and then slammed it shut when Samuel headed towards it. Why could no one understand his need to help his mother?

"Thank you for the advice," Samuel finally said. "And thank you for letting me be the first to bid on the farm. I really do appreciate all that you have done for me."

"Don't mention it, Samuel. You always have been, and always will be, one of our own, and we never let our own suffer in silence. Whatever you need, you only have to ask."

He patted Samuel's cheek affectionately. Samuel guided him out of the woods in the deepening twilight, then made his way to the stark house he had called home his entire life.

UNINVITED GUESTS

She had decided. She was going to tell him tonight. Betsie knew how she felt about Samuel, and she didn't need to wait for him to make the first move. She would go to his house after dinner, coax him out of his rooms for a stroll in the woods, and propose.

It was a solid plan, and it had put Betsie in an excellent mood. She hummed as she got dinner ready. It was a simple dinner of pea soup and biscuits, with baked fish and asparagus and sweet potato mash. Betsie had just finished seasoning the mash when the front door opened.

"Dinner's just about ready, *Daed*," Betsie called from the kitchen.

"That's good to know," Leroy's hearty response came from the living room. "We're all starving."

"That smells nice."

"*Denke* for having us over, Mr. Hershberger."

Betsie froze at the sound of strange voices. They weren't the voices of her brothers-in-law Ben and Ivan, and neither did she recognize them as the voices of Leroy's friends. She stopped laying the table for two and peered out of the corner of the kitchen door.

Otto Beiler and Uri Bontrager shuffled from one foot to the other, their hats in their hands, while Leroy urged them to sit and feel at home. Perplexed, Betsie tamped down the panic in her throat. It was just like *Daed* to bring people over for dinner without informing her. There was only enough food for two people; how was she going to stretch it to four servings? Their work in the fields meant Amish men had hearty appetites and by the looks of Otto and Uri they could pack away a feast.

Thinking fast, Betsie started cleaning potatoes. She broke some eggs and pulled out sausages from the smokehouse. She was in the middle of making a sausage bake when Leroy came into the kitchen.

"How much longer, *dochder*?" he asked, as if disappointed by the delay.

Betsie had to control herself from screaming in frustration.

"Another five minutes, *Daed*," she said instead.

"You know Otto and Uri, right?" Leroy asked.

"Hmm." Betsie was only half listening to Leroy as she brought out some strawberry preserves, eggs, and milk to make a quick dessert.

"They're nice boys," Leroy said. "Unfortunate that they have to find work off their father's farm to buy a farm of their own. But it shows great enterprise, just like Ben."

"You can call them in for dinner now, *Daed*," Betsie said, washing her hands at the sink.

The conversation flowed freely at dinner, but Betsie's mind was going over what she would say to Samuel later in the evening. She smiled and laughed automatically, and ate sparingly so she would leave enough for their guests.

Otto was the third son, but taller than the rest of his brothers. He had a vacuous face that gave the impression of stupidity, but his conversation proved otherwise. Uri, on the other hand, was as wide as he was tall, his girth threatening to become wider still. He was the second born and had eyes that kept flitting from object to face, never sitting still.

Betsie would have made it through the dinner blissfully ignorant of Leroy's plans if it hadn't been for Otto's passing comment.

"The barn will be the first thing I fix after the wedding," he said. "It needs an extension if we're going to keep some calves."

"That's mighty presumptuous of you," Uri said, swallowing a large bite of sausage. "What makes you think you'll get the farm?"

Otto ran a disparaging look over Uri's belly and Uri flushed.

"*Gott* asks us not to indulge in physical beauty," Uri mumbled.

"He also asks us not to indulge in gluttony," Otto sneered.

"I will not have such a vulgar discussion at my table," Leroy said with such finality in his voice it made Betsie jump. "This is still my farm."

Uri and Otto threw dirty looks at each other over the table for the rest of the meal. Betsie had lost her appetite. Why was *Daed* selling the farm? It was their home, where he had been born and Betsie and her sisters had been born and where their mother had breathed her last. Why would *Daed* sell it all?

Maybe he needs money. The thought struck Betsie. But what for? From what she knew of the household, there was no financial crisis. Her sisters were healthy, as were their husbands and children. Leroy, though tired and grumpy, was also healthy, as was Betsie. Then why sell?

As her gaze roamed from Otto to Uri she wondered if they even had enough money to buy the farm. It wasn't a very large farm, but it was still expensive. Otto and Uri had been working on other farms for two years and six months, respectively. Amish farmers didn't pay more than $3 a day, Samuel had told her, so neither of them had enough money to buy.

By the time *kaffe* and dessert were finished, Betsie had a raging headache. She tried to push the thoughts away and concentrate on meeting Samuel. She cleaned the dishes while Leroy saw the men out, her hands moving fast so she could leave for Samuel's house as soon as she was done.

"So," Leroy walked into the kitchen and sat at the table, placing his hands in front of him. "What do you think?"

"What do I think?" Betsie tamped her hands dry on a tea towel. "I didn't even know you were selling the farm till Otto mentioned it."

"I'm not selling the farm," Leroy spread his

hands.

"Then what did that conversation mean?"

"I'm not selling the farm," Leroy repeated. "I'm giving it away."

"What? Why?"

"I can't give it to any of my daughters. It's against the *Ordnung*. But I can make sure it stays with one of my girls."

"You're not making any sense; how..." Betsie began, but then it dawned on her. She had always been quick at putting two and two together, even when she was very little. It had always surprised her sisters how much she could glean from scraps of information in random conversations. "I'm going to marry Samuel, *Daed*. You know that."

"Has he proposed?"

"*Nee*, he..." Betsie stopped mid-sentence. The calculated gleam in her father's eyes had given her pause and her mind whirred again, back to yesterday and that look of concern he had given her. "You know very well from my conversation with Sarah and Kathy you eavesdropped on the other day that Samuel hasn't proposed."

"Maybe he never will," Leroy said.

"Of course he will," she said. *Will he?* "If Samuel didn't want to marry me, he would have said so. And I thought you liked Samuel? Why the sudden need to see me married off to someone else?"

Leroy's hands were steepled under his chin as he regarded Betsie steadily. After what felt like an eternity, he lowered his gaze and sighed.

"I no longer think Samuel is a suitable match."

"Why?"

Her face was hot, her eyes were burning, but she refused to shed the tears.

"I just don't think he'll be able to keep you happy."

Betsie watched Leroy's mouth press into a thin line. A few times her father had disappointed her. His lack of attention had been a looming shadow in her childhood. But she had never resented him like she did at that moment.

"And what would you know about keeping people happy?"

The words left her mouth before she could collect them and stuff them in a box she kept at the back of her mind. Leroy grimaced as if he had been struck. His pale, lined cheeks blazed.

"How dare you talk to me that way?"

"What are we to you? Toys? You have always resisted every decision that had the potential to make your daughters happy. You resisted Sarah marrying Ben till you no longer could, you were against Miriam moving to Indiana to follow her passion, and you thought Ivan was too short for Kathy."

"He is too short for Kathy."

"So I should marry Otto the tree to make up for it?"

"Samuel already has a farm he will inherit," Leroy said, pinching the bridge of his nose. "I want to leave this farm to one of my daughters so Miriam will always have a home. Is that too hard for you to understand?"

"That's nonsense and you know it. Miriam will always have a home with her sisters, and she knows that. What are you not telling me? Why the sudden change of heart towards Samuel?"

At first it looked like Leroy wouldn't answer. He chewed the inside of his cheeks and stared at the table.

"He isn't Amish enough."

Betsie sighed and rubbed the back of her neck. Suddenly she felt exhausted by the fight.

"You've always known of his passion for machines," she said, placing the tea towel on its hook beside the stove. "You've known of the kind of home he comes from. If Samuel had wanted, he could have left the community after his *Rumspringa*. He is as much Amish as you and I."

"But what if he's changed his mind and wants to be shunned once and for all?"

"Maybe. What if. Perhaps. These are all conjecture, *Daed*. We don't know what's in his heart. That's for *Gott* to know and for us to trust. And I trust Samuel."

"Be that as it may." Leroy stood up from his chair. The sharp dragging of wood on wood scraped on her already shot nerves. "This union will not have my blessing. If that's something you can live with, then be my guest. I won't have any part in this."

He stalked off towards the kitchen door, halted, and turned his head so Betsie could see his face in profile.

"I love you, and I will miss you when you leave. But if you leave with Samuel, know that you will no longer be my daughter and there won't be a place for you in this home when he leaves you high and dry."

Betsie stared at the back of her father's head as he walked away down the corridor. Time seemed to have slowed down with the beating of her heart. No longer trusting her legs to hold her weight, she sunk into a chair and let the tears come.

BETRAYAL

He counted his first week's earnings. The bills were old, like wilting lettuce leaves, and one had a grease mark on it, but the value they held for Samuel was great. He folded the bills and hid them within the pages of his Bible.

In everything I did, I showed you that by this kind of hard work we must help the weak, remembering the words the Lord Jesus himself said: "It is more blessed to give than to receive."
Acts 20:35

Samuel stared at the words. They sang to his soul like a benediction. All he did, all he was doing, was to help his mother. Constant worry over her well-being had him perpetually anxious and on edge. Nothing he did felt like it was enough, and he had woken from his sleep violently, drenched in sweat with an urgent need to work, and work, and then work some more so he could give her the treatment she needed.

This state of mind had made him lonelier, and he knew Betsie must feel it too. He was no longer mentally present in her presence, yet he found it hard to share his problems. Deep down he was ashamed that he still feared his father and lacked the guts to just walk out of this toxic home. Every time push came to shove, Selma would opt to stay and Samuel would accept her decision, never pushing her to choose an alternative. He didn't want to show Betsie this compliant boy who couldn't save his mother because he was weak. He didn't want to see it himself. So he worked, and worked and worked, because at least that felt like he was doing something.

He closed the Bible, and he placed it on his bedside table. Then he put his aching head in his hands. He cleared his mind of all thought and concentrated on the silence of the house. He could hear Melvin's heavy tread coming from the front room. The sound of the front door closing shut meant that Melvin had just come in for dinner. Samuel could hear the musical high notes of cutlery as Selma set the table.

Breathing slowly, Samuel was just beginning to relax when the sound of crashing china assaulted his meditation. He bolted off his bed and rushed towards the kitchen, his heart in his throat, visions of an unconscious or dead Selma floating in his mind's eye.

When he reached the kitchen, he saw Melvin sitting at the table glaring at Selma, who was crouched on the floor alternately picking up shards of broken glass and holding her belly. Her face was milk white and drenched in sweat even though it was the middle of winter. She looked in great pain, and bit on her lip not to scream because of it.

"*Mamm*, let it go." Samuel strode forward and took the broken pieces of glass from her trembling hand. He helped her to a chair and finished cleaning up, his temper rising as Melvin ignored the entire incident and served himself dinner. "Come on, *Mamm*." Samuel dumped the glass in the trash and walked over to Selma. "Let's take you to the doctor."

She looked up at him from her seat and Samuel's heart constricted. She looked frail and childlike, and he wondered if she had felt the same flood of love for him when he was a small child, looking up at her with boundless faith and trust. This was how *Gott* changed the places of the caregiver and the caretaker.

"She's not going anywhere," Melvin said, chewing on his baked potato.

"She's in pain," Samuel said through gritted teeth.

"Are you in pain?" Melvin asked Selma. He didn't spare Samuel a glance.

Selma's hand trembled, and she winced.

"*Nee.*"

It was a mere whisper, but they all heard it.

"*Mamm.*" Samuel hunkered down, so he was face to face with Selma. "You don't have to be afraid of him anymore. I will care for you. Come with me."

Selma wouldn't meet his eyes. She picked at an invisible crumb on the table.

"*Mamm*, please," Samuel begged. "You'll die!"

"*Och*, Sam," Selma moaned. "Why do you have to be so dramatic? Your father says I'll be fine at home, so I will be. Can't you just let things go? All I want is for us to sit and have a nice dinner like a family for once. Why do you have to ruin it?"

Samuel flinched as if he had been slapped.

"*Mamm...*"

"*Nee.* I am fine. It's just a little cramp. It will go away. Come sit. I made your favorite."

Samuel might have sat down to please his mother if he hadn't looked across the table at that moment. Melvin's malevolent pleasure at the scene made Samuel's blood boil. He stood up and stormed out of the back door. Selma kept calling for him to come back, but he paid her no heed.

He stalked aimlessly along the dirt path, kicking stones out of his way to vent his anger. Melvin's influence over Selma was boundless, and he couldn't understand how he could save Selma from it. His own fear had hobbled him as a child, but then Betsie Hershberger had come along and unfettered him from it. She had done what no one else had ever done for him. She had cared, and she had taken action.

Just thinking of Betsie helped him relax a little. His stomach growled in protest. His last meal had been a dry, chewy sandwich at the garage hours ago. Rubbing his belly, Samuel turned towards Betsie's house. If he were lucky, they would still be at dinner. He could always be sure of an invitation to dinner at the Hershberger house. Leroy liked him well enough and talked enough to cover Samuel's silence.

A few feet from the Hershberger house he was

contemplating an excuse to explain his presence when Leroy stepped out of the front door and two men followed him. Samuel recognized Otto Beiler and Uri Bontrager and wondered what they were doing at Betsie's house so late. He came closer, half hidden by the cherry tree that grew in the front yard.

"...a lovely dinner. She would do any man the honor of being his wife," Uri's voice floated down to where Samuel stood stalk still.

"Are you sure she is no longer walking out with Samuel?" Otto asked.

"*Ja*," Leroy said. "He hasn't proposed. Betsie is getting on in years and needs a reliable man in her life. I will ask for her decision and let you know."

"*Gut* night," Uri said.

"*Gott* be with you," Otto said.

They walked off the porch and disappeared into the night. Leroy watched them go, his hands in his pants pocket. He looked stooped in the lantern light, oddly diminished. Samuel wondered if it was a trick of the light or of his own mind, because Leroy and his daughter had fallen from grace in his eyes.

Samuel turned away and retraced his footsteps, his heart hammering like a fist into his ribs.

This wouldn't be the first time Betsie had gone behind his back to walk with another man, so it didn't come as a surprise to him. What came as a surprise was how it still hurt, as if he had been stabbed repeatedly in the guts.

BITTER WORDS

"It was kind of you to take me to the bakery," Sarah said. "I feel like a house."

"You look like one too," Ben joked. Sarah slapped his arm, and he laughed as he helped her climb into the buggy. Betsie watched as Ben lovingly placed a warm rug on Sarah's lap, and she felt envy.

"It was no trouble," Betsie said. "I had to go in town anyway."

Sarah had been giving baking lessons at a bakery in town for the past few months, but found it difficult to get there in her pregnant state. Betsie and Ben took turns to ride her there and back. Today was Betsie's turn.

GRACE LEWIS

"Ride safe." Ben waved. "And be back before sundown!"

"We'll be fine." Sarah waved back.

"It's not you I'm worried about," Ben laughed. "I'm worried for my poor ears."

As if on cue, the children came screaming into the yard chasing a goat. Eli was in the lead. Amos was close on his heels, and Joy trailed behind like a sad dog's tail.

"*Gut* luck." Sarah laughed at the look of alarm on Ben's face. "Ride on before the children start screaming to come along!" she urged Betsie.

Betsie slapped the reins, and the buggy trundled forward onto the dirt road. She smiled for the first time in hours. Leroy hadn't spoken to her at breakfast, and she hadn't spoken to him. She had cried herself to sleep last night and her eyes were puffy and painful. She hoped Sarah wouldn't notice.

"So, are you going to tell me why you look like a bloated pumpkin or do I have to beg?"

Betsie had to smile at Sarah's uncanny knack of reading her mind.

"It's been three years since *Daed* forbade one of his *dochders* anything, so now it's my turn."

"What do you mean?"

"He says I can't marry Samuel, that he won't give his blessing if I do."

"I thought he liked Samuel."

"He is no longer suitable," Betsie said in a remarkable impression of Leroy and made a face. "Suddenly the farm's inheritance obsesses *Daed*, and he wants me to marry Otto Beiler or Uri Bontrager so they can inherit the farm and his *dochders* can still live in it. He says it was a way to ensure that Miriam always has a place to stay in Jamesport."

"Miriam has a place to stay in Jamesport. She has three places to stay in Jamesport. Four once you marry Samuel."

"That's exactly what I said!"

Sarah lapsed into a thoughtful silence. Betsie felt much better having spilled it all out. It was a comfort to have sisters to talk to. She couldn't imagine what people did without sisters. Fathers, brothers, husbands and sons were all right, but there was no bond deeper, and more meaningful, than that of a sister. It was second only to that of a mother, and Betsie hadn't had the chance to get to know her mother well.

She had the image of a frail doll in her mind's eye when she thought of her mother, a doll with large blue eyes and dark brown hair. She remembered the mole beneath her left eye, and the snatch of a song. These were the few memories she had of her mother, but they were enough. Sometimes she had felt the loss of her mother, but then her sisters had rallied around her, and she had felt like the luckiest girl in the world.

"Don't worry about it," Sarah finally said. "I'll talk to *Daed*."

"*Denke*."

"Can we go to the post office first? I've run out of envelopes and stamps. I asked Ben to pick some up weeks ago, but you know how men can be."

"I'll bet he said you never told him to."

"*Ja!* Looked completely blank when I asked where my stamps were, as if I had gone mad."

Sarah's animated anecdotes of her family life kept Betsie amused all the way to town. She felt relieved now that Sarah had taken over the problem. She drove into town laughing at Sarah's jokes, her spirits rising as she envisioned herself in Sarah's place a few years from now, juggling children and chores with Samuel's help.

She stopped the buggy outside the post office and made to get out, but Sarah placed an arm on her wrist to stop her.

"It won't take me very long. I can walk to the

bakery from here," Sarah said. "It's just around that corner." She tilted her head down the street in the bakery's direction.

"But that's a block away," Betsie said.

"I can manage," Sarah smiled. "Plus, a little exercise keeps the limbs supple for when the baby comes. You go on. I'll ask Janice to drop me off at the diner once the class is done and we can go home."

Betsie still felt she should wait for Sarah and then drive her to the bakery, but Sarah was adamant about a brisk walk, so Betsie went her way.

She usually spent these afternoons at Andy's diner with a new book from the library and a steaming hot plate of French fries. She parked the buggy outside the diner, hooking up the reins against the special posts for Amish folk in the parking lot. This was one of the reasons Amish folk loved the diner so much.

"Hiya, Betsie!" Andy Gleeson, the owner of the diner, called from the front of the shop. She was signing for a delivery package, her short hair falling in her eyes. "We missed you! The usual?"

"The usual." Betsie grinned. "I just have to return this to the library. I should be back in ten minutes."

"I'll ask Nathan to keep the taters hot for ya." Andy winked.

Tucking *Misery* under her arm, Betsie walked down the street and took a left. The library was a ten-minute walk from the diner if you followed the main road. But Betsie knew of a shortcut that would shave off five minutes. Walking briskly to keep herself warm, Betsie took a right down a side street.

She was thinking of Sarah and Ben talking to Leroy, and the color she would wear on her wedding day, when she passed the 24/7 pharmacy. Absentminded, Betsie glanced inside the pharmacy, her gaze traveling to the garage beside it. Two men were working on it. Betsie's casual gaze slid over the corkscrew curls of one man, and the chestnut hair of the other that stood out distinctively in the gloom. Betsie looked back, startled by the familiar hairline. Samuel, wrench in hand, was tightening the bolts on a car engine, grease marks on the side of his face and on his arms. A tall black man stood beside him, drinking coffee and giving instructions.

Betsie's shock had turned her to stone.

He isn't Amish enough.

I just don't think he'll be able to keep you happy.

Leroy's words came back to her, bludgeoning her numb brain, battering it into action.

Samuel had lied to her. He had led her to believe that he was working at the Yoder farm when he had been working in an *Englischer* garage all this time. She had always been understanding of his liking for machinery and *Englischer* study of engineering, but this was taking it too far. What would the community say? Did Samuel even want to be part of the community, or was he trying hard to get shunned? And if so, what about Betsie? Was this why he hadn't proposed?

I no longer think Samuel is a suitable match.

She had just convinced Sarah to help *Daed* agree to the marriage. If Leroy saw Samuel he'd refuse to agree to the union and Betsie wouldn't have any grounds to disagree.

Anger took hold of her, thawing the frost of shock. She marched forward and into the garage. The man standing behind Samuel looked up first. He had deep pockmarks across his face, but he looked honest and kind. Samuel glanced up, then froze. He straightened slowly, placing the wrench on a table full of tools.

Betsie had expected him to look guilty and remorseful. Instead, Samuel looked offended, as if she had done something wrong.

"What's going on?" she asked. "What are you doing here?"

"This is where I work."

"I thought you worked on the Yoder farm."

"Not for a week now, *nee*."

The stranger, who had been looking between Samuel and Betsie, came forward, extending his hand in greeting.

"Hi, I'm Jason. I own this garage. You must be Samuel's girlfriend."

"Betsie," she said shortly, shaking his hand. "Samuel, what's going on? Why didn't you tell me about this? Why are you even working here? The elders will never understand, and you'll be shunned from the community."

"Why do you suddenly care?" Samuel asked, his arms folded across his chest. His face was an impassive mask, but his eyes were flinty and cold.

"Of course I care!" Betsie snapped. She was already angry at the deceit, but his aloof reaction was grating on her nerves. "Don't you care? Didn't you think even once what your actions will do to me? *Daed* is suddenly against the marriage. How do you expect me to convince him to give his blessing if you are sabotaging our marriage plans?"

No expression passed across his face. Samuel remained impassive.

"I never asked you to marry me."

Betsie flinched, as if he had slapped her.

"Ouch, that's harsh," Jason said. "I'll leave you two alone to hash this out."

"*Nee.*" Betsie was already stuffing the pain and humiliation inside the box at the back of her head to sift through and examine later. Samuel might think nothing of making a scene in front of an *Englischer*, but Betsie would sooner die than let that happen. "There is nothing left to discuss. Samuel's made himself very clear. *Gut* day, Jason."

"You too," Jason said. There was regret in his eyes, and a beseeching apology. Samuel's behavior embarrassed Jason. Even in the midst of her heartbreak, she considered this a sweet gesture.

She never looked back at Samuel.

I no longer think Samuel is a suitable match.

She turned and stormed out of the garage, *Misery* tucked under her arm, and misery stabbing her heart.

SHAME

Samuel lay in his dark room listening to Melvin snore in the room down the hall. Selma never snored. She slept silently, hardly moving through the night. She had been happy tonight. They had had a pleasant meal with no incident. Samuel had respected her wish for pretense at a happy family.

It was like poking a bruise thinking about Betsie, a dull ache that spread and pulsed.

He had been abominably cruel to her. Yes, the cruelty was unlike him and had stemmed from a place of hurt and betrayal on Betsie's part, but if he believed that was all it was, he'd be lying to himself. He had taken all his anger at Melvin, his frustration with Selma, and the need to lead a double life and dumped it all on her unsuspecting head.

He no longer believed she had been complicit in Leroy's plans to see her marry Otto or Uri. Her words, her deep concern and admission of Leroy's reluctance absolved her of any crime Samuel had imagined on his part. He had been so preoccupied with self-pity and his family's disregard of him that he had imagined offense where there was none.

And how could he accuse Betsie of keeping things from him when he had done exactly the same? He hadn't told her of Selma's illness, hadn't confessed his concerns for her or his financial state. Betsie was completely in the dark, hoping for a proposal that she had a right to expect. His disdain must have blindsided her.

He wondered if he should go talk to her. In the same instance, he recognized his reluctance to explain himself as another form of cowardice.

Stepping nimbly out of bed, Samuel tiptoed out of his room. He peeked into his parents' room. Melvin took over most of the bed, his face frowning even in sleep. Selma lay on her side, breathing gently. Samuel gazed at her serene face for a while, then turned to leave through the front door.

He had to make amends.

HEART TO HEART

Betsie's eyes were itchy and her throat raw from all the crying. Leroy had seen her red-rimmed eyes and blotchy cheeks at dinner and had had a smug expression on his face throughout the meal. Betsie hadn't known her *Daed* had such a mean streak.

She sniffled into her pillow, praying for peace and a better day tomorrow. She shut her tired eyes, hoping for sleep to come. She had nearly drifted off when someone tapped on her window.

Betsie didn't open her eyes. She knew who it was, and though her heart was leaping in her throat with joy, she made no move to open the window, or even acknowledge his presence.

"Betsie." Samuel knocked again. "I'm sorry. Please open the window."

She pretended to be asleep. As much as she was itching to hear his apology she wanted to make him suffer a little for putting her through so much pain.

"I know you can hear me."

Betsie sighed and sat up in bed, her back to the window. She sat like that for a moment, fixing her face into an impassive mask, mirroring his from earlier in the day. When she finally turned to face him, she had steeled herself to accept whatever came next.

She opened the window but made no move to step outside.

"Hi," Samuel said, resting his hand on the windowsill.

"Hi."

"I came to your house yesterday. You had guests for dinner."

"*Daed* had guests for dinner," she said shortly. "I only cooked and served."

"I heard them conversing on the porch," Samuel continued. "They were talking about marriage. Your marriage and how I was no longer suitable."

"And you thought I was complicit in that

farce?" Betsie snapped. "You think I would betray you again? I love you, Samuel, I would never do that to you."

"I didn't know what to think." He ran a hand through his disheveled hair. "I haven't been thinking straight for months now. Nothing is going as I planned. I've worked hard, but have nothing to show for it. And no matter what I do to make them happy, both the women I love only get upset with my decisions."

Alarmed by the bitterness and frustration in his voice, Betsie's impassive mask fell. She turned her face so she could see him properly in the moonlight. Tears streaked down his face, and he looked miserable.

"Samuel, what's wrong? What have you been hiding from me?"

"*Mamm's* dying." His voice shook. "She's dying, Betsie, and there isn't anything I can do about it."

Betsie was shocked. She had always thought Selma King was frail, but she hadn't known things were so bad. The last time she had seen Selma was at Christmas and she had been struck by how much weight the older woman had lost.

"How…? I don't understand. I didn't know Selma was ill."

"She's had a debilitating condition for years. It

causes her intense pain in the abdomen. Sometimes it used to get so bad that she couldn't stand up and I had to cook for her. Haven't you ever wondered why I never had any siblings? It's because *Mamm* can't carry them full term, if she's lucky enough to conceive."

Betsie held Samuel's hand, squeezing it gently.

"Her sister used to visit us often when I was younger," Samuel went on, staring in the middle distance as if the memories were playing before his eyes. "*Daed* never liked that. He felt *Ant* May was rubbing the abundance of her children in his face. He became so rude that they stopped coming. They moved away when I was seven."

"Is that why you've been working at the garage?" Betsie whispered, wiping the tears from his cheeks. "To pay for Selma's treatment?"

Samuel nodded, and fresh tears spilled out of his eyes.

"It's no use though," he said, the tone of bitterness raw and aching. "*Daed* has forbidden it, and *Mamm* is too scared of him to disobey him."

"Oh, Samuel." Betsie felt his pain and she could feel his helplessness. "I'm so sorry. I'll try to help with the housework. Selma shouldn't have to be on her feet all day. I'll come by first thing in the morning once Melvin is out of the house. Don't worry, we'll make her better."

An expression of relief passed across his face and he looked much younger than he did a minute ago. His shoulders slumped down from their tensed heights and his face relaxed.

"But Samuel," Betsie pressed on. "Promise to share these worries with me. You're not alone. I'm with you through thick and thin. Trust me. Make use of my concern and friendship. What use am I if you won't rely on me in your time of need?"

"You're right." He flinched and rubbed the back of his neck. "I should have told you, which is why I think I should be upfront about another thing."

Betsie's heart stopped beating for a minute as she anticipated what Samuel was going to tell her. He was avoiding her eyes, and he looked ashamed, as if what he was about to say would change the way she looked at him.

"I'm not getting the farm," he finally said. "*Daed* has told the elders that he wants to sell it after his death. I don't have an inheritance; I don't have a house to keep you in."

Betsie burst out laughing. She was relieved. Her mind had jumped to leaving the community, and she had panicked at the thought of losing him. She had always wondered what Samuel would choose if ever given the choice between her and machinery. This told her she came first.

Samuel looked bewildered, but her laughter was so infectious that soon he had joined her and they both laughed till tears of joy leaked out of their eyes.

"Oh, Samuel, you're so silly," she said once the laughter had subsided. "I don't care about your inheritance."

"But it matters," Samuel said, caressing the back of her hand with his finger. "Leroy already has objections to me. What will he say once he finds out that I don't have an inheritance or a home to keep you in? No father approves of a pauper for their daughter."

"We'll make a home," Betsie said. "*Nee*, listen. We'll work hard, both of us, and we'll buy a small house in the community. You can talk to the elders about your job at the garage, and if they approve, that will be our main source of income. Selma can live with us, and she won't have to do any work while she gets her treatment."

"It will take me some time to make that much money," Samuel said, his smile lazy and relaxed. "Can you wait that long?"

"I've waited this long." Betsie grinned. "I think I can wait a few more months."

"I never asked properly."

"You didn't have to."

"I still think I should. Will you marry me, Betsie Hershberger?"

Betsie held her breath, memorizing the moment: the slanting moonlight, the traces of silver in Samuel's hair, the way his eyes shone and the smell of frost.

"*Ja*, Samuel King. I will."

THE BIG SLEEP

Samuel felt like he was floating a few inches off the ground. A great weight had been lifted off his shoulders, and he wondered at his own stubborn stupidity for not sharing his worries and concerns with Betsie. Betsie had been his first friend, his support and his companion. He had loved her for as long as he could remember, baptizing into the faith because he knew he couldn't live without Betsie. He was glad it was all out in the open between them, and now they were engaged.

He could still see the way her face had glowed when he had proposed, like she had swallowed a star and its muted beams animated her face.

Samuel stopped himself from running all the way home the way the blood in his veins wanted him to. The engagement didn't feel like a burden as he'd imagined, but emancipation. Yes, there was a greater sense of responsibility, but it carried none of the strain or encumbrance Melvin had always expressed.

The sky lightened from charcoal to wool gray, and Samuel hurried his pace. Selma would be up and making breakfast. She had been eager for him to propose. He couldn't wait to see her cheerful smile when he told her the news.

Samuel took the route to the back of the house so he could enter from the kitchen. He passed the barn and saw that Melvin was already at work, milking the cows. This was better than Samuel had hoped. Melvin had never liked Betsie, going as far as to forbid Samuel to walk out with her three years ago. He wouldn't be too happy to hear about the wedding. It was best that he was out of the way while Selma and Samuel celebrated.

He went in to the kitchen but it was empty. He had expected pots on the stove, bread in the oven, but the kitchen was deserted and cold.

"*Mamm?*" Samuel called.

Maybe she had been too tired to get out of

bed. This had happened many times before, so Samuel wasn't too worried. He put the kettle on to boil for *kaffe*, set out a few eggs, and fished out the stale bread from yesterday. He'd whip up a quick batch of French toast before Melvin came in for his breakfast. He whisked the eggs, milk, and sugar, then set the mixture aside.

Making sure not to rouse her, Samuel walked gently towards Selma's room to check on her. She was lying in bed, the wool gray light of dawn falling on her closed eyes. A tiny smile tugged at her lips as if she were having a pleasant dream. Samuel placed a hand on her forehead to check for a fever. She felt cold to the touch. Too cold.

"*Mamm?*"

The first wings of fear fluttered like a moth inside his ribs. He touched her cheek, the skin cold and yielding. Her cheeks had sunken in over the years as her condition had taken its toll. Her mouth was slightly parted as if she were about to say something to him but couldn't remember what it was.

"*Mamm*, wake up." He shook her gently. "*Mamm*, come on now. *Daed* will come in for his breakfast any minute. Please, *Mamm*. *Mamm!*"

His hot tears fell on Selma's forehead, on her eyelids and her nose, but she did not stir. Her spirit had left her mortal shell and moved in *Gott's* glory to where Samuel couldn't follow till his own time. Samuel held his mother's hand, and cried for all that could have been, if he only had more time.

INTERVENTION

Leroy was having a terrible day. It had all begun with breakfast, or the lack thereof. When Betsie wasn't pointedly ignoring him, she was off at the King house making their meals. It was tragic what had happened to Selma. He felt bad for the entire family, especially Samuel, who had been so close to his mother. The funeral had been somber. Melvin had sat there with his usual disdain, and Samuel...

Poor Samuel! It broke one's heart to look at him. He wasn't weeping or crying, or shaming himself in any way. He sat there, straight-backed, accepting condolences and murmuring thanks. But when no one was talking to him, when he was free to look in the distance and contemplate his loss, he looked like a small boy who has lost sight of his mother in a crowded place. It was the look of edging on panic, and it hurt Leroy's kind heart to see it.

It hadn't broken his resolve, though.

When Betsie had come to him after the funeral and told him of Samuel's proposal, Leroy had said that his decision had not changed. He liked Samuel, but not enough to let him ruin his daughter's life. A farm and barn were not the only things he looked for in a son-in-law. They must have integrity and a love for the Amish way as well. Samuel didn't have enough of either, in his opinion.

Yet now he had just found out that Samuel wasn't getting the farm after all. The elders had called a meeting this morning and Leroy had attended. The subject of the meeting was a mystery till Joseph Miller had announced the sale of the King farm, barn, house, furniture and all.

"But what about Samuel?" Uri had asked.

Leroy had smiled in triumph. He had known it all along! Samuel was going to leave the community. Why else would he put up his inheritance for sale? Betsie might be naïve but Leroy wasn't born yesterday. He would not let Samuel dupe his daughter and be shunned with him.

Joseph Miller looked uncomfortable.

"We all know that Melvin is a hard man," he said. "He's had no love for his son. This is just an extension of that. He has refused to give the farm to Samuel."

It surprised Leroy, but in hindsight he wouldn't have put it past Melvin to be so petty.

"We offered him the first right of sale," Joseph continued. "But Samuel refused. He has integrity; I'll say that much about him. He didn't want his father's handout and is saving for a home. He was also saving for his mother's treatment, but there is our plan and *Gott's* plan, and surely *Gott's* plan is better."

Shame had stolen over Leroy then. He had only seen Samuel in the garage and assumed it was because the man couldn't control his urge to be near machines. Not once had he questioned why Samuel would feel the need to do something he knew the *Ordnung* frowned upon. Of course it was for Selma's treatment. Samuel doted on her, would have moved mountains for her, because he loved her.

He loved Betsie too.

Leroy's mind was full of the revelations of the meeting. He climbed the porch steps and rubbed his temple to dispel the headache. He felt like an old fool who thought he was wise. It just went to show that silver strands in your hair didn't mark an intelligent man.

Hungry for some good food, he opened the front door hoping Betsie wouldn't be too cold with him. The smell from the kitchen was mouthwatering. He walked in expecting to see Betsie with her back to him, working at the stove. Instead, he found the shock of his life.

Betsie was nowhere to be seen. Instead Sarah, Kathy, and Miriam sat at the table laid for lunch.

"Miriam!"

"Hallo, *Daed*," Miriam stood up to greet her father. "You're just in time for lunch."

"Where's Betsie? What's going on?" he asked, taking a seat.

"Betsie's at my house," Sarah said, serving salad. "She's taking care of the children so we can have a brief chat."

"What's happened?" Leroy asked Miriam. "Are you all right? Did they fire you? Are you here to stay?"

Miriam laughed. "Don't you wish that were the case? *Nee, Daed*. My job is secure and I will leave at the end of the week. I came because Sarah sent me a telegram saying you needed my help."

"What?"

"With Betsie, *Daed*." Kathy poured water in his glass. "She's told us about Samuel's proposal."

"And your rejection of it." Miriam arched an eyebrow.

"We can understand your need to secure the farm with one of your daughters, but that's no excuse to refuse Samuel," Sarah said.

"Did Betsie tell you he was working in a garage?" Leroy asked. He had felt a little less rigid towards Samuel after the meeting with the elders, but being accosted by his daughters like this had hardened his resolve. "Did she tell you that?"

"*Ja*," Miriam said, "and she also told us why. If you went back in time and working in a garage was the only way you could save *Mamm*, would you?"

"Miriam." Kathy was shocked.

"That's a bit harsh." Sarah placed a hand on Miriam's.

It was harsh, but trust Miriam to get to the heart of it. Leroy had often wondered if he could have saved Mabel. The *Ordnung* didn't forbid seeking *Englischer* healthcare in times of grave need, but it didn't encourage it either. The option was always there. They never had the time to take it.

"Samuel did what he did to try to save his *Mamm*," Kathy said gently. "Surely his intentions were pure."

"He was working on the Yoder farm," Leroy said, his fist balled in his lap. He hadn't touched his food. "They were paying him. He didn't have to seek employment in the garage."

"The Yoders were paying him $3 a day." Miriam's rejoinder cracked like a whip. "The garage paid $5 an hour. He didn't just have to save, and quick, for a treatment. He had to save for a home as well. That boy has stretched himself thin to meet his responsibilities towards the women in his life. You can't tell me that isn't important in a husband."

"But the *Ordnung*..."

"The *Ordnung* states that we shall not use electric machinery to plow our lands, or use it in our homes," Miriam interrupted. "It doesn't ask to refrain from touching or fixing machines, so don't use that as an excuse. What are you really afraid of?"

Leroy stared at her, his face carved out of stone. Out of all of his daughters he had often wondered why *Gott* hadn't made Miriam a boy. She had all the delicacy of a sledgehammer, and the sharp wit and mind most men lacked. She would have been a great asset to him, no matter how much she exasperated him by chipping away at his arguments to get to the bottom of things.

"I'm afraid that when I die you will no longer have a home," he said. "I'm afraid of my last few years without a companion to share my meals. I'm afraid that this house will become sad and lonely to suit a sad and lonely man. I'm afraid."

"I will always have a home in Jamesport as long as my sisters live here," Miriam said, her tone gentle now that Leroy had confessed his fears. "Our bond did not break just because we left home, *Daed*." She got up and walked to be by his side, leaning down so he would have to look into her eyes. "The answer to your prayers is the man you have been rejecting all along. Samuel doesn't have a home, you do. You wanted to marry Betsie to someone without an inheritance, Samuel was denied his."

"He loves Betsie." Sarah smiled.

"And he admires you." Kathy patted his hand.

"That man has lost his mother, don't make him lose his fiancée, no matter how afraid you are." Miriam squeezed his shoulder.

Leroy sighed. He rubbed the back of his neck, shook his head, and smiled.

"I give up." He raised his hands in surrender.

"You win. I will meet with Samuel. Now, let me eat my lunch in peace!"

"Of course, *Daed*."

"Wouldn't dream of disturbing you, *Daed*."

"More peas, *Daed?*"

Leroy sat back and let them fuss over him. He had thought giving in to their demands would leave him bitter, but he felt oddly at peace now, as if *Gott* had taken matters in His hands, so Leroy could relax in his old age.

BEQUEATHED

S amuel squirmed in his seat. He felt nervous sitting on the porch of Betsie's house being stared at by Leroy. He had always admired Leroy Hershberger, and envied Betsie a father that was concerned about his children's welfare, but trusting them enough to make their life decisions. Yet now, sipping on his *kaffe*, he felt like an insect under the gaze of an eagle, the superior species deciding if the bug was worth eating or not.

"Why didn't you leave?" Leroy asked suddenly.

"I'm sorry, but what do you mean?"

"The community. Why didn't you leave the community? You have no love for farming or animal husbandry. You like machines and from what I've been told you're a natural at it. Why didn't you pursue an education in the field and leave the village? Melvin wouldn't have missed you."

"*Mamm* would have," Samuel said simply.

Leroy didn't look pleased with the answer.

"So if Selma was all that kept you from leaving the village, how can I be sure you won't do it now she has been taken to the bosom of our Lord?"

"*Mamm* wasn't the only reason I didn't leave." Samuel shrugged. "I stayed for Betsie too."

Leroy chewed the inside of his cheek, observing Samuel.

"I talked to Tim Yoder," Leroy said. "He said you were a decent hand around the farm, so you know how to run one even if your heart isn't in it. My concern is what will happen when you're forced to do it for the rest of your life."

"I don't understand…"

"Many men do things they don't love for their loved ones, and the misery of that manifests itself differently with everyone. Your father loved to farm. He did not love your mother."

Samuel winced as if he had been slapped.

"He loved your *Ant* May, but she rejected his proposal. Selma had been in love with Melvin for as long as anyone could remember. He was a fool to think May would marry the man her sister loved. That rejection and marrying your mother made him bitter."

Long buried memories of his childhood came back to him in blinding flashes. *Ant* May's face falling when Melvin entered the room. Melvin having eyes only for *Ant* May, the shouting and screaming. *Ant* May leaving, saying she'd never come back. Melvin pushing Selma out of his way in anger, his mother's screams and the blood. The nights he could hear his mother sobbing, he peeked in to find her in the spare room with his old baby clothes clutched to her chest.

"I know that is hard to accept..."

"*Nee*, you are right," Samuel said, the clarity of his parents' failed marriage dawning on him like the answer to a mystery he had long puzzled over. "My mother and I were the chore my father despised. And you fear that if I am denied an education in machinery, or the chance to work with it, I will become bitter like my father and make Betsie miserable."

Leroy nodded, and Samuel saw a hint of shame in the man's eyes. It made him like Leroy more. He was trying so hard to appear tough and ruthless for his daughter's happiness, yet he was a kind man who did not indulge in such reprehensible tactics.

"I love Betsie very much," Samuel said. "I have already given up on a college education for her, and yesterday I quit my job at the garage. Betsie thought it would be unseemly to buy a home in the village from money made through machines. I agreed. I'm hoping the Yoder family will take me back."

Leroy looked surprised.

"You're still working towards buying a home?"

"*Ja*," Samuel said. "My aim is to have a home by the end of the year and work towards buying the surrounding land over the years."

"And how do you expect to do that and feed my daughter on three dollars a day?"

"We'll manage. I have money saved up. It's not enough to buy a house just yet, which is why we have to wait till the end of the year to get married."

"That won't be necessary."

The finality in Leroy's voice dashed any hopes of gaining his support for the union. The Amish custom didn't necessarily demand the couple get parental approval before marriage, but Samuel had really hoped to wed Betsie with Leroy's blessings.

"You'll be inheriting this farm." Leroy waved

his hand across the fields and toward the house. "Save that money for emergencies."

Samuel wasn't sure he had heard right. He kept waiting for Leroy to burst out laughing and claim it was all a cruel joke. He had never known such generous kindness from his own father; he hadn't expected it from Leroy.

"I… I don't understand."

"One of the conditions I placed before Uri and Otto, given that one or the other would inherit the place once they married Betsie," Leroy said, "was that Miriam and I will always have a place to stay here, no matter what. Do you agree to those terms?"

It sounded too good to be true. His own farm, the price of which was marriage to Betsie. He would gain a family and a farm in one go, not to mention the respect of the community. And as always when he thought of how wonderful life was being to him, Melvin's jeering face rose in front of his eyes. The feeling of elation was deflated immediately, replaced by bile burning his throat, and his cheeks flaring with shame.

Of course the community wouldn't respect him; he was a fool to think they would. They would think him opportunistic, a lesser man for marrying to get a farm. They wouldn't see that the farm was given to him out of Leroy's generous heart, or that his love for Betsie was true. No. They would think like Melvin, that Samuel didn't deserve the favor Leroy was bestowing on him because it hadn't been earned.

"With all due respect, sir," Samuel said solemnly, "I want to make it on my own."

"I understand your need to prove your father wrong by getting on your own two feet with no one's help. But you will help me out, not the other way around. Please, accept my offer."

Samuel was a little shocked at how accurately Leroy had guessed his thoughts. Was his mind so easily readable?

Samuel looked at the fields and tried to alter his vision of the future. He could see himself in those fields next to Leroy, learning his trade secrets. He could imagine sitting by the fire, listening to Leroy's stories of his youth. He could see his children sitting at their *grossdaed's* feet, and Samuel realized how much he needed a father right now, so soon after Selma's death.

Leroy wasn't only accepting Samuel's marriage to Betsie, but offering his home and, more importantly, himself as Samuel's family.

All that remained was his answer. Would he accept Leroy's generosity and open himself for love and friendship, or would he let Melvin ruin the only chance at happiness that came his way, just because he felt he had something to prove?

"I'm honored." Samuel smiled.

Leroy's prickly demeanor fell, and he smiled.

"Welcome to the family."

EPILOGUE

The sun kissed her hair, and it shone like the brown pebbles at the bottom of the river in summer. Her delicate hands felt tender and fragile in his, but their warmth was a comfort in the chill.

"Do you, Samuel King, take Betsie Hershberger to be your wife in the sight of *Gott* and all His creation?"

"*Ja*, I do."

"And do you, Betsie Hershberger, take Samuel King to be your husband in the sight of *Gott* and all His creation?"

"I do."

Samuel hadn't been this happy in his entire life, as Joseph Miller placed his hand on their entwined hands and gave his blessing to the union. The ceremony was small, as tradition dictated. Only their close friends were in attendance. Their families would wait for their arrival at the Hershberger farm for the reception.

Giving their thanks to Joseph Miller, Samuel and Betsie stepped into David Stoltzfus' buggy. They rode towards the Hershberger farm, giddy and laughing. They arrived amidst cheers and cries of congratulations.

"So, how does it feel to be Betsie King?" Kathy asked, rocking her baby son, Jasper.

"I don't feel different," Betsie said. "I thought I'd feel different."

"Wait till nightfall," Kathy laughed.

Samuel turned as red as Betsie did. They avoided looking at each other, but it comforted him when Betsie took his hand. They were guided to the head table where they were served. Sarah and Kathy managed the children. Miriam served the food with the help of Ben and Ivan, while Leroy played the harmonica.

He looked around, but saw no sign of Melvin. He wasn't surprised. He was about to go back to his food when he saw someone enter the barn. She was older than he remembered, but he would have known her anywhere. She looked so much like his mother.

"I wrote her a letter," Betsie said by his side. "I told *Ant* May that Melvin wouldn't be joining us for the wedding."

Samuel was lost for words. Watching *Ant* May walk into the wedding celebrations was like having a part of his mother in the room.

"Oh, Samuel, look at you!" *Ant* May said, reaching the table and holding Samuel's face in her hands. "You've grown to be more handsome than I had hoped! And such a beautiful bride! Your children will be little angels."

"*Ant* May, it's so *gut* to see you!"

"I wouldn't have missed your wedding day for the world. Selma must have been so proud of you." Tears stood out in her eyes. "I wish we hadn't moved to Pennsylvania. But Mark inherited his *grossdaed's* farm, and it was too *gut* of an opportunity to pass."

"She missed you," Samuel said with no malice. "She would talk about you often in the last few weeks."

"Was she in great pain?"

"*Gott* was merciful. She passed away in her sleep."

"Praise be to *Gott*," *Ant* May wiped her eyes

with a handkerchief. "I'm sorry I wasn't here. I should have stayed in touch."

"I know why you didn't, *Ant* May, and I understand."

She looked relieved, yet he could tell his words had done nothing to wipe away her guilt at leaving her sister with Melvin. Samuel supposed he could do nothing to assuage it, that it was a struggle his aunt would have to see to alone. But he prayed that *Gott* would grant her peace like He had granted him.

"*Gott* bless you and your union. May you have many children, and each a blessing from *Gott*."

"*Denke, Ant* May," Betsie said, kissing her hand.

The music grew louder as evening fell and people began to dance. Samuel guided Betsie across the floor. She looked more beautiful as the day waned and evening fell. It was as if she was made up of a galaxy of stars, each shining its brightest.

"So, Mr. King," Betsie teased. "Are you ready to start a new journey?"

"*Ja*, Mrs. King," he grinned. "I think I am."

THE HEART OF FORGIVENESS

BOOK DESCRIPTION

Betsie and Samuel married for love, but only three years down the line, their relationship has been forced to take a backseat to children, and other responsibilities. Their marriage is already strained when Melvin, Samuel's father, comes to stay with them. He's a crotchety old man who brings misery wherever he goes. Matters come to a breaking point when their first child is kidnapped without a trace.

Will Betsie and Samuel's marriage survive this turmoil? Will they ever get their daughter back? And will Samuel finally find it in his heart to forgive his father?

"Be kind to one another, tenderhearted, forgiving one another, as God in Christ forgave you."
~ Ephesians 4:32

THE VISITOR

The shop smelled of lemon and wood varnish. Bolts of cloth in rainbow colors were stacked on wooden pegs along one wall; ribbons and glass jars of buttons festooned another wall. Betsie King touched the blood-red silk gingerly. The fabric felt as soft as a baby's downy hair. Samuel, her husband, glanced at her, and she snatched her fingers away, rubbing them against her sensible cotton skirt.

"It's beautiful, isn't it?" Mary Miller asked, pushing her glasses up her thin nose. "It's a shame *Gott* doesn't approve of fine silks."

"At least, He approves the sale of them," Betsie laughed. "If He'd instructed the sale of only

cotton and gingham in plain colors for us Amish
folk, you'd have gone out of business."

Mary laughed. Her family had owned the local
dress shop for as long as anyone could remember.
It had been small before, with only the odd
flowery print for the *Englischer* customer. But
little by little, the shop had expanded, and the
stock infused with brighter, non-Amish prints
and colors.

Betsie glanced across the shop at Samuel. He
had his back to them, but she could see he was
infinitely bored. Emma, their nine-month-old
daughter, was in his arms, trying to reach a spool
of bright purple ribbon, but Samuel didn't lean
forward to help her grab it. In fact, he looked distant, like his mind was elsewhere. Betsie felt a
flash of annoyance towards him.

"You know," Mary whispered, leaning forward. "Sometimes, when I'm all alone in the shop,
I like to drape a yard of silk around my skirt and
walk about. Oh, Betsie! The sound it makes is
dreamy."

Betsie giggled. It felt good to be out of the
house. She had been cooped up for three weeks,
tending to the household and to baby Emma. It
didn't help matters that she was also expecting
another child. Her belly, not yet recovered from

the first pregnancy, was already bloated and showing in her third month.

"You know," Mary said, placing a thoughtful finger on her pointed chin. "It's too bad you can't wear silks. It would have done wonders for your complexion. Not to mention it would have hidden that paunch. Doesn't Samuel say anything about your weight?"

Betsie's face flooded with blood. Heat radiated off her as she stammered an explanation. "It's the pregnancy…"

"Emma's what, nine months now? Surely that's enough time to lose the weight you put on. Stop eating French fries." Mary laughed good-naturedly. There was no malice in Mary, that much Betsie knew, but Mary was tactless and clueless as to how much her words hurt sometimes.

Betsie was humiliated. Mary had just said what Betsie had been feeling for the past few weeks. Her hands had come to rest on her belly, as they often did these days, as a reminder that it was home to a baby and not evidence of her gross eating habits.

Betsie was saved from searching for a reply when the shop door opened, clanging the bell attached to the top. A young *Englischer* girl with ash blonde hair came in, a stack of papers in her hands. Her jean-clad legs were long and lithe, her waist tiny. Betsie watched Samuel glance at her, his gaze lingering a moment too long before he looked away. She didn't want to know what he was thinking in that moment. She didn't think she could bear it.

"Excuse me." The girl looked from Betsie to Mary, not sure who the proprietor was. "May I have a word?" She had pretty pink lips and perfect white teeth.

"Of course." Mary stepped forward.

"Our neighbor's son went missing two days ago." She flipped her hair back from her freckled shoulders. "We're helping out by placing these flyers in town. Would you mind putting these posters up in your shop window?"

She handed Mary the flyers with the picture of a boy about six years old standing in front of a tree. He was wearing a Cardinals baseball cap over his red hair, his toothy grin missing three teeth, his green eyes full of joy. There was a smattering of freckles across his button nose, and his left hand clutched a catcher's mitt. Dylan Brice was written underneath, along with a phone number and a reward.

"Bless his heart!" Mary cried. "His parents must be devastated."

"They are." The girl nodded, her hair swinging with the motion. "They were at the Kmart doing their weekly grocery shopping. Dylan wanted a ride on that rocket ship they have outside the store."

"The kiddie ride?"

"Yes. So his dad gave him a few cents to get him out of his hair. They never found him when they came outside. They suspect he was taken because a few people saw a man talking to Dylan shortly before he disappeared, one of those army winos fresh out of the war."

"Oh, *Gott* help us if our veterans are stealing our children."

"They should never have gone to war," the girl sniffed. "Muhammad Ali got our hostages back from Iraq. Why go to war after that?"

Mary was out of her depth, as was Betsie. Neither had followed the infamous Gulf War; the village was cut off from such news. The Amish did not take part in politics or war. Their way of life was peaceful and dedicated to the glory of *Gott*.

"I'm sure you're right," Mary said. "I'll put these up right away."

"Thank you." The girl smiled brightly at them

both and left, her glorious hair swinging about her waist.

"*Englischer* and their wars." Mary rolled her eyes. "Oh, but poor child. I hope they find him soon."

"*Ja,*" Betsie murmured.

"And you'd best start on that drink Nancy Hilty swears by," Mary cautioned. "No man likes a plump wife."

"I'm pregnant, Mary."

"*Och,* congratulations!" Mary exclaimed. "Let's hope it's a boy this time, eh?"

Betsie's smile was small, and she fingered her purse, showing she wanted to pay for the fabric she had chosen for Emma and herself. Mary led her to the till in the shop's front. Samuel looked relieved that the trip had ended.

Tucking her purchase under her arm, Betsie followed Samuel out into the spring air. The sun was glowing, but there was an occasional cool breeze to soothe the harsh touch of the sun's rays. It was perfect weather for a picnic next to the river or in the woods. Too tired to prepare a picnic, Betsie decided on a scoop of ice cream instead.

"It's the perfect weather for ice cream, isn't it?" she asked, smiling up at Samuel.

He kept walking as if he hadn't heard her.

"Can we stop at Frankie's for a scoop?" She tried one more time, raising her voice a little.

"No."

It was the abrupt way he had said it, not making eye contact, that made Betsie cringe on the inside. She felt ridiculous for asking. Of course he would say no. Mary had just made it very clear men didn't prefer plump women. Samuel had to be thinking about her bloating belly, and how it disgusted him.

Biting the inside of her cheek, Betsie slowed her pace, so she was just behind Samuel, not walking beside him. She looked at his broad shoulders, his straight back, and the soft curl of his chestnut hair at the back of his neck under his hat. Emma had placed her head on his shoulder, her tiny hand clutching the fabric of his coat. Betsie felt an intense love for both of them, a love marred by her own insecurities.

Their buggy was a block down, next to the pharmacy where there were posts for horse buggies. As they approached, Betsie saw a young boy standing by the buggy, a bright green balloon in his hand. He was wearing a red baseball cap, his red hair poking out from underneath the rim.

Betsie gasped. It was Dylan Brice, the missing boy!

She hurried forward and clutched the child by the shoulders. He jumped and whirled around to face her.

"Betsie, what are you doing?"

But Betsie didn't hear Samuel. The boy wasn't Dylan Brice. It wasn't a boy at all.

"I was just looking," the little girl said. "I wasn't gonna touch him, promise."

Her red hair was cut short, and she had scrapes on her knees and scabs on her elbows. She was much older than six, and there was a smudge of dirt across her pointed nose. Her confused eyes were a firm brown. Even the baseball cap wasn't the same. It was a generic red cap, not a Cardinals cap.

"Oh, that's all right," Betsie said, taking her hand back. Her heart was racing in her chest. She had thought she had found the missing child. This girl wasn't Dylan Brice, but she looked lost just the same. "Are you lost?"

The girl nodded. Samuel came forward and handed Emma to Betsie.

"We'll help you," he said, kneeling down, so he was face-to-face with the child. His smile was kind and warm. For the fraction of a second, Betsie felt envious of the girl.

"There you are, Mary Anne!"

An old woman in cream slacks and a pink button-down shirt came striding out of the pharmacy clutching a paper bag.

"I've been looking all over for you, missy! Have you been bothering these good people? I apologize for my granddaughter," the woman said. "She can be a handful."

"*Nee*." Samuel stood up. "She was no trouble."

"She was just admiring our horse," Betsie added.

"Mary Anne loves animals. Ponies are her favorite, aren't they?" The woman smiled down at Mary Anne, who was wearing the biggest frown Betsie had ever seen on a child so young. It made her want to giggle.

"I don't…" Mary Anne protested.

"Oh, hush now," her grandmother admonished. "What will these good people think of your manners?"

"We can give you folks a ride, if you like," Betsie offered. She found the pair endearing and wanted to get to know them better. Mary Anne stopped frowning and looked eagerly at the buggy.

"No," Samuel said abruptly.

Betsie stared at Samuel, her cheeks blazing. She hadn't felt this embarrassed in years. Samuel was red in the face as well, and he looked angry.

"We have to get back to the farm," he said, his tone curt and brisk.

"Oh, that's all right," the woman smiled. "Mary Anne and I live nearby. Thank you for keeping an eye on my granddaughter."

"Don't mention it," Betsie mumbled.

She climbed into the buggy awkwardly and sat down. She avoided looking at Samuel as he took his seat beside her. The buggy pulled away from the sidewalk, and Betsie glanced at the grandmother and daughter, the pair they made on the sidewalk. As she watched, a young couple emerged from the pharmacy and hailed Mary Anne. She watched the red balloon bobbing in the girl's hand as she ran to her parents.

Losing sight of the pair when they turned a corner, Betsie wondered if the grandmother made the difference in that family's life. Maybe if her own father were still here, Samuel wouldn't neglect her the way he did.

Leroy's death had been unexpected. He had finished planting the barley with Samuel one day and spent the evening singing to Emma. He had gone to bed after their Bible reading and had never gotten up. Samuel had found him in bed, smiling serenely.

Betsie knew it was the only way Leroy would have wanted to meet the Lord, and she was happy he got a dignified end; but it had left her with a hole that needed filling, but Samuel didn't seem up to the task.

Betsie glanced sideways at Samuel's face. There was a slight frown in the crease of his eyebrows, a permanent feature that hadn't been there before. The sole responsibility for the farm had fallen on him since her father's death a few months ago, and she knew it took a toll on him. Mathematics and science came naturally to him, farming not so much. But he still plowed on. Betsie wondered, not for the first time, if he resented her for the choices he had to make to be with her.

It didn't help that she was no longer as beautiful as she had been when they had married. She often felt him turn away from her when she approached him for a kiss goodbye, or to hold his hand as they sat side-by-side at night reading the Bible. In her three years of marriage, she hadn't felt more distant from her husband as she did now.

~

THE BUGGY TRUNDLED across the dirt road that passed throughout the village from homestead to homestead. They passed a group of young *Englischer* walking beside their bikes, packages from the goods they had bought at farms in their bike baskets. Betsie spied some Amish *Rumspringa* children amongst them. Betsie held Emma close so the jostling wouldn't disturb her sleep. Emma's wispy chestnut hair shone almost red in the sun. It tickled Betsie's nose, and she sneezed.

The road approached their house from the east, so visitors saw the back of the house first before the road bent and approached the front. It had been in Betsie's family for three generations. Leroy Hershberger had four daughters and no sons. He had bequeathed the house and farm to Samuel when he had married Betsie.

Betsie admired her home with childlike wonder. Samuel had made no changes after Leroy's death. The chicken coop was whitewashed to look like a part of the house. The barn was a sedate brick red against the azure sky. Their vegetable patch was a slash of fresh green in the brown yard, and the fields of wheat nodded under the sun.

The buggy turned with the road, the horse's clip-clopping hooves muffled by the dirt. Betsie felt a lull overcome her, the swaying motion making her drowsy. Her eyes lingered on the cherry tree in front of the house, and her mind played with the idea of tying a swing to one of the branches for the children.

Her drowsy eyelids snapped open when the front of the house finally came into view and she saw a buggy parked by the porch.

Who could be visiting at this time?

Betsie wasn't sure who it was, but she knew it didn't bode well. People didn't wait for you to come home to give you good news. She saw that the man sitting on their porch step was the village elder Joseph Miller; it confirmed her suspicions.

BITTER MEALS

Melvin King had found a gear last night. It was wedged between the floorboards in Samuel's room. Samuel's *old* room, he reminded himself.

He sat at his dusty kitchen table in his quiet house eating a burned piece of toast. The gear lay flat on the table, its spiked edges like burrs attached to his eyes so they couldn't look away. The toast was dry and hard to swallow. There was no cheese in the panty, no cream to sprinkle with sugar, no butter freshly churned. He ate his toast and sipped his bitter *kaffe* while his mind chewed on the events that had led to his present condition.

Melvin King had always felt lonely, but he had never felt alone before.

He had felt no connection to Selma, his wife, when she was alive. Their marriage was a mixture of spite and convenience. He had been in love with her younger sister May, but she had refused him, saying he should ask Selma to walk out. Humiliated, Melvin had sworn never to ask Selma, but no other girl in the village would have him. They all knew how much Selma loved him.

It used to enrage him, how the village girls had manipulated his match to Selma. As for Selma, she was a fool who would follow him around the house, her moon-face bland and idiotic in its love for him.

He supposed he did love her in his own way. It was impossible not to. She was compliant, had his meals on time, and was an excellent cook. She stayed out of his way and anticipated his needs before he was even aware of them himself. She had been a good wife till she had died. Now the house was in disrepair, and he had to fend for himself in the kitchen.

The women who had forced his marriage to Selma had been of little help after she had gone. A few of them baked cakes and brought meals once or twice a month. But that soon stopped. The community's abandonment hurt Melvin, but he would never show it. He supposed he could have bought the cheeses, the yogurts, and the creams he was fond of like most *Englischer* tourists did on their walks in town, but his pride prevented it. Why must he, an old Amish community member and contributor, go about buying things like an *Englischer*, an outsider, a stranger?

Melvin finished his breakfast, his body held taut from getting up, but his mind still focused on the old memories the gear had awoken. All he had time for now were the memories that spilled into the restful cracks of his day, making him slow and absentminded.

The gear was stark black. There were still pieces of dirt and grime in it. Melvin's wrinkled finger touched the edges of it, his brittle yellow nails tapping a rhythm.

What did Samuel find fascinating about these darn things?

The young, unlined face of his infant son rose in front of his eyes. Samuel running ahead in the path through the cornfield, his laughter high-pitched as his plump baby legs propelled him forward, looking back mid-run, his full smile showing four small teeth, his hazel eyes shining with love and joy.

Melvin snatched his hand away, unprepared for the intensity of the memory.

His breathing was suddenly labored, and he couldn't distinguish between the present or the past. The gear came into focus and Melvin blamed the cursed thing for his confusion. He swiped it off the table, dust rising up, dancing in the sunlight as it settled back on the wooden surface.

Samuel.

His only child. His only son.

How much Melvin had loved him. He was a precocious boy. He had learned to walk by eleven months, was talking by a year and a half, and was ahead of all the other *kinner* his age. Melvin had taken great pride in his son. But then Samuel had grown out of his infancy, asking questions Melvin had no answer to. At the same time Selma had gotten sick, and it became apparent that no more children would be forthcoming.

He didn't know which had hurt most: Selma's barren womb denying him children through no fault of his own; or that look in Samuel's eyes when he asked about the workings of lights and telephones, and Melvin didn't know. It wasn't easy watching helplessly as your child realized you weren't the all-knowing hero they had thought you were.

He was losing the unquestioned trust and adoration of his son, without the blessed hope of replacing it with another child who would love Melvin in the way only children could.

Melvin had tried to curb the curiosity, hoping that if Samuel thought machines were a sin, he would go back to believing Melvin was the only man he had to look up to. But if he had taken his sweet nature from Selma, he had taken his stubbornness from Melvin. Samuel's curiosity only grew with age, and Melvin's love became bitter.

He's probably running that farm into the ground, Melvin thought, getting up on his feet with some difficulty. His knees had been aching more often than not these past few months. *Leroy was a good man, but too taken in by his stupid daughter to see what was right and wrong. Samuel has no heart for farming.*

Placing his dirty plates in the sink, he looked out at the back yard of the house and the fields that needed tending that day. Out of necessity, he had had to hire help around the farm. Mark Graber would be there any minute. Melvin turned towards the screen door but had to stop when the entire floor bucked. He grabbed the sink to stop from falling, his eyes falling on the gear he had swept to the floor. His head was spinning, his heart hammering against his chest, and unbelievable pain shot through his body.

Please, Gott, Melvin thought, his eyes fixed on the gear. *Not like this. I don't want to die like this!*

Darkness engulfed him.

HOMECOMING

M ark *Graber found him unconscious on the*
kitchen floor.
We thought he was dead.
He is too old to live alone.
Will you do a son's duty?
I wouldn't ask, if he had anywhere else to go.
Samuel's mind resonated with Joseph Miller's
news as he rode down the dirt path in his buggy.
The old man had waited till Betsie went inside
the house to put Emma to bed, then he told
Samuel about his father's collapse. None of that
had surprised Samuel. Joseph was known for his
tact, which is why he was the head elder in the
village. What had surprised him was his own
reaction.

At first his throat had tightened, expecting the news, but after he was told of Melvin's collapse there had been absolutely nothing. No reaction, just the echoing hint of relief. Melvin hadn't died. This had surprised Samuel, who had no love for his father.

Leroy's death had penetrated Samuel, because Leroy Hershberger was the father he had never had. A little absentminded and heavy-handed with his favors and gifts, Leroy had managed to make him see farming with the eye of an engineer. There was a system to everything. If one thing went wrong on the farm, it would affect everything. Farmers were the engineers of nature, trying to mend the system to work for their benefit. It had developed a passion for farming in Samuel that Melvin's bitter taunts never had.

Before he had passed away in his sleep, Leroy had been a boon. Always ready with encouragement to show Samuel the right way, Leroy had taken to the role of Samuel's father as if it came naturally to him. This hadn't surprised Samuel. Leroy had nurtured four daughters after the death of his wife. His own expectation of a rocky relationship had surprised him. Melvin had engrained the thought of worthlessness so deeply in

Samuel's heart he had expected no one to want him as a son.

Now that the farm completely depended on Samuel, he felt like he was floundering in the deep sea. One task wasn't complete before another needed attention. He was up long before dawn and slept long after the owls had taken flight for their nighttime hunt. Yet every day it felt like the farm was failing, that it was unraveling at the seams. There weren't enough hands to work the farm, but the mouths to be fed off it kept growing.

He frowned at this thought, reining the horse into a slow trot. It was true that he was happy with Betsie and Emma. It was also true that the news of another baby on the way so soon had been bittersweet. More bitter than sweet, if Samuel was being honest. He had hoped Betsie would recover from Emma's pregnancy and help with the farm. But in her condition it would be callous to ask for help. It also annoyed Samuel that she was blind to their financial situation, or to how hard Samuel worked to save the money that they had. He couldn't well be expected to squander it on ice cream.

Samuel shook his head at the angry thoughts. *It's the thought of Melvin and going back to that farm that's got you thinking negatively,* he thought. *Betsie is a wonderful mother, and she does more than her duty as a wife. If I go to sleep late, she goes to sleep much later, and the baby disturbs her sleep. If I rise before dawn, she rises before me to make my breakfast. She is my rock.*

Feeling much better at having regained his emotional equilibrium, Samuel urged the horse on. The King house rose from behind a copse of trees, hitting his vision like an unexpected sore. The site left Samuel physically breathless.

So much about his childhood home had changed, yet nothing had.

Paint was peeling away, and the garden Selma had tended so lovingly was dead brush. The windows of Samuel's room were thick with grime, and the porch swing creaked noisily on rusting hinges.

It was like a ghost house where nothing but the memories of his horrid childhood lived, forever doomed to repeat themselves.

Taking a shaking breath, Samuel parked his buggy next to Joseph Miller's. Samuel sat there for a minute, trying to compose his thoughts, to compose himself to meet his father. He hadn't seen him in three years. Not since the day he had gotten married and left home. They had avoided each other at church, and Samuel had had no reason to come back home.

Until today.

He is too old to live alone.

Climbing the stairs was difficult. Samuel's legs felt like deadweights. He managed to reach the front door with some effort, but found that he could not bring himself to knock. He was like a stranger on the door of his own childhood home.

The door swung open anyway. Joseph Miller stood there with a kind smile.

"He's being difficult."

If the snarling voice that came down the hall was what Samuel thought it was, then Melvin King was being more than just difficult. Samuel walked down the hall and entered Melvin's bedroom. It was in disarray. There was a pile of laundry on the chair, old plates of food were sitting on top of the dresser, and the place hadn't been dusted in a while. Melvin was struggling out of the bed, barking threats at Mark Graber, who looked bored.

"Melvin, look who's come to see you," Joseph said.

Melvin stopped struggling and regarded Samuel with narrowed, distrustful eyes. Samuel saw that his beard was unkempt and was a solid white, not the chestnut shot with silver the son remembered. His face looked lined and unwashed as well. The house hadn't been the only thing suffering from neglect.

"Come to see my corpse, have you?" Melvin growled. "Well, I'm not dead yet!"

"Now, Melvin!" Joseph admonished. "Your son has come to take you home with him."

"This is my home. I'm not going to his wife's house to live on his charity."

"You can't live on your own, Melvin. Someone needs to care for you, and who better than Samuel, your own son, to do so?"

"He doesn't want me, though, does he?" A shrewd look crossed Melvin's ferocious face. "I bet you had to persuade him to take me because no one in this ungrateful village wants to care for me."

Joseph balked, his mouth opening and closing in guilt and embarrassment. Samuel felt sorry for the head elder. It wasn't easy being at the receiving end of Melvin's conniving insults.

"*Ja*, Joseph told me of your collapse," Samuel said, stepping forward into the room. "And it's true that you and I have no love for each other. Nor do we want to spend more than a minute in each other's presence. But it's also true that you are my father, and I will do my duty by you."

Melvin's lips puckered in distaste, as if he had licked a lemon.

"I don't need your charity," Melvin spat.

"It isn't charity." Samuel shrugged. "It's decency. What would you rather have, dying in comfort in my house with my wife and children? Or here, in squalor, alone till someone thinks of dropping by and eventually finds you stiff and dead for *Gott* knows how…?"

"Enough!" Joseph Miller looked between father and son, horrified. Samuel envied him the shock. It meant Joseph had a loving relationship with his children. Samuel hadn't known that from Melvin. "Melvin, Samuel's right. You can't live alone. It's not that you are not physically able, it's not that," Joseph said tactfully. "I'd sleep better at night knowing that you are cared for."

Melvin eyed Joseph then Samuel, thinking.

"Fine," he said, raising his arms. "I'll go. But only because you asked, Joseph."

"Great!" Joseph clapped his hands together and rubbed them. "Excellent! Why don't you go with Samuel right away? Mark and I will deliver your things once they're packed."

Melvin snatched his hand away from Mark,

who had been holding it, and stood up on his own. He swayed on the spot for a fraction of a second, but regained his balance. He took a few stolid steps, but then had to lurch to hold the door frame to keep from falling to his knees. Samuel watched, fascinated, as the larger-than-life father of his childhood was reduced to this stooped, bumbling old man fighting for a foothold.

Pity flooded him, but he made no move to stretch out his hand and help his father. He knew Melvin's nature well, and Melvin would not appreciate any form of help he deemed weakness. So Samuel let him have what was most precious to Melvin, his dignity and his pride.

Slowly but surely, Melvin made it to the porch, then to the buggy. It took him the best part of half an hour, but no one rushed him. Joseph and Mark got busy sorting through the mess in the room and packing Melvin's clothes while Samuel went ahead and brought the buggy closer to the porch for Melvin.

As they headed back down the dirt road, leaving the old King house in their dust, Samuel felt his trepidation grow. The burden of his childhood had lived in that house, and it had been a source of misery for him. Now he had extracted the reason for his misery and was bringing him to his untainted home for it to fester in the happiness he had built with Betsie. The thought twisted like a knife in his side.

Yet what was he to do? He couldn't leave his father to die alone. That wasn't Christian, and it wasn't Amish. Selma had taught him better than to abandon the people *Gott* had assigned for you to love and be responsible for. Samuel didn't love Melvin, but he had a duty towards him, and he would perform it well, *Gott* willing.

Melvin was quiet throughout the ride, a small mercy Samuel was grateful for. When they turned into the front yard of his home, he saw Betsie sitting on the porch with Emma. It was their favorite spot to sit and play. Emma would often crawl to the front door, begging to be let out on the porch amidst the potted flowers and the slanting sunrays.

A smile crept across his face, as it often did at the sight of his daughter. He stopped the buggy by the porch steps and jumped out to hold Emma, who was raising her arms to him to be picked up. He was about to turn to assist Melvin but stopped; he had just looked up and seen Betsie's shocked face, and his extremities had turned to ice.

Samuel had neglected to tell Betsie of Melvin's coming, or his agreement to Joseph's plan to allow Melvin permanent residency at their house. Fresh guilt erupted inside him and he couldn't meet his wife's eye. He turned to introduce Emma to Melvin instead.

I'll talk to Betsie later in private, he thought.

"I see you didn't tell the Mrs.," Melvin chortled, his malevolent eyes darting gleefully between Samuel and Betsie. "Good. I see you took my advice about keeping your wife in her place."

Samuel's face blazed scarlet with fury at Melvin, but more so at himself for allowing the situation to come about. He tried to save the situation by shaking his head at Betsie, trying to communicate that none of what Melvin said was true, but Betsie had turned away from him. The set of her shoulders and the lift of her chin told him she was furious.

Samuel sighed. Less than a minute at his home and Melvin was already ruining their lives.

THE LAST STRAW

The plate had broken neatly in two, but the food had done none such kindness. It had splattered the wall and stained the rug. Betsie had cleaned up as much as she could; the smell of damp carpet still clung to her nose. Melvin had kept up a litany of his disappointments and Betsie's failings while she picked up his mess.

She sat on the front porch now, planting azaleas in small pots while Emma played with a rattle. While her hands worked, her mind drifted to the past week and how it had strained the very foundations of her marriage.

Samuel had told her of Melvin's collapse, and she had bid him farewell as he had driven away to check on his father. She had never questioned his going. It was expected of him, no matter their past relationship. She had waited with Emma on the porch, a roast in the oven for dinner, her eyes on the dirt road. When Samuel had arrived with Melvin in the buggy with him, it had come as a shock. Melvin's admission that it had been the plan all along was a slap to her face.

Why hadn't Samuel trusted her with that information? Did he think she would oppose him? Yes, Melvin was a horrible father, and she feared he might be just as horrible to Emma, but she wouldn't deny Samuel the chance to do his duty. Did he think her petty and heartless?

And now where is he when his father is throwing around plates of food and terrorizing his daughter? Betsie frowned and stuffed pots with rich black soil. *Yes, the farm demands all his attention, but he should have thought of that before he brought another mouth to feed in the house. Or, at the very least, asked me if I was willing to care for Melvin in my condition.*

Emma giggled and cooed, shaking her fists to make the rattle sing. Leroy had made it for her with a hollow piece of wood filled with hard seeds and fitted the wooden pieces together. He had painted it a pale eggshell blue, and it was Emma's favorite possession.

Tears filled her eyes at the memory of her father.

Leroy Hershberger had been a good man, a little absentminded, but his heart had been in the right place. None of his daughters had wanted for anything, and he had given them more than just a roof over their heads and food to eat; he had given them the freedom to be themselves, to choose their own destinies.

He never imposed himself on anyone, she thought, rubbing her hands clean on a rag. He had even died in the least inconvenient way, going to sleep after a long day in the field with Samuel, and after kissing Emma goodnight.

Emma's fussy wail brought Betsie out of her reverie. Bored with the rattle and hungry, Emma was alternately sucking on her fingers and rocking back and forth, a monstrous frown on her forehead. She was late crawling and could only wiggle on her diaper-covered bottom to get close to Betsie.

"Oh, my love!" Betsie laughed. "*Mamm* is sorry! We forgot all about your lunch. I'll just be a minute. It's your favorite custard."

Scattering a few wooden blocks that Sarah, her sister, had given her on the porch in front of Emma, Betsie put the gardening tools on a hook on the wall far from Emma's reach. Making sure the new toys suitably occupied Emma's attention, Betsie sprinted inside to grab the bowl of custard she had set out before Melvin had thrown his tantrum.

"She frowns just like her *grossdaed*," Betsie muttered, a giggle escaping her lips. She mixed the custard with a spoon and walked back to the porch, looking forward to feeding Emma. She was a good eater, not picky like Kathy's children had been. Emma would devour her own pureed food and still want bites from Samuel's supper.

"Here you are, sweet pea," Betsie sang, as she came through the front door.

The porch was empty.

Blocks lay scattered where she had left them, the rattle lay on its side. The garden tools were in their basket, the basket was on its hook. The flowers were undisturbed, and traces of soil were still lingering where she had worked. Everything was there, everything was accounted for.

Except Emma.

Betsie's grip tightened on the bowl of custard just as her grip on reality loosened. Colors became over bright and she could smell the turned soil and the sap from the cherry tree nearby. The sky seemed to press on her eyes, so she couldn't keep them open for too long. Her vision was rippling, like she was seeing everything from the bottom of the river in the woods. For the fraction of a precious minute, her mind was in freefall.

"Emma?"

Timid and hoarse, her voice was barely audible to her own ears, but it snapped her body out of its temporary paralysis. The bowl tumbled from her lifeless fingers and crashed on the floor, shards and custard flying in all directions. She stumbled forward on feet that had grown numb and a scream ripped through her constricted throat.

"EMMA!"

She lurched down the porch steps, frantically searching the bushes and under the porch. Maybe Emma had tried to crawl and fallen under the porch. Maybe she had grown tired and fallen asleep, that's why she wasn't replying. Maybe she had hurt her poor head... maybe she had crawled inside the house... maybe Samuel had her... maybe... maybe... maybe...

Any possibility was acceptable to her, even if it meant Emma was hurt but somewhere nearby, because the other possibility was unacceptable. Dylan Brice in his Cardinals cap, his red hair shining in the muted shade of the tree, was at the forefront of her mind. Dylan Brice, who had been taken and not returned home to his weeping mother and father.

"Emma!" Betsie's sobs grew hysterical as the panic she had kept at bay seeped into the back of her spine and her entire body.

"What are you screaming for?" Melvin's malevolent face peeked from his bedroom window that faced the front of the house. "Lost her, have you? I expected it."

"You!" Betsie screamed, relief flooding her like warmth. "You took her!"

Yes, it must have been Melvin. He wanted to see Betsie panicking, to prove that she was a careless mother. Emma was in Melvin's room. Why hadn't Betsie thought of this? Her Emma was home, only a few feet away.

"Of course I haven't got her!" Melvin snarled. "You've lost her. You had one job, and you muddled it up."

"What's going on?" Samuel came marching to the front of the house from the fields. His hat was off and his hair rippled in the wind.

"Your wife has lost your child," Melvin said. "And she's accusing me of kidnapping. I told you she was a bad egg." Having said his piece, Melvin shut the window and left Betsie and Samuel alone.

"He's lying," Betsie cried. "He has Emma. I know he does!"

"What does he mean, you lost her?" Samuel asked.

The question stung, as if Samuel had slapped her. He had just taken Melvin's word over hers. Was this how things would be from now on?

"She was on the porch," Betsie snapped. "I left to get her food. I wasn't gone for more than a minute. She has to be in his room. Where else could she go in such a short time?"

Samuel climbed the porch steps and entered the house. She heard the door to Melvin's room open and her heart thudded in her throat. She expected to hear Emma's giggles, to see Samuel walk out, Emma in his arms, a relieved look on his face, mingled with guilt and shame for having doubted her.

Samuel walked out alone, his face pale with worry. Betsie's knees gave under her and she fell to the ground, scraping her left palm on a small rock, but she didn't feel the pain. The aching sense of loss and the physical need to have her child in her arms dominated her senses.

"Why did you leave her unattended?" Samuel accused. "You should have taken her with you."

His words hammered at her. They sparked a flame inside her; it burned to ashes any love that she had for the man in front of her. It gave her the strength to climb to her feet and face him, her shoulders back.

"How could I have taken her with me?" she screamed. "After breaking my back cleaning up after your father's tantrums, keeping the house in order, and your needs in check, how do you expect me to carry two children at one time all day?"

Samuel took a step back, alarmed by her ferocious response.

"I have no help. Yet you didn't ask me if I could care for Melvin," she accused him. "You don't help with him. You just expect me to care for him. But why would I expect you to do anything different when you have been neglecting Emma and me?"

"I have not..."

"*Ja!* You have." She wouldn't let him put a word in edgewise. "You spend all day on the farm, all night in the barn, and I say nothing because I know you work hard for us. But even when you are with us, you aren't with us. You don't play with Emma like you used to. You don't feed her or help with her. You don't even talk to me!"

A spasm of guilt crossed Samuel's face, and Betsie felt bitter triumph.

"There is no point in arguing," Samuel said shortly. "I'll look for her."

"Find her," Betsie begged. "Oh, *Gott*, please bring my *boppli* back home!"

She collapsed on the porch steps, finally giving in to grief.

THE SEARCH

There had been a moment, a long moment, after he had left Betsie prostrated in grief on the front lawn that Samuel stood in the back yard, his mind completely blank. A house separated him and his wife, and he stood in the middle of the back yard torn between the simple choice of walking in search of Emma or taking the buggy.

Walking would be faster, but it wouldn't take him far or fast. It would take a few moments to hitch the horse to the buggy, but that time would be made up soon by the beast's speed.

Samuel still found it hard to believe that Emma was taken, kidnapped as Betsie had hysterically put it. But if there was even a remote chance of this being true, he needed to be fast to apprehend them, whoever they were. A dim memory of an *Englischer* boy came to mind, and he remembered the missing posters in town when they had gone to the dress shop a couple weeks ago. A cold sweat broke on Samuel's body. Kidnapping wasn't such a far-fetched idea, now that he thought about it.

"I want to go with you," Betsie panted, running up to the buggy when Samuel led it to the path in front of their house. "I have to go with you."

"One of us must stay home with *Daed*," Samuel said, hating himself as he did, but there was no way of avoiding it. Her words were still fresh in his mind.

"Then you stay home, and I'll go look for Emma."

"Don't be ridiculous, Betsie," Samuel snapped, desperate to be away, conscious of time slipping by. The kidnapper could be out of the village by now. "I'll be back soon."

He snapped the reins, and the horse trotted forward. Samuel avoided looking at Betsie's despondent face, or that of Melvin peeking through the curtains in his bedroom window.

His first port of call was their neighbor

George Lengacher. He was one of the few pig farmers in the village, and he ran a roaring trade with *Englischer* customers now that the elders had decreed it was acceptable for the townsfolk to purchase fresh produce directly from the farms.

Samuel found George in the large wooden kiosk he had built in the front yard of his home. Smoked and fresh meat hung from hooks in the ceiling, rashers of bacon and pork belly lay in trays covered with cloth to keep the flies away. George was old, and stooped, but he had the strength and agility of a younger man.

"*Gut* to see you, neighbor." George raised his hand. "I was just going to take a lunch break. Care to join me?"

"*Nee*, but *denke*, George," Samuel said. "I've come for something else."

"Bacon?" George asked, scratching his chin. "A shank perhaps?"

"*Nee*, I wanted…"

The sound of clip-clopping hooves had captured both Samuel and George's attention. Isaac Hilty was bringing his horse-drawn buggy to a halt next to Samuel's. He was frowning down at Samuel, but Samuel returned his gaze coolly. Isaac had never liked Samuel, and he did not try to hide it. As far as Samuel was concerned, the feeling was mutual.

"Hallo, Isaac!" George waved. Isaac jumped off the buggy and strode towards the kiosk, his broad shoulders slightly hunched. "The usual?"

"*Ja.*" Isaac said shortly.

George got busy fixing Isaac's usual order. Samuel didn't feel comfortable discussing his troubles in front of Isaac Hilty, but there was very little time.

"As I was saying, George," Samuel continued as if Isaac wasn't there. "I wanted to know if you've seen anyone around with a baby. Our Emma is missing. She was playing on the porch when Betsie went to get her custard. She was only gone a minute, but when she got back, Emma wasn't there."

"*Gut Gott!*" George stopped wrapping a shank of pork in brown paper. "But where could she have gone?"

"She didn't go anywhere," Isaac snorted. "She's too young to walk off. She was taken, I suspect, and by an *Englischer* no less."

"What makes you think it was an *Englischer*?" Samuel asked.

"Are you suggesting someone from the village

did it?" Isaac asked, his beard bristling. "We're *gut* Christian people who live by the words of the Bible. You can't say the same for an *Englischer*. You know what?" Isaac frowned suddenly, as if remembering something. "I just came back from the town and I saw a man on the path. He was carrying a large bundle in his arms. His army jacket covered it."

"Oh, I saw him as well!" George said. "He passed by the farm not ten minutes ago!"

"I bet he had Emma under that jacket," Isaac said with certainty. "I said it would come to mischief, allowing *Englischer* folk to prance up and down the village. It was an invitation to their sordid ways to corrupt our way of life."

"*Denke*, Isaac!" Samuel held Isaac's hand, squeezing it in gratitude. Isaac was so surprised, he forgot to look displeased. "*Denke*, George!"

Samuel didn't wait for their response, but jumped into his buggy and rushed the horse back onto the path.

Ten minutes ago! If Samuel hurried, he might yet catch him on the road to town. Samuel struck the reins again, and the horse trotted faster. He kept his eyes peeled for any stranger on the dirt road or the fields and lands besides it, but he met no one. The buggy jolted a little as it always did when it came on the asphalt road that led to town.

Samuel slowed the horse down to a trot, perplexed. He was disappointed and panic was lacing his throat. Where was his daughter? Who took her and why? He wasn't rich, he had no money to spare for ransom. He didn't own jewels or a fancy car. What would the kidnapper gain by abducting his child?

The horse, unguided, trudged into town. Samuel wondered what to do and thought to consult his friend Hector, the librarian. At least that would alert the people in town to keep a look out for Emma.

He was passing by the main commercial district when he saw posters of the kidnapped boy. But the poster wasn't alone anymore. Beside the picture of the smiling boy was a sketch of a man. It wasn't detailed, but the face was narrow and bony, the eyes tiny slits in the sallow face. Written beneath the sketch was a description of the suspect and the clothes he wore. Samuel saw the words 'army jacket' and his heart leaped in his throat. Isaac Hilty had seen a man with an army jacket.

Dread seeped within Samuel at the implications. This tore to shreds any last hope that this was all a misunderstanding, a bad joke being played on him and Betsie.

His breath shuddering in and out of his lungs, Samuel turned the buggy towards the police station.

"WHAT WILL I TELL HER?"

Samuel hid his face in his hands. He was sitting in front of a neatly organized desk in the small office in the town library. His friend Hector, the head librarian, patted his knee gently. Samuel had been wandering the town aimlessly after his disappointing visit to the police station. The site of the library had been a welcome reminder that he had friends in the *Englischer* town, and he had made a beeline for the comforting presence of Hector.

"You will tell her the truth."

"But what if she hates me?" Samuel moaned. "You didn't see her this afternoon, she was furious. She said… she said some things."

"She has lost her child," Hector explained, his tone soothing. "Anyone would be half out of their mind with grief and worry."

"I'm worried too." Samuel's hands shook. "The

police said they still have no idea where the Brice boy is. All they did was take down the details on Emma; they said they couldn't file a missing persons report till twenty-four hours had passed. I have nothing to give Betsie, no hope, nothing. I'm going out of my mind!"

"Of course you are. This is your daughter, your baby girl. But you can't pit your grief against each other. In this time of crisis, you need to forget about your own pain and help support your wife. She said some awful things…"

"True things," Samuel murmured.

"Be that as it may, Sam, she didn't mean them. It's her fear talking. She needed someone to lash out against. Go home now. Go, be with your wife. The townsfolk have been searching for Dylan and they won't mind adding Emma to the search. The townsfolk have a favorable opinion of our Amish neighbors, and we'll do everything in our power to help."

"Thank you, Hector."

Hector squeezed Samuel's hand.

"Don't thank me yet. Drive safe."

Samuel walked out of the semi-gloom of the library into the fading light of twilight. The sun would sink in another hour and the very worst night of his life would start.

Our life, he corrected. *It will be horrendous for both me and Betsie.*

Walking on leaden feet, Samuel didn't see where he was going. He turned the corner sharply and bumped painfully into a woman. She stumbled, her grocery bag crashing against the concrete sidewalk. Cans of beans, baby formula, and boxes of macaroni and cheese scattered at Samuel's feet.

"I'm so sorry!" He bent to help her up, then retrieved her shopping for her. "It was my fault. I wasn't looking where I was going."

"Oh, now, dear." The woman was middle-aged, her hair a dusty, faded auburn with heavy streaks of silver. "I'm sure there's no harm done. Thankfully, I didn't buy the tomatoes, or else they'd have become ketchup on the sidewalk."

She laughed, a pleasant musical laugh. Samuel found he was responding to her kind smile.

"Let me walk you to your car," Samuel said, holding her groceries.

"I don't have one." The woman smiled. "I'm just passing through the town, you see. My grandchildren and I were taking a train trip to St. Louis to see the Gateway Arch then on to Mark Twain National Forest. My grandson loves Mark Twain! But my little granddaughter got ill on the train ride, so we stopped over here till she gets well again."

"I'm sorry to hear that," Samuel said, only half listening. "Where are you staying, with relatives?"

"Oh, no," the woman laughed again. "All our family is back in Des Moines. No, we're staying at the motel by the woods. A very pleasant place, indeed. I'm hoping my little Grace will recover sooner in the fresh air."

"I know the place. I can give you a ride there. It will be hard for you to manage the walk and the groceries,"

"That is very kind of you…"

"Samuel King."

"Thank you, Samuel. My name is Maude Teller, and I will take your kind offer."

Samuel led her to the buggy and helped her settle in. He climbed in beside her and set the horse trotting towards the Green Woods inn at the far end of town. It was closer to the Amish village than the town center, on the other side of the woods that were a natural divide between the two.

"Are you a married man, Mr. King?"

"Please, call me Samuel. Yes, I am married."

"Any children?"

A lump constricted Samuel's throat and he couldn't speak.

"I'm sorry for the personal question." Maude bit her lip. "My son always says that I let my mouth run on."

"It's all right."

"Children are such a blessing from God, Samuel. Yet they can be trying too. Believe me, I know. My son hasn't spoken to me in five years. It's his wife, of course. She never liked me being around Eric. But I finally convinced him that he needs to let me see my grandchildren. They need to know their grandmother. It builds stronger relationships, don't you think?"

Samuel thought of his own father, frowning in a corner in his room, barking orders at Betsie. Somehow he doubted that would help anyone build better relationships. Melvin's addition to the household had destroyed Samuel's hard-earned relationships.

"Well," Maud said, a note of sweet triumph in her voice. "My son called me three days ago to say that his wife had broken her leg after she slipped on an ice cube in the kitchen, and could I please care for the grandchildren while she was in the hospital? I jumped at the opportunity, of course. I don't believe in gloating and holding 'I-told-you-so' over my child's head, I'm not one of those mothers…"

Samuel was only half listening. His mind was on the dreadful encounter at home. He didn't think he could bear Betsie looking at him with her miserable eyes devoid of love and faith in his abilities as a father.

"… so I suggested a trip instead, and the kids fairly jumped at the opportunity. I suppose Jennifer keeps them closeted in the house. Poor things were pining to be let out. Here, I have pictures!"

Samuel glanced at the pictures in Maud's wallet. The boy was about six, wearing a zebra costume. His front two teeth were missing, and his nose was heavily freckled. The girl – Maud had said her name was Grace – looked about a year old, dressed in a flowery pink tutu, a flowery bonnet on her head.

"Very cute," Samuel said, clenching his fists around the reins. "Here's your motel."

"Oh, thank you!"

Maud got off lithely and smiled up at Samuel when he handed her the groceries.

"May God bless you with lovely children, Samuel King, and give you your heart's desire."

Her wish took Samuel aback, and he fervently

prayed for it to come true. Not wanting to go home yet, he watched her walk upstairs. She stopped at number twenty-four, turned, and waved goodbye. Samuel did the same and turned his buggy back home, his mind on the baby formula in Maud's groceries, wondering if the kidnapper would be kind enough to give his Emma milk.

My darling girl will be hungry, he thought. *She won't be there to share my food. Oh, where is my baby? Is she being taken care of, or will that monster let her starve?*

Halfway back to the village Samuel had to stop the buggy on the side of the road and succumb to the tears and jagged sobs that were threatening to choke him to death.

THE WALK BACK HOME

The screen door slammed shut behind him, and Melvin walked as fast as his aching legs would carry him. He leaned heavily on the walking stick Joseph had given to him and trudged towards the dirt path. He could hear Betsie wailing even on the road. He walked faster, wishing to outdistance her cries because he knew if he had to hear them for a minute longer, he'd go insane.

It had been two days since Emma went missing, and it had dashed to pieces the peace of the house. Betsie was always crying. Her sisters were always with her, making a hash of calming her down. Samuel was out of the house from sunup to sundown, looking for their child in the town and its surrounding areas. They couldn't expect Melvin to tolerate such an environment.

He wanted peace to think. His brain function wasn't what it used to be, and he had grown accustomed to silence in the past three years. He had never thought he'd miss the sweet sound of nothing, but he did. So when the morning had started with Betsie crying over Emma's milk bottle, he had decided to go back to his quiet house to think things through.

Emma's disappearance was bothering him. A lot of things were bothering him, but that was at the top of his mind. His left leg felt heavier than his right, but the rest of his body coordinated nicely.

Everyone's a suspect, Melvin thought, *and if Samuel weren't such an emotional fool, he'd see it.*

Melvin had stopped thinking in positives long ago and had seen a face of the village only a man thoroughly jilted by it would. Samuel might believe that all Amish folk were good Christian, *Gott*-fearing folk, but Melvin knew better. Amish folk were human, and where there was human flesh, there was access for the Devil.

Hadn't he seen Arthur Troyer add water to the milk he supplied the *Englischer* dairy shop in town? Hadn't he seen Jacob Stoltzfus kick a cat because it was in his way? Hadn't Francine Yoder stolen two sheep from the herd her son shepherded to teach him a lesson? Hadn't Isaac Hilty bullied and hit his fellow pupils in the school?

Oh, Melvin had the village dead to rights and knew evil lurked here as much as it did in town. But the question was, who? Who could steal Emma, and why? Melvin had a low opinion of Samuel, but he had to admit that Samuel was doing a good job at his farm. He was responsible and wasn't henpecked as Melvin had suspected. But he was still a fool who didn't see the evil in his fellow men.

It was to ponder on these thoughts that Melvin made his way back to his farm. He'd fix himself a mug of *kaffe* and sit in the porch swing and think.

Melvin saw the corn was coming along nicely, as he drew abreast with his fields. He could see the house beyond it, and some activity going on within. As he came closer, he saw Otto Beiler rushing down the cornfield. The stalks almost reached his knees, and Otto was a tall man. Otto was waving and hollering at the woods. Melvin squinted his eyes against the sun and saw a young boy dart behind a tree. His face was dirty and his red hair matted. He looked like an urchin.

You keep those no-good Englischer *thieves out of my fields, Otto,* Melvin thought, grimly satisfied to see the boy run back into the woods.

"*Gut* job, Otto!" Melvin crowed. Otto jumped in surprise. He looked at Melvin as if he had seen a ghost, but then his large face broke into a pleasant grin.

"Can't have the little ruffian stealing the crop."

"I worked my back too hard on it to allow that to happen."

"Are you enjoying Samuel's farm?"

"Humph," Melvin grunted noncommittally.

"Samuel is doing an outstanding job on it. I didn't appreciate how much effort it took to manage an entire farm on your own. Now that I have my own farm, and my boys are still too young to help, I can see how much toil it takes to keep your head above water."

"And what farm would that be? Far as I know your older brother got your father's farm."

"Oh." Otto looked alarmed. He darted his eyes towards the house, then back at Melvin. Melvin turned to see Mary Beiler, Otto's wife, and his twin sons traipsing around Melvin's backyard, feeding Melvin's chickens.

"And just what do you think you're doing on my farm?" Melvin growled.

"It's not your farm, Melvin. I bought it from the village church."

"I'm not dead yet!" Melvin screamed. "I'm not dead yet!"

"But Joseph Miller said you bequeathed your farm to the church to do with as they will. Technically, it's the church's farm, and you vacated it. What would you have – that the farm go to seed, the crop be lost while you convalesce in your old age..."

"I'm not dead yet!"

"You're not young either," Otto shot back. "Look at the farm. Go on, look at it. I put a fresh coat of paint on it. I fixed the pens in the barn and the leak in the roof. My wife has cleaned and polished the inside of the house. She tends to the vegetable garden and has started a small dairy business. What was there when you were taking care of it? Weeds and cobwebs."

"It's still my farm!"

"It is *Gott's* farm, Melvin King." Otto raised himself to his full height. "You don't own the land, you were just assigned the task of tilling it and tending it for *Gott's* glory. Now, if you have any problem with this, you can take it up with Joseph Miller. I am a busy man."

Hadn't he said it? The Amish were just as

crafty as anyone, and didn't this just prove it? Joseph Miller had orchestrated Melvin's ousting from his own home, so he could sell Melvin's farm from under his nose. Yes, Melvin had bequeathed the farm to the church, but he was still alive. The least Joseph and the elders could have done was to inform him!

No one in this community had ever done right by him.

Melvin turned back towards the path but stopped when he saw the urchin boy looking from the trees. Melvin couldn't tell what the boy looked like exactly, but his round face was filthy. In a fit of malice, Melvin yanked out a few ears of baby corn and marched up to the boy.

"Here!" Melvin growled, thrusting corn in the boy's hands. "Steal as much as you want."

Petty deed done, Melvin trudged back to his son's house, muttering under his breath.

DISAPPOINTMENT

The house was eerily silent. Samuel helped Miriam Hershberger down from the buggy. The noon sun was right overhead, shrinking their shadows to their heels.

"Are Sarah and Kathy inside?" Miriam asked. The second eldest Hershberger sister, she was a teacher in Indiana.

"They are a great help."

"*Ja*, but they can't neglect their own homes for long. I'll care of the house now till we find Emma."

Samuel said nothing but turned to retrieve Miriam's luggage. A heavy hand touched his shoulder. Miriam squeezed gently.

"We will find her, Samuel. *Gott* willing."

Samuel nodded his appreciation of her support, then guided her inside. The front room was aglow with cheerful sunlight. The door to Melvin's room was slightly ajar; the creaking thud of a rocking chair came from inside. Samuel saw Miriam frown. He knew how it must look. Melvin had taken Leroy's old room, as well as Betsie's mother's rocking chair, for his own comfort.

"We've put you up in your old room."

"I thought you would convert it into a nursery."

"We changed our minds," Samuel said. "Betsie's old room was closer."

"How is she?" Miriam asked.

Samuel stopped. He stood inside the door to Miriam's room, and even though the sun was blazing in the first hot day of spring, he felt cold.

"She blames me."

"She couldn't possibly."

"She does."

"Well." Miriam bit her lip, and Samuel knew she was trying to think of an excuse for Betsie's behavior. "She's in shock. Of course she'll lash out."

Samuel didn't disagree. It was the same response everyone had, but he knew better. He knew something had snapped between him and Betsie, and things would never be the same. He set Miriam's baggage by the dresser and followed her to the master bedroom. It was the biggest room in the house and had belonged to Sarah, the eldest Hershberger sister, before she had married.

They could hear voices coming from inside. Low murmurs and soothing tones. Sarah and Kathy had come, as they did every morning, trying to persuade Betsie to eat a little, to get out of bed and take a bath. Samuel turned the knob to open the door, but a sudden scream of anger stopped him.

"Samuel doesn't care! He won't find her because she doesn't mean as much to him as she does to me. We aren't important to him."

Miriam glanced up at his stricken face. She touched his chilly hand, squeezed it.

"I'll talk to her."

"*Nee*," Samuel said. "It's the only thing that's keeping her from completely giving into depression. Let her have it."

"But Samuel, this isn't healthy!"

"It's what she needs right now."

Samuel opened the door. Sarah and Kathy looked up from their chairs. Betsie swung her face towards the door. Their eyes met. For a brief second Betsie looked ashamed, but then her eyes became hard chips of ice. Her chin jutted out. Samuel didn't look away, trying to pass along his own steady love for her in his gaze.

Betsie turned her face away from him, turning towards Miriam, who embraced her.

Samuel closed the door behind him, gently. He sighed and walked off to the kitchen. Melvin's lunch had already been set out on a tray on the table. Sarah and Kathy had tried to give Melvin his meals, but Samuel had insisted it was his job to do so. He picked up the tray of baked fish and collard greens and took it to his father.

Melvin sat in the rocking chair with his fingers steepled in front of his nose. His narrow eyes followed Samuel as he set the tray down and cut up the fish in bite sizes.

"I see Betsie has finally got the right measure of you." Melvin chuckled. "How does it feel to be surrounded by things you don't love?

"I love my life." Samuel shrugged. "It's taking a bad turn at the moment, but I believe *Gott* will see us through."

"*Gott* will not see it through if you don't help yourself, Samuel." Melvin chortled. "You fail at everything you touch. You're running Leroy's farm into the ground. Your marriage has failed.

You say you love your life and those in it, but you don't know how to care for them."

Samuel's clutched the knife and fork in his fists.

"Huh, you couldn't even care for your own daughter. They stole her right from under your nose."

Samuel set the knife and fork down. He got up and set the tray in Melvin's lap. He leaned close to his father, a pleasant smile on his lips.

"Just like you couldn't keep your farm? Joseph Miller sold it from under your nose and made you rely on your son's charity. How does it feel to be a burden, Father?"

If he had thought he would gain any satisfaction from his father's livid face, he had been mistaken. Samuel felt tainted, as if he had compromised on the values Selma and Leroy had taught him. He was acting like Melvin, and he had sworn never to do that.

He stood up abruptly and left the room. The sound of crashing plates followed him out of the house. Samuel unhitched the horse, jumped into his buggy, and rushed to town, trying to drown out the sound of Betsie's accusations, and Melvin's malevolent disappointment.

SPYING

The front door closed, and Betsie opened her eyes. She lifted her head slightly from her pillow to see if someone else was in the room. She was alone. Hurrying so she wouldn't miss *him*, Betsie picked up her shoes and tiptoed out into the front room. She could hear her sisters' low voices coming from the kitchen. She eased open the front door and slid out of the narrow opening, closing the door gently behind her. She put on her shoes and ran down the porch steps to catch up with her quarry.

Hiding behind the blueberry bush near the Zook farm, Betsie peeked out to see where Melvin was headed. She was convinced Melvin had taken Emma to spite Samuel and Betsie, and that was where he went each afternoon. She had urged her sisters to follow him, but none of them had believed her.

She watched as Melvin walked on slowly, encumbered by his walking stick. The heat pooled sweat under her arms, and she felt her scalp itch and prickle. In her haste, she had forgotten to put on her *kapp*. She was beyond worrying about basic propriety now. If people thought she had gone mad, so be it. She would appear unhinged if only it would get her daughter back.

Sarah had told her of the village's efforts at finding Emma. The villagers were taking turns, helping scour the highway and the adjoining area, looking for the man in the army fatigue jacket. Betsie was sure that man was responsible for whatever had happened to Dylan Brice, but not Emma. Her own grandfather had stolen her.

Melvin walked into the woods, and after a few heartbeats so did Betsie. There was more cover in the woods, and she could walk faster behind Melvin without being detected. As she walked, she wondered if Melvin had a hut in the woods no one was aware of, and if so was someone else helping him in the kidnapping? Surely, Melvin didn't leave Emma alone at night in the dark.

The thought was too horrible to bear, so Betsie pushed it away. No, someone else was helping. That was the only explanation. Why would Melvin go for a daily walk if not to check on Emma? His legs were too weak from the fall. He was always complaining about his knees hurting, so why would he take a walk in the sweltering sun?

The sound of the river reached Betsie's ear. She stumbled into a clearing and had to jump back behind a tree. Melvin had turned his face towards the clearing in that instant, and she was sure he had seen her. She bit her lip, praying to *Gott* that Melvin hadn't. After a couple of minutes, she peeked from around the trunk of the tree.

Melvin was walking up and down the river, poking at trash and bloated bags with his walking stick. Betsie frowned. Maybe he had seen her and was stalling. Maybe he thought if he would pretend to traipse up and down the river she would get bored and go away. Well, Betsie would not do that.

Melvin poked open a black trash bag. A mess of old fast food cartons spilled out.

"Oh, thank *Gott*!" Melvin said.

Betsie hid behind the tree again as Melvin

turned. The high cries and laughter of children were coming from the woods. A host of them came to the riverbank, fishing rods fashioned of slim pieces of wood in their hands.

"Hey, boys!" Melvin called.

The group of boys stopped in front of Melvin.

"Have you boys seen a large man hereabouts? A tall *Englischer* with an army jacket?"

"*Nee*, sir."

"What about a little girl? She's a *boppli* still. Doesn't walk or crawl, or say a word, but she babbles like a brook, and her hair shines red in the sunlight."

"*Nee*, sir."

"Ah, well," Melvin sighed. "You keep an eye out for her. There's a piece of candy in it for the one who finds her. Her name is Emma, and she belongs at the King farm."

"The old King farm or the new one?"

"The new one," Melvin muttered. "Now off with you!" he bellowed.

Betsie's knees had given way long before Melvin had finished talking. Tears streamed down her face, but no sound would come out. Melvin hadn't kidnapped Emma. His daily walks were a search for her. He had been poking at refuse on the bank to make sure it wasn't…

Betsie clutched her hand to her mouth to stifle her agonized cry.

Oh, her poor *boppli*! If Melvin didn't have her, then who did?

A CLUE

He had dreamed of running through tall cornfields in the dead of night. Selma's voice was calling him, but he couldn't see where he was going. There were no stars to guide him, only the murky black night, the dew-laden itchy leaves of corn, and loamy earth between his toes.

And dread. Dread chilled the back of his neck, because there was something else in the field with him. Something sinister was lurking in the stalks, watching, waiting to pounce.

"Samuel!"

"*Mamm!*" Samuel cried, his eyes opening wide, the last vestiges of the dream blowing away like wisps of smoke from his mind.

He turned in the bed, groping for Betsie's hand, but found only cold sheets. The darkness outside the window was slowly turning opaque, gray touching the receding black. Betsie was staring out at the changing gloom, her chin resting on her hand.

Samuel felt the aching need to call her to bed or to hold her. They were hurting and miserable. They needed each other. But his courage failed him. What if he tried to touch her, and she backed away, or pushed him away? Samuel didn't think he could take that kind of rejection from her.

Quietly, he slipped out of bed and put on his clothes. Betsie seemed to rouse at the noise he was making. She glanced at him as if from far away, then gathered her skirts and stood up. She left the room, leaving behind a chilling cold.

How had they come to this? He couldn't remember a single time when they had been so distant. Yet now, the tolls of marriage, responsibility, and parenthood had alienated them in their own room.

Samuel washed his face from the basin by the window, touching the back of his neck with wet hands. His back was curved, his shoulders stooped against the weight of the coming day, the coming weeks and years. Sighing, he prayed for strength, and straightened his back.

Breakfast was sizzling on the stove. Miriam was making pancakes, a pained expression on her face. Samuel recalled that Miriam hated cooking. Emma loved pancakes smothered in honey. She would devour tiny bites within seconds, her four little teeth grinning through honey-covered lips. She would never let Samuel clean up her fingers afterwards, always insisting on licking each digit clean.

Samuel took Melvin's breakfast to him, but unable to stand the smell, or the memory and how it twisted his heart, Samuel left without having any breakfast. He tended to the farm as he did every day now before he left for the town in the afternoon.

From sunup till midday, Samuel worked like a man possessed. Not that he was trying to make up for the time he would spend looking for Emma and Dylan. He found the physical work an excellent release for his own pent-up frustrations and fears. He had visited the police station every day, but they had nothing to report. No leads, no clue.

Drenched in sweat by midday, Samuel went into his room to change his shirt. He found the water in the basin replaced, a bar of soap and a folded towel on the windowsill. Touched by Betsie's thoughtful gesture, Samuel cleaned himself up as best he could and changed his clothes.

"Do you want me to starve?"

Rolling his eyes, Samuel picked up the tray of freshly baked bread, salad, and cheese and took it to Melvin. He was just setting the tray down when there was a loud knock on the front door. He heard rapid footsteps, then the front door opening.

"Oh, *Gott*," Miriam gasped. "Have you found her?"

Samuel nearly ran out of the room. There were two *Englischer* police officers in the front room and a young man holding a large folder. Miriam was twisting a kitchen towel in worry. Betsie walked into the room, her face alight but her eyes dark tunnels. Samuel wanted to hold her hand.

"No, we're here to get a description of the girl, Emma King," one of the police officers, a young woman, said. She looked around nervously, her eyes darting from Miriam's *kapp* to Betsie's haggard appearance.

"We discussed how it would be easier to find Emma if there was a picture." The second officer was male, dark-skinned, and infinitely polite. Samuel had seen him during the search.

"Yes," Samuel said through dry lips. "But I told you we don't have a picture. I left an accurate description."

"It's not the Amish way," Miriam added.

"I understand," the male officer said. "That's why we asked the police officers in Kansas City to send their sketch artist. There are some points in the description he didn't understand. If you could answer some of his questions, he can sketch a likeness. It'll be easier to post the sketch across the county for a broadening of the search."

"Okay." Samuel nodded. "Betsie, would you please answer their questions?"

His voice trembled slightly, and he physically stiffened, waiting for the rebuke.

"Okay."

Samuel relaxed. It was the first word she had said to him since Emma was taken from them. He sat across from her, listening to her describe their daughter.

"She has a heart-shaped face, and her chin will be pointed once the baby fat disappears," Betsie said. "Emma has her father's eyes, and his hair

GRACE LEWIS

color, though it shines red in the sun. She has four teeth, two at the bottom and two at the top. She has a mole on her neck, right here," and she pointed under her chin.

While Betsie spoke, the sketch artist was busy with his pencil. He asked questions to further refine the sketch, and Betsie answered with a composure Samuel hadn't expected of her. Samuel watched, fascinated, as a picture emerged on the paper. It didn't look exactly like Emma, but the resemblance was striking enough. Betsie teared up a little when the artist showed her the result.

"Yes," Betsie nodded, "that's her."

"Josh," the male officer said. "Do you think you could make an extra copy of that for the family? I'm sure they'd appreciate it."

"Sure, Dom," Josh, the sketch artist, said.

"We should get back to the station." The female officer had been leaning against a wall, her arms folded in front of her chest all this time.

"In a minute, Ruby. Let Josh finish."

Ruby rolled her eyes.

"Why don't you get a few copies of the Dylan boy's posters and sketches of the suspect? We can give them to Samuel to distribute in the community."

Ruby left, her hand resting on the handle of her baton. Josh was frowning as he worked, his tongue lolling out of his mouth.

"You have a sketch of the suspect?" Betsie asked.

"Yes," Dominic, the male officer, said.

"Could I have one?"

Samuel was a little concerned at Betsie's request. Why would she want the suspect's sketch?

"Sure."

Ruby came in with a stack of posters. She handed them to Dominic, a deep frown on her face. She looked like she wanted to be anywhere else but here. Samuel wondered at her attitude, but it was soon cut short when Betsie got up and strode into Melvin's room.

"What do you want? Can't a man eat in peace?"

"Who is that?" Ruby asked, her hand back on the handle of her baton. Dominic touched her shoulder to stop her from taking it out.

"It's just my father," Samuel said, walking forward.

"He can be a bit disagreeable," Miriam explained. "He's old."

Curious, Samuel walked into Melvin's room,

leaving the door wide open. He sensed more than saw the others crowding the door frame. He found Betsie sitting on her knees in front of Melvin, the sketch of the suspect held up.

"This is the suspect we're looking for."

"What do I care for a suspect?" Melvin growled, glancing at the sketch, then back at Betsie.

"I know you care. I know where you go when you leave the house."

Samuel's frowned deepened. Now what had his father been up to?

"I don't know what you mean," Melvin said, gathering his hands on his knees. "I never cared much for girls."

"I saw you in the woods," Betsie said. "I saw you looking by the bank of the river and asking the children to keep a lookout for Emma. I know you care, and I know you want to find her. I'm helping you to do so." She stood up, placing the picture of the suspect on Melvin's lap.

Samuel was torn between pride for his wife and a sense of wonder at his father. He would never have seen Melvin as a caring grandfather, more so because Melvin wouldn't want to be seen as such. He had seen nothing but good in Leroy, even when Betsie had pointed out some of his faults.

He wondered why children could never understand their parents.

"Wait."

Melvin had picked up the poster, and another one had slid from under it. He leaned down with some difficulty, his wrinkled fingers groping for the poster. Once it was in his hands he squinted at it, his face lined with the effort. Then his eyes opened wide, and it was as if he had grown younger by ten years.

"I know this boy!"

Melvin held the picture of Dylan Brice.

"What?"

Everyone was shocked. Betsie stopped in the middle of the room while the police officers crowded in.

"You've seen Dylan Brice?" Ruby asked.

"*Ja,*" Melvin said. "He was in the woods by my farm. The boy was filthy, and the cap was missing, but I know this is him. I never forget a face."

"You saw him on *your* farm. You mean this farm?" Dominic asked.

"*Nee,*" Melvin said tetchily, "my farm. Sold under my nose!"

"He means his old farm," Samuel said. "It was

sold to Otto Beiler a month ago. I can take you there."

"What was he doing?" Betsie asked. "Why was he there?"

"I don't know." Melvin shrugged. "I saw him peeking out of the woods, and Otto Beiler was shooing him away. He said the boy had been stealing corn. I gave him some when Otto wasn't looking. The boy looked hungry, but he said nothing."

"When was this?"

"Two, maybe three days ago."

"Why didn't you inform the police?" Ruby said accusingly. "They could be anywhere now!"

"Well, I didn't know he was missing, did I?"

"There's very little time to lose," Dominic said. "Could you take us to the farm, Samuel?"

"Yes, of course."

"Josh, head back to the station. Ruby, radio the station that we need a search team in the woods near the Amish village. Let's go!"

Samuel followed. So did Betsie.

"I'm coming as well." Her face was stony, daring him to refuse her. "I will not stay at home. I want to help."

"Sure," Samuel nodded, holding the front door open for her.

"I'll stay with Melvin," Miriam assured them. "Go find Emma!"

"*Denke* for being here for us, Miriam," Samuel said.

She waved them off from the porch. The curtains in Melvin's bedroom twitched as he watched them go.

INTO THE WOODS

Betsie still felt a little overwhelmed. The number of people that had turned up to look for Emma and Dylan Brice was staggering. Samuel had introduced her to Tom and Alice Brice, Dylan's parents. Both were slight of build and red of hair, Alice's bespectacled eyes were green like Dylan's, and Tom's button nose was smattered with freckles, like his son's. She wondered if they had seen Emma in her, as she saw Dylan in them.

Samuel's friends Hector and Jason Fleming had also come to help, bringing their friends with them. Betsie had even run into little Mary Anne, the tomboy girl, and her grandmother, Polly. Her sisters Sarah, Kathy, and their husbands had all come, as had Betsie's friends. They had all left their farms and stoves untended to help find her daughter.

They had begun the search slowly, calling out the children's names. The volunteers had broken into pairs, and Betsie still remembered how Tom and Alice had held each other's hands as they had gone along a chosen path. It made the loneliness of her sorrow more pronounced.

She was alone now, half-a-mile north of the apple grove. She was looking for any sign of habitation, ash from a campfire, a child's footprint in the mud, discarded wrappers or trash. She didn't call out, even though she wanted to. Her intuition said if she called out to Emma, her kidnapper would know she was nearby and he would run away.

She passed by the apple grove and saw the bright red remains of a Coke can nestled amidst the roots of an old tree. She was bending to pick it when she heard voices. They were angry and came from across the grove. Betsie stiffened as she recognized the voice of police officers Ruby and Dominic.

"… I don't buy it. Have you seen the way they treat their women?"

"What are you talking about?"

"The veils and the high collars in such oppressive heat. And not to mention their gendered roles. Why must the woman cook and sew?"

"Ruby," Dominic sighed. "What does this have to do with their child's kidnapping?"

"I just think it's convenient the little girl was taken in such a short time. No one saw anyone near the King house. Isaac Hilty saw the suspect on the dirt road to town."

"What are you saying?"

"I think the father did it."

"Samuel?"

Betsie's blood turned to ice.

"Well, why not? She gave him a daughter. He was displeased, so he got rid of her. I bet the little girl is in some shallow grave..."

"That is ignorant and prejudiced. If that's how you feel, then I'm taking you off the case."

"Hey! That's not fair!"

"What's not fair is your biases coloring your performance as an officer of the law. As a police officer, you pledge to protect and serve."

"These Amish don't even pay their taxes. So they aren't the citizens we promised to protect and serve. I mean, just look at the situation. We're busting funding on an Amish kidnapping, suspecting a US veteran who served his country in Iraq!"

"Just because he was a soldier doesn't mean he is automatically a hero, Ruby." Dominic sighed. "Go back to the precinct. I don't need you on this case anymore."

"Mark my words, Dom." Ruby's voice was fading, and Betsie knew she was walking away from the clearing. "It will be the father, or that cantankerous old nut in the rocking chair. Probably the only true thing he said all day was that he didn't care for girls."

Betsie's hands were shaking. She felt an anger so violent she could have chucked the crumpled can in Ruby's face and felt no remorse. How dare she accuse Samuel of such a heinous crime? How dare she think of Amish men as heathens and women as oppressed chattel?

After she heard Dominic's heavy footsteps walk away from the grove, she emerged from behind the tree and wandered for a while. She still held the can, although she didn't know why. Her mind was grappling with hard questions and had no time to spare for trash she had found in the woods.

If some of the *Englischer* police were biased, and didn't believe someone had kidnapped

Emma, were they really doing all they could to find her? How had someone stolen her baby from under her nose without leaving a trace, without being seen or detected?

When she finally stopped, it was in a section of the woods close to the Lambright farm. A creeper of lush, green ivy climbed on an old oak, falling like a waterfall from its branches. Betsie's eyes filled with tears. It was a relic of her childhood. She had spent countless hours in the Green Room, the interior of the green ivy waterfall, playing house and hide and seek.

She entered it a little awkwardly. She wasn't a little girl anymore; the entrance was narrow, and she didn't want to break the leaves. Sunlight became an emerald beam inside, dust moats looked like tendrils of moss floating in the air.

Unbidden, the memory of Sarah's wedding day came to her. She had stolen a plate of cookies, while Samuel had nicked a bottle of milk, and they had sat and talked in the Green Room. It had been the moment that had cemented their friendship. Tears pattered on her cheeks, and a little sob escaped her lips as a new longing opened within her; a need to be held by Samuel, her friend, her husband.

As if he had heard the silent wishes of her

heart, Samuel broke into the room from the narrow opening. He said nothing, no word of reproach. He simply held out his hand, his expression forlorn, but reaching out to her. Betsie took his warm hand and held it to her cheek as the dam broke. She let herself go in his arms and cried.

When she looked up, it was to see Samuel's face drenched in tears, trickling down his chin to mingle with hers. Their pain was one, just as their daughter was a product of them, the thing that united them irrevocably. How could Betsie have thought her pain was her own, her loss only felt by her? How could she have pushed Samuel away?

"I have failed you. I have failed Emma," Samuel sobbed. "You were right. I was so caught up in keeping the farm from failing, I neglected the one thing that meant the most to me, my family."

"*Nee*, Samuel." Betsie wiped his tears. "We're both responsible. I should have forced you to talk to me; I shouldn't have waited for you to tell me your troubles. And they aren't your troubles, Samuel. If this has taught me anything, it is that our burdens are no longer our own. I am here to share yours, and you must bear mine."

"I just miss her so much." Samuel sniffed.

"I do too. It's like a hole…"

"In my chest," Samuel finished her sentence. He held her closer to him and kissed her hair. Betsie clutched onto his shirt, promising to never leave him alone again.

They left the room together, Samuel holding the entrance wide for Betsie. They had entered it alone, heavy with burdened hearts. They left it united in their grief, lighter than before and full of love to face the ordeal ahead.

CLUTCHING AT STRAWS

He was in the cornfield again, but this time he wasn't alone. Betsie was beside him, but she was just a child, her chin barely reaching Samuel's shoulder. They were walking down a narrow path between the tall stalks. Betsie clutched his sweating hand. His ears were cocked for any sound. They were looking for a kitten that had gotten separated from its litter.

"Do you hear anything?" Samuel asked.

"No," Betsie whispered. "But I can feel something."

"What?"

"Something is following us."

"Are you sure?" Samuel turned to look at Betsie, but she wasn't alone. A woodpecker sat on her head, and as Samuel watched in growing horror, it pecked at Betsie's skull.

Tap tap tap.

"*Ja*, I'm sure."

A trickle of blood ran down Betsie's forehead.

TAP TAP TAP!

Samuel awoke with a start. It was still dark, but Betsie's side of the bed was empty. The bedroom door was ajar and voices were coming from the front room. Putting on his robe, Samuel hurried out. Betsie was standing in the front room with Miriam, who was holding a candle. Tom Brice stood with them, a very keen expression on his face.

"What's happened?"

"They caught him!" Tom said. "They caught the suspect. I came to collect you because I know you'd want to know where he took your daughter. Alice is at the station."

"I'll be out in a minute."

Samuel rushed inside the room and dressed in haste. Betsie came in as he was buttoning his shirt. She was clutching at her nightgown, and Samuel could see the dark circles beneath her eyes. She placed a sobering hand on his shoulder.

"Whatever happens, I love you," she said. Her lip was trembling, and Samuel saw fear in her eyes. The gruesome image from his dream came to him then, and he shuddered. He understood that she expected the worst, and his legs trembled. He didn't think he had the strength to see his fears made real, but Betsie was relying on him to be strong for them both.

He wouldn't fail her.

"I love you too, my Betsie."

She kissed his cheek and hurried him along.

THE POLICE STATION was dimly lit with the skeleton crew busy manning active stations. Alice was sitting in the waiting area, her glasses flashing in the overhead light so for a moment she looked blind.

"Has he said anything?" Tom asked, approaching his wife.

"Not yet." Alice pushed her glasses up her nose. "Inspector Jackson said he'd let us know as soon as they have something. Would you like some coffee, Samuel?"

"That's kind of you."

"I need to stretch my legs." Alice's smile was small and nervous.

Samuel took a seat beside Tom and waited. Alice appeared with three Styrofoam cups of hot coffee and they sipped and waited. After an hour, the station doors opened and a female officer Samuel recognized as Ruby walked in, pushing two teenaged boys ahead of her.

"I caught these two making a mural on the train tracks," she told the man at reception. She glanced towards the visiting chairs and her mouth curled in a sneer.

"Tom, Alice, Samuel."

Dominic Jackson came out of a room to the far left of the station and approached them. He looked haggard, as if he hadn't slept in days. There was a small swathe of stubble on his left jaw just beneath the chin where he had forgotten to shave it that morning.

"What does he say?" Tom asked, his hand clutched tightly in Alice's. Samuel suddenly wished Betsie were here.

"I'm sorry," Dominic sighed. "It looks like we've been chasing the wrong man."

"What do you mean?" Samuel asked in a tiny voice.

"His name is Charles Monk, and he was honorably discharged a few months ago. He lost an eye in Iraq." Dominic rubbed his tired face. "Eyewitnesses saw him talking to Dylan on the day he went missing, but Monk was in the Brewing Room the rest of the day. That's where we found him. It's a bar three miles out of town. Shady place. Mostly a biker den." Dominic waved his hand and sighed again. "The bartender and the owner both saw Monk there that day."

"But Emma…"

"He says he was in the Amish village looking for work. He saw a man named Yoder who gave him a melon, but no work. He hitchhiked to the Brewing Room and gave the melon to the owner. There are witnesses. I'm sorry, but he just isn't our guy."

"But then where did our children go?" Alice screamed. "Did they vanish into thin air?"

"We're trying our best…"

"No, you're not!" Alice was inconsolable. Tom tried to hold her, but she beat at his chest, her face crumpling, sobs wrenching out of her.

"I'm sorry," Dominic sighed. He took a step forward and touched Samuel's shoulder. "Please tell your wife we're doing the best we can. I'm sorry, Samuel, I really am."

Samuel felt deflated and suddenly exhausted,

as if he had hoed an entire field by himself. They had been chasing a shadow all this time. Emma could be anywhere, and they didn't have the first clue where that could be.

ACCEPTANCE

Samuel had arrived with the sun, his disappointed face the only announcement Betsie needed. He was in the backyard now, cutting wood for the stove. Betsie sat on the porch amongst her flowers and her sisters, thankful for the women's presence, but at the same time wanting them to leave her alone.

She and Samuel had been looking one way, while their daughter had been taken another one. Where was she? Who had taken her, and why?

"… too sour, don't you think?"

"Sorry?" Betsie was startled out of her reverie by Miriam.

"I said we could make a lemon cake, but the

lemons are too sour for the amount of honey we have in the house."

"I suppose," Betsie said, her eyes losing focus again.

"Betsie, stop it!" Miriam warned. "Stop doing this. I know it hurts, and your pain is inconsolable, but you can't lose your grip on life like this. Think of Samuel, think of your unborn child."

Betsie's lip trembled. She knew what Miriam said was true, but it was such an ultimate act of betrayal to Emma. To even think of trying to move on was giving up on her daughter, and Betsie couldn't do that. She wouldn't abandon Emma that way ever again.

"Look," Miriam said, placing a gentle hand on Betsie's shoulder. "All of us are here for you, for as long as you want. But you need to gather up your life and make something of it. We can't do that for you, I wish we could, but we can't."

"Miriam's right, Betsie," Sarah said, tucking a stray strand of hair back in Betsie's *kapp*. "You have to at least try."

"What's that?" Kathy blurted.

They all looked down the dirt path Kathy was pointing to, and Betsie saw it too. It was a large cloud of dust, hurtling towards them.

Betsie squinted at it and saw sunlight reflected off glass.

"It's a car," Betsie said.

"Could be the Brices," Sarah said.

"I'll set a pot of tea." Miriam got up from the porch.

The car came closer and Betsie saw the black and white paint. She stood up suddenly, her heart in her throat. If it was the police, maybe they had some leads. The car stopped on the dirt drive that led up to the porch. Betsie was displeased to see Officer Ruby in the front seat. She was alone. She didn't step out of her vehicle. She rolled the window down and spoke to Betsie without looking at her.

"Captain Jackson sent me to inform you they've found Dylan Brice."

"What?" Betsie's mouth had gone suddenly dry. "Where? Emma?"

"At the train station," Ruby said, stifling a yawn. "There was no trace of your daughter. Now, if you'll excuse me."

Before Betsie could blink, Ruby had put the car in first gear and was racing back down the dirt path. Betsie ran anyway. She ran to the backyard where she could hear the swish and thud of the axe.

"Samuel! Samuel! They've found the Brice boy. They've found Dylan!"

"Emma?"

Betsie shook her head.

Samuel dropped the axe, narrowly missing his toes. He snatched his shirt from the peg next to the barn door and put it on it as he ran to the stables. Betsie was with him every step of the way. She helped hitch the horse up and buttoned the last two buttons on Samuel's shirt. Samuel urged the horse out forward, then stopped.

"What are you waiting for?" Betsie asked, incensed. "Go!"

"Come with me." Samuel extended his hand. "She's our daughter. We should look for her together."

Betsie smiled for the first time in weeks, her face brightening as it did so. She took his hand and jumped into the wagon with him. As they trundled down the road as fast as they could go, Betsie realized that unbeknownst to her, she had already started to heal.

TRACKS

The police station was a stark opposite of what Samuel had seen only a few hours ago. The desks were full of officers, and more came and went all the time. Samuel went to the reception desk and asked if he could see Captain Jackson. The man behind the desk picked up the telephone on his desk, but at that moment Officer Ruby came inside the precinct.

"I told you we haven't found your daughter," she said.

"We still want to see Captain Jackson."

"He's a busy man." Officer Ruby folded her arms. "Greg, give these folks an appointment and send them on their way."

"Hello, Samuel."

Officer Ruby's face lost its gleeful expression and turned sour. Captain Dominic Jackson was standing at the other end of the hall, a large coffee in his hand. He ushered Samuel over.

"Please excuse Officer Cox," Dominic said. "She was on the graveyard shift and it still hasn't ended. Why don't you get these nice folks coffee, Officer Cox?"

Dominic closed the door on Ruby's frowning face.

"She told us you'd found Dylan Brice," Betsie said, taking a seat in front of the captain's desk.

"We didn't find him." Dominic rubbed his tired eyes. "God landed that child in our lap. Officer Cox apprehended two teenagers last night from the train station. Minor misdemeanor. They were painting graffiti art on an unused platform. One of our officers was stationed at the train station, just to keep the kids away. It can be dangerous with trains coming in."

He took a long sip of his coffee, and Samuel wondered if he had burned his tongue.

"It was a little after dawn when our officer saw an old lady and a young boy walk up to the station. They were carrying no bags, and the officer wouldn't have given it much thought if the kid hadn't fallen to the ground. He says the kid looked drugged, and he saw enough description points matching Dylan Brice to take a closer look."

Dominic pinched the bridge of his nose and gave them a tired smile.

"It's a good thing he did because the old lady was planning on leaving the state. That's how we found Dylan."

"But where was he all this time? What old lady?"

"We're still grappling with the final details. It turns out there was a missing persons report filed in Des Moines for a Maud Teller. That's our kidnapper. She escaped her facility a month ago, and Des Moines police had been looking for her."

"Des Moines?"

A bell was clanging in Samuel's head. He had heard someone mention that city recently, but who?

"That's where she's from. She's criminally insane. She stabbed her daughter-in-law in the leg when she was refused visitation with her grandchildren. She genuinely believes that Dylan is her grandson."

"What about Emma? Did she mention Emma?" Betsie asked, placing her hands on the desk.

"I'm sorry, Mrs. King," Dominic spread his hands. "She wasn't with Dylan."

"How is he?" Samuel asked.

"Drugged, dirty and disoriented, but physically fine. He's in the hospital right now, but his parents are just relieved to have him back."

"But where were they living all this time? It couldn't have been the woods. We searched every inch of it. But then, how did Dylan escape to the woods?"

Samuel was only half listening. Des Moines was stuck in his brain like a stubborn piece of spinach stuck in the very back teeth. He knew he had heard the name of the city recently, and his intuition told him it was important.

"She isn't cooperating. We've questioned her again and again, but she doesn't recognize the sketch of Emma and keeps insisting we give her grandchildren back."

"Grandchildren? Not child?"

"Yes, we'd hoped that meant something as well, but we think it's her condition that confuses her. She has three grandkids, but it is possible that she only kidnapped one. Till she cooperates, or her son comes to help us, we're trying to do the best we can. For now, all she says is 'Where are Neil and Grace?'"

Grace…

Des Moines…

St. Louis…

The Gateway Arch…

Green Woods Inn…

It came flooding back to him in sharp images. Samuel stood up so suddenly he knocked the chair back. It fell with a loud clatter on the floor.

"What's the matter?" Betsie asked, clutching his arm. "Samuel, you're as white as a sheet!"

"I need to see her."

"What? No!" Dominic shook his head emphatically. "I can't allow that."

"You don't understand," Samuel said, earnestly. "If I'm right, I think I've seen this woman before and I know where she was staying."

"What?"

"Yes. But I can't say that for sure till I see her. I don't have to talk to her, I just need to see her face."

Dominic stared at Samuel for two quick beats, trying to take the measure of him. He then nodded tightly and led Samuel and Betsie out of the room. Dominic led them through a passage, then through a door made of metal bars. Betsie held Samuel's hand, and he gave her a nervous smile. His heart was beating in his throat, and he felt a little nauseous. What if he was wrong, and this wasn't the woman he had met the day Emma had been kidnapped?

"No talking," Dominic warned, before he opened a nondescript door.

Samuel followed Dominic inside, Betsie close on his heels.

She was just as Samuel remembered her, but a little frazzled around the edges. Her dusty red hair was in place, but her smile had gone. She looked hostile, and there was a mad gleam in her eyes.

"Where's my granddaughter, you witch!" Maud Teller screamed. She jolted out of her chair and scrambled for Betsie, her sharp nails clawing at the air. "Where's Grace?"

"Out!" Dominic roared, ushering Samuel and Betsie outside. He slammed the door shut. Maud was still screaming on the other side. "There, you saw her. Now explain," he said to Samuel.

"I know where Emma is," Samuel said, running back down the hall.

"How?" Dominic asked, running beside him.

"I'll explain on the way."

"We'll take my patrol car. It'll be faster."

The whole precinct watched as Captain Dominic Jackson and an Amish couple rushed out of the office and into the parking lot. Samuel sat in the passenger seat while Betsie sat in the back. Adrenaline was rushing in Samuel's veins, matching the speed of the car they were in.

"Where are we going?" Dominic asked.

"The Green View Inn," Samuel said. "It's on the far side of town, near the woods. I think that's how *Daed* saw Dylan. That inn is right across the woods from his old farm. Dylan must have escaped into the woods, but he was too drugged to ask for help."

"But how can you know that?" Dominic asked.

"I met Maud Teller on the day Emma was kidnapped."

Betsie gasped, but Dominic put his foot on the pedal and the car went faster.

"I had just come out of the library after talking to my friend Hector," Samuel continued. "It was hours after Emma had been taken, and I bumped into an old lady. Maud Teller. She was carrying groceries, bags full of boxed meals and baby formula. I offered to give her a ride to the motel. She talked about her grandchildren. That they were from Des Moines, and how her young granddaughter, Grace, was ill, which is why they had to stay in Jamesport for a few days till she recovered."

Betsie's intake of breath was a painful hiss. She was thinking the same thing that was at the forefront of his mind. If Emma was Grace, then she had been ill. Emma must have been drugged as well, but she was so little, so young. What if she couldn't stand it? A more dangerous thought followed this one. If Maud wouldn't be parted from her grandkids, what had induced her to leave Emma behind?

Samuel clutched his hands together and prayed for *Gott's* mercy.

The car finally reached the large clearing of the Green View Inn. It was a shabby establishment at the edge of town. Dominic left the car to go talk to reception. Samuel didn't follow. Instead he walked towards the building and took the stairs to the upper level, where he had seen Maud go that afternoon a few weeks ago.

"It's room 219!" Dominic called from below.

Samuel stationed himself before the door and waited for Dominic to reach him. Keys jingled as Dominic climbed the stairs, the proprietor on his heels. Betsie sat in the car, and Samuel understood that she couldn't face whatever was inside this room. Samuel noticed the whorls in the wood, and places that had been chipped over the years. Time seemed to stand still, as Dominic placed the key in the lock and turned.

The room was in disarray. There was a strong smell of refuse, cloyingly sweet, yet rotten. The queen-sized bed was unmade; syrup bottles and pills cluttered the bedside tables. Samuel sent up a prayer for strength and walked inside.

"She checked out a few hours ago," the proprietor was stammering. He was a skinny man with an even skinnier mustache on top of his generous lips. "We usually clean within the hour. The housekeeper's husband died."

"I don't care if you never clean the rooms," Dominic said in a warning voice. "I need to know everything you know about the woman who was renting the room."

"She was just a sweet old lady. That's all I know."

Samuel picked up a sheet from the floor. He looked under the bed.

"Emma?" he called tentatively.

No reply.

"What about the kids?"

"Kids? What kids?"

"Her grandkids."

"She didn't have any grandkids. I would have noticed. Kids make a lot of noise."

Samuel's hands shook as he opened the small fridge underneath the desk while Dominic checked the bathroom. Both were empty. Samuel went for the closet. The smell was strongest here.

"You don't have to do this, Samuel." Dominic's hand was comforting on Samuel's shoulder.

Samuel stood back and watched Dominic open the closet doors. A few empty hangers hung like bats from the clothes bar, an ironing board rested against the inside wall, a tower of soiled diapers nestled beside it.

"She isn't here," Dominic sighed. It was an odd sound, part relief, part disappointment.

"I'm telling you, man." The proprietor shifted from foot to foot. "There were no kids. Those are probably the old lady's."

"Come on, Sam," Dominic said kindly. "You did well! We'll run forensics on the room and see if we can find a trace of Emma."

Samuel's shoulders were hunched. He had really thought he'd find Emma in here.

"No one is to go in or out of here," Dominic said to the proprietor. "This is a crime scene. Come on, Sam."

Samuel made to step out of the room, but a

soft thudding sound made him stop. It had been so low and discreet that for a minute Samuel thought his ears were ringing. But there it was again.

thud

Like something substantial knocking against wood. Samuel turned back to face the room. The closet door was open; Dominic had swept the bathroom. Samuel had found nothing under the bed or in the fridge. Where was the sound coming from?

thud

There was a drawer in the desk. It wasn't very large.

Thud.

But it was large enough to fit a small child. Like a baby.

THUD!

Samuel grabbed the handles and slid the drawer open. It was deeper than it looked. Some-one, probably Maud, had lined it with sheets to make it soft. Within these sheets lay Emma. Her face was pale, and she could barely keep her eyes open, but she was there. Her left leg was kicking slightly as it always did in the early hours of the morning when she was hungry, but too sleepy to cry out for it yet.

Samuel picked his daughter up with trembling fingers. Tear fell unheeded down his face as he held her to his chest and felt the gentle pulse of her heartbeat.

He was so happy, so relieved. He had found her. He had found his daughter, Emma!

FORGIVENESS

Betsie had never been taken by *Englischer* medicine, but she had to admit that some of their ways made sense. They had encouraged her to hold Emma, to talk to her, sing her favorite lullaby. The doctor and nurses had even given her privacy to hold Emma skin to skin, Betsie's warmth transferring to Emma's cold cheek till her baby was toasty warm.

She was sitting with Alice and Tom Brice now. Samuel was in with Emma, doing his fair share of holding her. Officer Ruby Cox was in Dylan's room. He had woken up an hour ago, and she needed his statement. Things finally felt right, like a piece of the puzzle had clicked in place. She realized how lucky she was. If they had reached the motel even a couple hours later, Emma might not have made it. The thought made her shudder, and she dismissed it quickly.

Samuel joined them after a while and they sat in the waiting room drinking *kaffe*.

"Why do you think she left Emma behind?" Alice asked.

"Who knows?" Samuel shrugged. "She has completely lost her mind. Captain Jackson told me that her son contacted the police a few hours ago. Apparently, Maud liked to medicate her children. Her son, Eric, said she had insisted he had asthma his entire young adult life, when he never had."

"Why would she do that? Why claim your healthy child is sick?" Betsie was very confused.

"For many reasons," Tom said. "One of them is control. If you can convince someone they're sick, and you're the only one who can care for them, you control their behavior and how they treat you. They will do whatever you want for fear that you'll stop caring for them."

"Also attention," Alice added. "Mothers of sick children get attention. I'm not saying it is always the case. But you will not be mean to a woman whose child is ill, will you?"

Betsie found all of this fascinating. She could

understand from firsthand experience the attention, and the control one had when one's child was sick or missing. But she would rather have her child safe and healthy than sick and dying.

Dylan's door opened suddenly and Officer Cox came outside. She sighed heavily and put away her notepad.

"Is Dylan okay?" Alice asked, getting up. Tom stared owlishly at the police officer.

"Yes," Ruby Cox said. "Dylan corroborates that he did take money from Tom, and he went to the ride outside the grocery store, where Maud Teller had asked him to assist her with some shopping. Then, she led Dylan to the motel where she offered him a can of Coke. It's safe to assume the drink was spiked because Dylan doesn't remember much after that."

Alice stifled a sob with her hands. Tom rubbed her shoulders in comfort.

"But he escaped at one point, didn't he?" Samuel asked. Ruby threw him a dirty look but answered begrudgingly.

"It was after Emma was taken," she said, putting her pen back in her breast pocket. "Dylan says he was locked in the motel room one day when Maud returned with a crying baby. Maud kept calling her Grace, saying she was crying because she was sick. Maud then gave Emma some cough syrup and Emma slept. He says he asked her where she'd got the baby from, and Maud had laughed. She told him about his parents' farmhouse, and how his stupid mother had left the baby on the porch. She knew because she had been watching them for a while from the bushes. She said she saved baby Grace."

Betsie gasped. So that was how Maud had taken Emma so quickly!

"That's why he went to the village?" Tom said. "He was looking for Emma's parents?"

"That was how it started." Officer Cox nodded. "Dylan had taken the keys out of Maud's purse while she was in the bathroom. Once she left, he ran into the woods looking for the farm Maud had mentioned. He found a farm, but the man over there shooed him off. He then thought of bringing Emma with him, just running away and hoping to be found, but by the time he got back Maud had returned."

"But why didn't Maud take Emma with her to the station?" Betsie asked, shaking her head. "I don't understand why she would leave her behind."

"We have to thank Dylan for that," Officer Cox said. "He says Maud was often forgetful; she kept talking about another baby and would sometimes forget about Emma. Sometimes Dylan had to feed and change Emma because Maud would be out of the room all day. When Dylan realized Maud was talking about leaving town he gave Emma some cough syrup and put her in the biggest drawer. He thought he could make a run for it once at the station and alert the authorities so he could save Emma. He fed Maud a story about Grace's mother taking her away, that he had stayed behind because he loved his grandmother more. Maud bought it and left Emma behind without even looking for her."

"My brave boy," Alice sobbed.

"We can't thank him enough," Samuel said, squeezing Tom's hand in gratitude.

Betsie held Alice's hand. Both the mothers cried out their anxiety over their children. Officer Cox stood there a moment, looking from one parent to the other as if she wanted to say something. Then she shrugged, gave a brief wave, and left for the bank of elevators down the passage.

"Mr. and Mrs. King?" The doctor assigned to Emma was a young female by the name of Amy Ram. Betsie had caught her giving Emma a quick kiss on the cheek and had instantly liked the young woman.

"Yes?" Samuel said.

"Emma's test results are back," she said. "I'm happy to inform you she is perfectly healthy, and this hasn't impacted her development. She has lost a little weight, but I'm sure she'll regain that soon."

"But she's sleeping too much," Betsie pointed out.

"That's the cough syrup," Amy said and nodded. "It isn't recommended for children as young as Emma, but the toxicology report came out clear. She should brush it off in a few more hours. But if you feel that her sleep cycles have become prolonged, you can always bring her back."

"Bring her back? You mean we can take her home?" Samuel asked.

"Yes." Amy grinned.

"Let's take our daughter home." Betsie smiled up at Samuel and took his hand in hers.

Miriam, Sarah, and Kathy had been busy in the hours since they had found out about Emma's recovery. The King household smelled of rich food.

Betsie's nieces and nephews played in the front
yard, waving and cheering when Samuel pulled
the buggy into the drive.

Betsie put a finger on her lips, and the children quieted instantly. Samuel helped her down,
and her sisters immediately surrounded her with
their husbands and children.

"How did they find her?"

"What happened?"

"Why is she sleeping?"

"Tell us everything!"

"Can we at least come inside?" Betsie asked.

"Of course." Ben Lambright, Sarah's husband,
laughed. "Go inside and have some food, Samuel.
I'll put the horse-and-buggy away."

They all walked into the front room, but
Betsie turned towards Melvin's room instead.
The door was slightly ajar, and she saw Melvin
sitting in the rocking chair by the window. When
she entered he looked up, and his eyes became
dewy. His mouth, however, caved into a grimace,
and his bushy brows furrowed in a mighty frown.

Betsie felt Samuel beside her as she walked in.
He stood with her as she bent down to show
Emma's sleeping face to Melvin.

Melvin sniffed, unimpressed, but the moisture
in his eyes was unmissable.

"I know you're careless, but don't make a habit of losing your children," Melvin snarled.

Betsie felt Samuel stiffen beside her. She hadn't taken Melvin's words to heart. She had got a measure of the old man now, how he pretended to be hard as nails, but on the inside he was just as vulnerable as the rest of them. Samuel, on the other hand, was always prickly when it came to Melvin. She hoped he wouldn't ruin Emma's homecoming.

She watched as Samuel bent down a little so he was face-to-face with Melvin. Melvin's face was a mask of eager aggression. Betsie spotted a dangerous glint in Samuel's eyes that she didn't like.

"Samuel," she began tentatively, but Samuel was completely focused on his father.

"I know what you're trying to do, and I will not let it happen," Samuel said pleasantly. The tone surprised Betsie, but the look on Melvin's face was thunderstruck. "Your days of controlling my moods are done. If there is one thing I've learned through this ordeal, it's I can't control everything. The only thing I can control is how I react to things. So I've decided I'm going to react to you with kindness, love, and forgiveness. Not because that is what you deserve, but because that is what my mother taught me."

Melvin chuckled, a nasty grin spreading across his face, though Betsie noted a hint of fear in his wide eyes.

"Then you're more foolish than I gave you credit for if you think your dimwitted mother taught you anything." Samuel only smiled and it irked Melvin. Rage made Melvin's face red, and he screamed, spittle flying from his mouth. "Your mother was the worst thing that happened to me. The second thing was you! You can't even keep your house in order, and you think you can ignore me?"

Samuel's smile was fixed, but he turned on his heels and faced the room full of adults and children watching the spectacle open-mouthed.

"Something smells nice," Samuel said. "What's for dinner?"

Betsie had never been more proud of her husband.

EPILOGUE (CHRISTMAS)

"Is there any more pudding?"

"Of course, Eli." Betsie ruffled her eldest nephew's hair. The dinner table was groaning under all the dishes. The feast was in honor of Miriam, visiting the family for Christmas. Betsie fetched Eli some more pudding, then fixed a plate of cranberry sauce and carrots for Emma.

"Betsie!" Sarah cried. "Look!"

Betsie walked over to where her sisters were sitting by the fire. Sarah held Rachel King, Betsie's three-month-old baby daughter.

"She just smiled!"

"I think you should have another baby, Sarah," Kathy laughed. "You get so excited by gassy smiles!"

"Oh, hush!" Sarah scolded and got back to admiring baby Rachel.

"Have you seen Emma?" Betsie asked.

"She was following Samuel," Miriam said.

Betsie scanned the room but didn't find Samuel. She noticed Melvin's food tray was missing from the kitchen, so she went to the front of the house. Emma was standing at Melvin's bedroom door. The door was slightly ajar. Tiptoeing closer, Betsie hugged Emma, who sunk back into her mother's arms and grinned up at her, placing a chubby finger on her own lips and Betsie's.

Betsie peeked into the room. The remains of Melvin's dinner lay on top of the dresser. Melvin lay in his bed, the left side of his face hanging loose, having lost all muscle strength in the last stroke he had had a few weeks ago. Samuel dabbed Melvin's chin gently with a soft towel, then got back to reading the Bible aloud.

Betsie felt a rush of love for her husband, and she hugged Emma close to her. A man who didn't abandon his aging parents would never abandon his wife and children.

She led Emma back to the kitchen and fed her dinner. After a while, Samuel joined them, diving into the conversation and festivities as if he had been there the whole time. He passed by her to get to the food and she clutched his hand.

Their eyes met, and she squeezed his hand, expressing all the emotion she felt for him. She didn't have to say she loved him because he squeezed her hand back. Their feelings for each other were obvious in their eyes.

Click here to get notification when the next book is available, and to hear about other good things I give my readers (or copy and paste this link into your browser: *bit.ly/Grace-FreeBook*). **You will also receive a free copy of *Secret Love* and *River Blessings*, exclusive spinoffs from the *Amish Hearts* and the *Amish Sisters series*** for members of my Readers' Group. These stories are NOT available anywhere else.

FREE DOWNLOAD

NOTE FROM THE AUTHOR

Thank you for taking a chance on the *Amish Hearts* series.

Did you enjoy the series? I hope so, and I would really appreciate it if you would help others enjoy this book, and help spread the word.

Please consider leaving a review today telling other readers why you liked this book, wherever you purchased this book, or on Goodreads. **It doesn't need to be long**, just a few sentences can make a huge difference. **Your reviews go a long way in helping others discover what I am writing**, and decide if a book is for them.

I appreciate anything you can do to help, and if you do write a review, wherever it is, please send an email at grace@gracelewisauthor.com, so I could thank you personally.

Here are some places where you can leave a review:

- Amazon.com;
- Goodreads.

Thank you for reading!
    Blessings,

Grace Lewis

PS: I love hearing from my readers. Feel free to email me directly at grace@gracelewisauthor.com (or to connect with me on Facebook here https://www.facebook.com/GraceLewisAuthor). I read and respond to every message.

OTHER BOOKS BY GRACE LEWIS

Click here to browse all Grace Lewis's Books (or copy and paste this link into your browser: *bit.ly/gracelewisauthor*).

THE AMISH SISTERS SERIES

This series is the sequel of the *Amish Hearts* best-selling series that you have just read, and tells the story of Samuel and Betsie's daughters.

The Choice, book One

Baptized into the Amish faith, Emma finds her heart divided between family, community, and forbidden love for an *Englischer* man.

Emma King is a respectful and hard-working Amish girl. It is no wonder that she has caught the eye of Luke Yoder, one of the most upstanding men in the Amish community. Her sister Rachel, by comparison, is reckless and foolish; she risks bringing the family shame. Yet all of this is nothing compared to the Amish community's censure of her father, Samuel King, a man with an obsession. But Emma has secrets of her own: mistrust of Luke Yoder, and a growing attraction to a stranger... an *Englischer* man.

Facing the accusations of her community, and the disquiet of her own heart, Emma King must make a choice that might devastate her happy Amish life. Will she follow her heart, or surrender herself to the will of *Gott*?

>> **Copy and paste this link: amzn.to/ 3QmrQFb into your browser to read it now.**

Faith, book Two

Three Amish women, three tests of faith. Will they persevere in their love for *Gott* or will their hardships harden them to *Gott's* benevolence?

Nestled in an Amish village, surrounded by friends, the King family is living the ideal life. Then sorrow comes to roost as one by one the pillars of the household are devastated.

Betsie King, severely ill, must rely on the help of her daughters and decide between her own mortality and the welfare of her family. Rachel must face her own sins and find redemption in the face of rejection. Emma has to deal with the dark secret of the man she is walking out with.

Will Betsie choose family over faith? Will Rachel redeem herself in the eyes of *Gott*? Will Emma be able to forgive Luke his human failings? Or will these trials tear the King family apart?

>> **Copy and paste this link: amzn.to/3O0ehtx into your browser to read it now.**

Heartache, book Three

The King sisters have come a long way, but life isn't done throwing obstacles in their path. While Rachel must find the man who will make her happy, Emma must overcome the daunting risks to her unborn child.

When Emma Yoder discovers she is pregnant with her first child, she feels like *Gott* has granted her every blessing she has ever wished for. Safe in the cocoon of her husband's adoration and her family's love, Emma is looking forward to motherhood. But a friend's miscarriage and her own checkup at the *Englischer* hospital turn her dreams into a nightmare.

A temporary teaching position at the local Amish school has become a boon for Rachel King. She enjoys teaching and loves the children, especially Elijah Lapp, a motherless child whose neglectful aunt can't seem to fill the void. Walking out with a man she finds annoying, Rachel finds herself hoping for the attentions of Elijah's father, but her past has a nasty way of catching up with her.

Will the two sisters overcome their hardships with the support of their families and the grace of *Gott*, or will their heartache engulf their peace of mind and happiness?

>> Copy and paste this link: amzn.to/ 3b8hHvn into your browser to read it now.

Torment, book Four

Emma Yoder's life is perfect. She has two children and another one on the way. She is married to the man of her dreams, and she is the darling of the village. But a tragic accident threatens to tear this blissful life asunder. Losing all hope and support from the community, Emma faces the toughest decision of her life.

Will Emma be able to pull her happiness out of the maw of death?

Rachel Lapp is worried for her sister Emma, but her own personal loss is too great to bear. Married for four years without a child, Rachel craves a *boppli* above all else. Her obsession has driven her to consider *Englischer* methods that might estrange her from the community but it is a risk Rachel is willing to take.

Is Rachel willing to lose everything, the love and support of family, husband, and community for a chance at motherhood?

A drought threatens the village and Samuel King pushes his solar panel powered machines as the only solution to the Old Order community. Though the community is against these advancements Samuel believes they are the only way forward.

Will Samuel's obsession with technology spell doom and shunning for the entire family?

>> Copy and paste this link: amzn.to/ 3O3o1D0 into your browser to read it now.

River Blessings, exclusive book for members of my readers' list

When the river blesses the King twins with its bounty the twins must go on a journey to find those *Gott* has deemed deserving of them.

When the King twins find a sack full of stray

puppies in the river, they know it to be a sign from *Gott*. Thus begins a quest to find homes for the dogs, but there are obstacles along the way: angry adults, haunted houses and bitter hearts. Will the twins find their furry friends new homes, or will they have to give them up to the *Englischer* dog shelter?

>> **Click here to read it now.**

THE AMISH CHRISTMAS
SEASON ROMANCES SERIES

An Unexpected Amish Thanksgiving, Book 1

Left to lead the family, strong-willed Emily Miller's skills are put to the ultimate test.

After losing her brother, Emily struggles to reconcile her faith in *Gott* with her feelings of abandonment and the responsibilities she's been left to handle. She must protect her family and save the farm, but the weight of her worries is too heavy and her confidence waning. Emily doesn't know how to run a farm, let alone care for her mother, her widowed sister-in-law, and her six-year-old nephew.

With the Thanksgiving holiday approaching, time is of the essence. She rushes to open a craft and woodworking shop. Her hard work appears to pay off until she goes nose-to-nose with the most despicable man she's ever met – her competitor Arthur Yoder. She'd do well to keep her distance, but unfortunately, that's impossible.

A large order stymies her. She doesn't want to, and yet she has no choice but to enlist Arthur's help.

Will working together cause more strife or will it lead to a surprising outcome?

>> Copy and paste this link: amazon.-com/dp/B09M8S7QJW into your browser to read it now.

A Surprising Amish Christmas, Book 2

Christmas is a time for rebirth and rejoicing. Can it be a time for healing too?

When a loved one dies, a part of us die also. Anna Miller has accepted her grief for her husband Michael, but she wants to live for her son, James.

Plagued by doubt, and guilt, Anna wants to become independent enough to provide a good life for her son James, but in the lonely hours, bent over her crochet table, she aches for something more.

Widower William Troyer cannot forget nor can he forgive. Disillusioned by the community he grew up in, he has moved his small family to Glenwood hoping to get a fresh start for him and his daughter. But can he trust again?

On this Christmas Day, can two grieving souls heal together?

A Blessed New Year's Eve, Book 3

** An Amazon #1 best-selling Amish Romance **

With the new year approaching, the joyful Gertrude feels a gap in her life.

Gertrude Stoltzfus is a mischievous young woman who finds the positive in everything. But she is also the only one single and without family responsibilities among her siblings, and she feels that something is missing.

When her great aunt gets sick shortly before Christmas and needs caring for, Gertrude goes to help, hoping this is her purpose in life. She arrives in an unknown community shortly after Christmas, putting her out of her comfort zone. But thanks to her sweet personality, she soon makes friends. Except for one person: John

Beiler, who took care of Gertrude's great aunt until she took over.

His attitude towards life is drastically different from hers. He shows his concern by being responsible and reliable, she shows her affection by making others laugh and brightening up their day with her jokes. Soon he confronts her.

In this new year, as Gertrude slowly unravels why John behaves the way he does, will she find a new meaning to her life?

38197815R00273